BLUEBELL WOOD

A DCI Tanner Mystery
- Book Ten -

DAVID BLAKE

www.david-blake.com

Proofread by Jay G Arscott

Special thanks to Kath Middleton, Ann Studd, John Harrison,
Anna Burke, Emma Porter, Emma Stubbs and Jan Edge

First edition published by Black Oak Publishing Ltd
in Great Britain, 2023

Cover Photograph ID 211260172 © Mreco99 | Dreamstime.com

ISBN: 9798865638599

DEDICATION

For Akiko, Akira and Kai.

DAVID BLAKE

THE DI TANNER SERIES

"To those who by persistence in doing good seek glory, honour and immortality, he will give eternal life."
Romans 2:7

- PROLOGUE -

Wednesday, 10th June

A GHOSTLY LAYER of early morning mist inched its way through the ancient trees of Bluebell Wood, hovering above its carpet of burgeoning blue flowers like a discarded wedding veil.

Frank Hall stopped for a moment to catch his breath. 'Where the hell is he?' he muttered quietly to himself, digging his hands into the pockets of his flimsy raincoat to shake his head in weary consternation.

'CHARLIE!' he shouted, endeavouring to mask his mounting frustration. 'HERE, BOY!'

Remaining still, he listened to his voice, echoing away into the disturbingly quiet woodland, tuning his ears for even the faintest of sounds. But there were none. No chirping birds, no scuffling rats. There wasn't even a breath of air to rustle the leaves above.

About to call again, the sudden snap of a branch had him spinning around.

Squinting his eyes against the sun's low early morning rays, he caught sight of a footpath, winding its way through the surrounding bluebells like a gently meandering river.

The sound came again, louder that time, reverberating through the woods from some unknown place directly ahead. When he heard the growl of a dog, he leapt suddenly forward, lifting his voice once more.

'Charlie! Here boy! Come on!'

Traipsing over the rarely trodden footpath, he plunged through the undergrowth, deeper and deeper into the mist-shrouded woods. As the trees began closing in around him, so did the mist, turning the sun's welcoming rays into an impenetrable blinding white light.

Barely able to see anything at all, he cast his eyes down at his feet, only to realise that not only had the path he'd been following disappeared, but so had the bluebells, and his boots were now being snagged by a twisted mass of razor-sharp brambles.

Regretting having worn his old khaki army shorts, he stopped again to listen, the skin on his face prickling against the cold misty air. He could still hear the sound of a dog's ominous low growl, but as he remained completely still, he began to wonder if it was *his* dog, or even if it was a dog at all?

Squinting his eyes against the sun's blinding incandescent rays, he was about to call his name again when the darker side of his imagination began to get the better of him.

Deciding that it was probably best to keep his mouth closed, he continued on, lifting his feet over the tangled network of thorns to place back on the ground as quietly as possible. As he inched his way blindly on, his hands held out in front of him for fear of walking head first into a tree, he continued to listen as the growl became more of a malevolent snarl.

With his mind becoming crowded by the petrifying image of a starving lion, recently escaped from a local zoo, he considered the idea of turning back when the ominous growl suddenly erupted into an over-excited bark, one he could recognise anywhere.

Drawing in a grateful breath, he plunged steadily forward to find himself stumbling out into a mist-shrouded clearing, in the middle of which stood a solitary tree, its base hidden by a layer of thick swirling mist.

Seeing the familiar silhouette of his dog, tugging at something behind it, Frank's face cracked into a relieved smile. 'There you are, Charlie! For a minute there I thought I'd lost you!'

But the dog didn't respond. Instead, it continued heaving back at whatever it had caught in its jaws with rabid determination.

'What've you got there, boy?' he asked, ambling cheerfully forward with a curious frown.

As if becoming aware of his presence for the very first time, the dog let go of whatever it was he'd found to present his owner with a threatening snarl.

'Cut it out, Charlie. It's me!'

But Frank's curt chastisement did nothing to improve the dog's brooding rage.

Watching him draw back his drooling lips as his lowered hindquarters spasmed and twitched, Frank took a precautionary backwards step. He'd been warned of the potential dangers of owning a Rottweiler, a dog bred for its exceptional strength, but more so with this particular animal. He'd been found beaten and abandoned on an old council estate, a few days before it was due to be demolished. When Frank saw him, cowering in the corner of a dog shelter, he elected to take ownership the moment he was told that he was due to be put down that very afternoon.

Remembering reading somewhere that the worst thing to do was to offer any indication that he was afraid, he stood up straight to step gingerly forward. 'Charlie, I'm warning you!' he stated, meeting the dog's demented gaze.

As the animal's rage only seemed to grow with hostile intensity, Frank pulled Charlie's lead out from his pocket to hold out in front of him.

The sight of it, or maybe just its scent, must have been enough for the dog to finally realise who was approaching, as he lifted his head to bark twice in a more playful manner.

Taking a breath, Frank relaxed his stance, just as the dog dug his paws into the dry crusty earth to twist around, charging off behind the tree to scamper into the woods.

'For Christ's sake,' Frank cursed, watching him bound away into the mist-shrouded shrubs. 'Not again!'

About to chase after him for what would have been the third time that morning, he remembered the tree, and that Charlie had been tugging at something behind it. Curious to know what it was, he turned to begin inching his way around the tree's thick grey trunk. When his boots slipped on its moss-covered roots, he rested a steadying hand on its coarse gnarly bark before continuing on.

Making sure to keep his eyes focussed on the ground directly beneath his feet, something warm brushed against his forehead. Looking up with a start, it took him a full moment to realise what it was; the remains of a human foot, its skin ripped partially away to leave bright crimson blood dripping from what was left of its three remaining toes.

Lifting his head up to see the body suspended

above, he stumbled back, his eyes unable to stop staring up into its ashen grey face, and the swollen purple tongue jutting awkwardly out from its twisted, crooked mouth.

Hearing Charlie's bark directly behind him, he spun around once again, only to become overwhelmed by a sense of nauseating disorientation.

Spiralling backwards, he placed a steadying foot behind him. But somehow he knew that there was nothing there. The ground his foot was stepping onto had disappeared. In its place was a gaping black chasm, filled with nothing but swirling mist and shifting shadows.

As his foot descended helplessly down, he tried twisting himself back, desperate not to fall against the hanging corpse behind him. But the lower half of his leg immediately pulled him up short. With it jammed inside the hole, his entire weight was thrown against it, forcing the tendons surrounding his knee to instantly tear.

Screaming out in pain, he flung his hands up to take hold of something, *anything* to help keep the pressure off his trapped twisted leg. It was only when he realised that the thing he'd grabbed hold of was what was left of the hanging body's foot did he snatch his hands away with disgusted repulsion.

As he continued to fall, his leg snapped in two underneath him, leaving him lying on the ground, staring in horror at a length of splintered bone, jutting out through his skin like a broken fence post.

- CHAPTER ONE -

'I DON'T SUPPOSE you've seen my car keys knocking about the place anywhere?' Tanner queried, glancing up to see Christine emerge into the living room.

With her tangled mop of greying-blonde hair hanging over her face like a dislodged wig, she lifted her chin in an effort to look at him more clearly. 'Why are you up so early?'

'I told you. I want to get in before everyone lines up outside my office to start their normal round of endless moaning.'

Christine raised a clump of hair out of her eyes to squint up at the clock on the wall. 'But – it's not even half-past seven? You don't normally leave before nine.'

'I know, but as I said last night, I want to make sure my desk's clear before Saturday.'

'I'm sorry, but what's happening on Saturday?'

Tanner stopped what he was doing to give her a scolding look of mock reproach. 'I do hope you're joking?'

'Oh, you mean our wedding,' she laughed.

'Ha, ha. Very funny,' he replied, fetching up a coffee mug from the kitchen's breakfast bar to drain the last of its contents.

'And that's this weekend, is it?'

'As hilarious as your remarks are, I need to find my

keys.'

'I think you'll find them where you left them,' came Christine's unhelpful response, stumbling towards the kitchen like a bewildered zombie.

'Which is where?'

'By your laptop.'

'And where's that?'

'Next to your phone.'

'They can't be.'

'Why not?'

'Because I've got my phone here,' he replied, holding it up.

Christine stopped her ambling shuffle to gaze over at it. 'So you have.'

'I assume that means you don't know where my keys are?' he continued, dropping it back down.

'Not a clue, sorry. But in my defence, I can barely work out where the kitchen is. Have you tried the sofa?'

'The sofa?'

'Well, that *was* where you collapsed, the moment you came back from work last night. That was where you fell asleep, as well.'

Leaving Christine to continue her erratic journey to the kitchen, Tanner hurried over to the furthest end of their L-shaped sofa. 'They're not here!' he announced, his eyes glancing fitfully about.

'Have you looked under the cushions?'

Tanner lifted one up. 'Found them,' he groaned, barely loud enough for Christine to hear. 'My laptop as well.'

'Whilst you're searching through the house, looking for your various personal items, there's something else I think you might need.'

'What's that?' he replied, heading back for his phone.

'A pair of trousers?'

Stopping where he was, he gazed down at his muscular hairy legs with a look of apprehensive bemusement.

'A pair of matching socks wouldn't go amiss, either.'

'What would I do without you?'

'Go to work in your underpants, apparently.'

Having retrieved the lower half of his suit from the bedroom, Tanner returned to the living area, hopping on one foot as he put his trousers on. 'How did you sleep, anyway?'

'Like a baby.'

'Really?'

'Well, when I say "baby", it would probably be more accurate to say a two-year old, one who'd spent an entire day being drip-fed a diet of ice cream, amphetamines, and crack cocaine.'

'I thought I heard you get up a few times.'

'A *few* times?'

'Did you get any sleep at all?'

Christine shook her head. 'I only ever seem able to if the Karate Kid decides to take time off from his busy training schedule.'

'I thought you said he was going to be a footballer?'

'Judging by the amount he was kicking me last night, I think his ambitions may have graduated up to becoming a Wing Chun grand master.'

'At least you've got some time off work, which is more than I have.'

'You mean, before Kung Fu Ken arrives?'

'I actually meant before the wedding.'

'After which he probably will.'

'Not immediately, I hope, at least not until we get back from our honeymoon.'

Christine cupped her hands around her bulging

abdomen. 'You never know!'

'Anyway, I'd better be off,' Tanner announced, fetching up his laptop and keys to hurry out to the hall. 'Call me if you need anything.'

'And how, exactly, am I supposed to do that?'

'Huh?' he replied, reaching the door to glance vacantly back.

'Your phone's still on the counter.'

Reversing himself around, he lurched back to the breakfast bar. 'I'd forget my own head if it wasn't screwed on.'

'At least you've got your trousers on this time.'

Tucking his laptop under his arm, he reached for his phone, only for it to burst into life the moment he touched it.

'I don't think it likes to be picked up,' Christine mused, watching Tanner recoil from it as if was a disgruntled rattlesnake.

Leaving the phone where it was, Tanner stared over at her with a look of nervous apprehension. 'That can't be good. Not at this time.'

'You won't know until you answer it.'

'Well, it's not going to be the cleaners, telling me that the toilets are blocked. For a start, I'm not sure they've got my number.'

'Do you want me to answer it? I can always tell them you're unblocking our own.'

Tanner smiled over at her before picking up the device. 'Tanner speaking!'

'Sorry to bother you, boss,' came an apologetic voice from the other end of the line, 'it's Sergeant Dixon.'

'Dixon?' Tanner repeated, endeavouring to put a face to the name.

'I'm the night-shift duty sergeant?'

'Oh, right. Sorry, I should have known that.'

'Don't worry, boss. I'm normally gone before you come in.'

'That's no excuse. Anyway, Dixon, how can I help?'

'A call's just come in. A body's been found at Bluebell Wood.'

Tanner cast a wary eye over at Christine to find her thankfully focussed on filling the kettle. Knowing that a body turning up just three days before their wedding could very likely put an end to their planned honeymoon, the one they'd both been looking forward to ever since he'd suggested it, he skulked surreptitiously out into the hallway.

'Are you still there, boss?'

'Sorry, yes. Go on.'

'The man who called said it looks like suicide.'

Tanner stopped where he was to draw in a relieved breath. 'Do you have any more details?'

'Only that it sounds like the person hanged himself, and that he found the body whilst walking his dog.'

'Do forensics know?'

'That was my first call.'

'And the medical examiner?'

'That was my second.'

'And you say the body is at some place called Bluebell Wood?'

'Yes, boss. It's a two-hundred acre area of ancient woodland near Bradfield.'

'Which is where?'

'Er...just up from North Walsham, boss. The body was found in a clearing, right in the middle. I've had a quick look at the map. I don't think it's accessible by car. I think the best way to get there would be via the footpath leading off Millbank Road. There's a carpark directly opposite, which should be empty at this time of day.'

'OK, thank you.'

'No problem, boss.'

'Before you go, can you do me a favour? Call Cooper and Gilbert? Tell them to meet me there.'

'Anyone else?'

'That will do for now. If it is a suicide, that should be more than enough to cover it.'

- CHAPTER TWO -

URNING INTO THE unfamiliar carpark Dixon had directed him to, Tanner pulled up to stare fitfully about. Apart from his own, there wasn't a single other vehicle there; no squad cars, no ambulances, no forensics vans, nothing! There wasn't even an abandoned shopping trolley. The only thing that could meet the description of being some sort of wheeled transport was an infant's faded plastic toy car, leaning at an odd angle against a bin in the far corner, one of its grotty yellow wheels being eyed up by a crow.

'Where the hell is everyone?' he asked himself, wondering if it was really possible that he'd come to the wrong place.

With considerably more choice than he was used to, he steered his dusty jet-black Jaguar XJS between the faded lines of the nearest space to climb slowly out.

Digging inside his coat for his phone, he was about to put a call back to the station to find out where everyone was, when his eyes were drawn to a slovenly sun-bronzed man wearing a stained florescent bib and a scuffed yellow hardhat, heaving himself up into the cabin of one of three diggers parked opposite the carpark's entrance.

'Excuse me!' he called, raising a hand to help garner the man's attention. 'Sorry to bother you. I'm looking for Bluebell Wood?'

'Wot about it?' the man huffed, looking Tanner up and down with an air of aloof indifference.

'I'm supposed to be meeting some of my colleagues there,' Tanner continued, already feeling his hackles rise. 'Am I in the right place?'

'Don' know, mate,' the man smirked back in response, 'but I'm not sure how I should, given that I don't know where you said you'd meet 'um.'

Tanner took a calming breath. 'The carpark opposite Bluebell Wood? Is that here?'

Tugging open the cabin door, the man took his time to climb slowly inside. Planting himself onto the dirty cracked vinyl seat, he finally looked back at Tanner. 'Well, there's a carpark over there,' he replied, pointing over to where Tanner's car was parked, 'and I think the trees on this side 'ave been known to go by the name of Bluebell Wood, so I s'pose you must be.'

Tanner offered the man a thin smile. 'Right, thank you!'

'Then there's the sign, of course.'

'Er...which sign is that?'

'The one right in front of ya.'

Following the man's gaze, Tanner stepped to the side of the digger's cabin to see what the man was directing his attention to. It wasn't a sign as such. More of a long, seven-foot high advertising billboard, depicting an artist's impression of dozens upon dozens of perfectly proportioned houses, all of which were surrounded by lime green cartoon-like trees.

Seeing the letters of something written over the top, he continued past the digger until he could read the development's name. "Bluebell Wood. A spectacular series of luxury two and three bedroom apartments."

'The job starts today,' he heard the man continue. 'Just so ya know.'

'I wouldn't get your hopes up,' Tanner mumbled, quietly to himself. 'Do you know if there's a way inside?'

'The main entrance is 'round the corner, but there's an access door right in front of ya, but you 'ave to get permission from the foreman before you go in.'

'I'll remember that for next time,' Tanner called back, shoving open the door to step lightly through.

- CHAPTER THREE -

HEARING THE MAN shout, 'Oi, mate!' in protest behind him, Tanner closed the makeshift door to find himself standing on a well-used footpath, leading the way through the trees ahead. With no idea where he was supposed to be going, he was about to recommence his phone call to the station when the sound of voices came echoing their way through the trees.

Recognising at least one of them, he began marching along the path to eventually find himself emerging into a clearing. In the middle stood a large solitary tree surrounded by various emergency personnel, half of which he'd been expecting to see back at the carpark.

Stepping to one side to allow a uniformed constable to walk steadily backwards, unspooling a reel of blue and white Police Do Not Cross tape, Tanner looked up to see DI Vicky Gilbert, stepping over a series of raised aluminium platforms towards him.

'Morning, boss!' she called out, offering him a tired but dutiful smile.

'Sorry I'm late,' came his apologetic response. 'The duty sergeant must have sent me to the wrong carpark.'

'Which one was that?'

'How many are there?'

'Three that I know of.'

'Well, it would certainly have been useful to know that before driving over. Is Cooper around?'

'I left him with the man who found the body.'

'And where is he?'

'Inside the ambulance.'

'Which is...?

'Back at the carpark.'

'Just not the one I was directed to.'

'Apparently not.'

'How about Dr Johnstone?'

'He's with the body.'

'And where's that?'

'On the other side of the tree.'

Remaining where he was, Tanner gazed hesitantly towards it. 'I was told it was suicide. Is that still the case?'

'Well, it's a young man, and it does look like he hanged himself,' came Vicky's non-committal response.

'So, it is then?'

'It *should* be.'

Tanner stared at her with a questioning frown. 'But not obviously so?'

'There would appear to be something missing.'

'And what's that?'

Vicky opened her mouth to answer, only to immediately close it again. 'It's probably easier just to show you.'

'Then I suppose you'd better lead the way,' Tanner replied, letting out an impatient sigh.

Ducking under the spooled-out tape, he followed Vicky over the platforms to eventually see what she had described: a young man dressed in jeans and a hoodie, hanging by his neck by a thick coarse rope. As his eyes dropped to the body's feet, suspended about twelve inches off the ground, a query crept into his mind, one which he knew to be the reason for Vicky placing a question mark over what should have otherwise been a clear an unequivocal cause of death.

'We've already had a good look around for it,' came the familiar voice of their medical examiner, Dr Johnstone.

Glancing up to find the short middle-aged man taking him in with a studious expression, Tanner continued to stare anxiously about.

'There's an impression in the ground,' he heard Johnstone continue, 'next to the discarded half-chewed Nike trainer, so something *was* there.'

'It just isn't there anymore?'

'Not that we've been able to find.'

'Are there any other signs of foul play?'

'It's too early to say.'

'I don't suppose you'd be willing to hazard a guess, it's just that I have a wedding to go to on Saturday, one that I really do feel I should attend. After that, I'd been hoping to go on holiday. So, if there's the slightest possibility that it's anything more nefarious, I'd be grateful to know sooner rather than later.'

'Who's getting married?' came Johnstone's spurious response.

'For some peculiar reason, I suspect you already know, being that you've been cordially invited.'

'May I ask who the lucky woman is?'

'Your mum,' Tanner replied, shaking his head with a wry smile.

'Really? How strange. You do know that she died last week?'

Tanner immediately regretted his glib remark. 'I'm sorry. I didn't know.'

Johnstone's eyes fell solemnly to the ground. 'I'm the one who should be sorry, Chief Inspector.'

'Why's that?'

'Because she's alive and well, and living in Bournemouth,' he announced, meeting Tanner's gaze with a conniving grin.

'Oh, right. Good one.'

'How's Christine?'

'Struggling to sleep.'

'Wait till the baby arrives.'

'That's what I keep telling her, which is why I'd rather not have to postpone our holiday. I think we could both do with the break before she gives birth.'

'By holiday, I assume you mean your honeymoon?'

'As they both involve going to Spain to do nothing more stressful than lying beside a private swimming pool for two weeks, I'm not sure I care what it's called.'

'Fair enough.'

'So...?' Tanner continued, bringing both the conversation, and Johnstone's attention, back to the body.

'Yes, of course. Well, apart from the lack of something for him to have supported himself with, on the surface at least, there's nothing to indicate that this was anything but self-inflicted. There are no signs that his hands had been bound, nor that he was involved in any sort of a struggle. I also can't see any immediate indications that he'd been drugged in anyway.'

'What about his foot?' Tanner enquired, pointing at its bloody remains.

'From what your officers have told me, it seems likely that the injuries are the result of the dog who found him.'

'So all that's missing is whatever he used to stand on,' Tanner mused, his attention returning to the base of the tree.

'If he had been hauled up by someone else,' came Vicky's voice, 'is it likely that they'd have taken the one piece of evidence that would have led straight to a verdict of suicide?'

Tanner lowered himself down onto his haunches to study the ground directly beneath the victim's torn, bloody foot. 'I suppose that depends on whether or not they thought leaving it behind may lead us straight to them. Clearly something *was* used.'

'Could the dog have taken it?'

'Something to ask the dog's owner, perhaps? I don't suppose there are any footprints where the rope was tied off?'

'Nothing obvious enough for us to compare against the victim's shoes,' came Johnstone's reply. 'Unfortunately, the ground is as hard as rock, which doesn't exactly help.'

Hearing the sound of someone creeping up behind him, Tanner turned his head to see Cooper approach, his hands shoved down into the pockets of his trendy dark grey city coat.

'Morning Cooper. How's our witness doing?'

'Apart from his leg, he seems alright.'

'What's wrong with his leg?'

'The idiot broke it,' Cooper smirked. 'He said his foot got caught in a crack in the ground, just after he found the body.'

'The crevasse in question is on the other side of the tree,' said Johnstone, directing their attention to a wide jagged fissure, creeping its way over one half of the clearing.

Tanner lifted himself up to step cautiously over to it. 'I don't suppose our victim could have kicked the log down there?' he asked, staring into its seemingly bottomless abyss.

'What log's that?' Cooper questioned.

'The one we think he must have used to stand on,' Vicky replied.

'I didn't know it was missing.'

'That's probably because you didn't bother to look,' Tanner muttered to himself. 'I don't suppose the witness said anything about seeing his dog run off with a piece of wood about a foot long, and six inches in diameter?'

'I can't say I asked.'

'And why should you have, being that you didn't know it was missing?'

'Exactly!'

Tanner rolled his eyes discreetly into the back of his head. 'What about a suicide note?' he continued; the question directed at Dr Johnstone.

'Not that we've found.'

'And his identity?'

The medical examiner pulled out a tablet from under his arm. 'A Mr Samuel Brogan, at least that's what was on the driving licence found inside his wallet.'

'OK, well, that's something I suppose,' Tanner replied, delving inside his coat to retrieve his notebook, only to realise that he must have left it at home.

Glancing around to find Vicky thankfully making a note of it, he saw his other detective inspector doing nothing more productive than to gawp voyeuristically up at the victim's puce, contorted face. 'Don't you have anything better to do, Cooper?'

'Actually, I don't,' he replied, his eyes meeting Tanner's with hostile belligerence. 'But I'm not sure that's my fault, being that I've yet to be given any orders.'

'I suppose you're unaware of the phrase, "using your own initiative?"

'I wasn't aware that was how the Police Force worked.'

'OK, well, what do *you* think we need to do?'

'Er...go back to bed?'

'How about trying to find whatever it was the victim must have used to stand on?'

'You want me to find a single piece of wood in the middle of a rather large forest?'

Tanner took a moment to glance about at their surroundings. As much as he didn't like to admit it, Cooper did have a point. If the dog had managed to carry the item off, the chance of being able to locate it would be like trying to find the proverbial needle in a haystack. Actually, it would be more like trying to find a piece of hay in a haystack.

'If I can't go back to bed, can I at least find myself a coffee somewhere?'

'You can have a look down that hole in the ground, first,' came Tanner's frustrated response.

'If you say so, boss.'

'I do say so, thank you, Cooper!'

With the portly DI slouching his way past, Tanner looked up to find Vicky staring at him.

'How about me?' she asked, in a more respectful tone.

'Maybe you can help forensics to make a cast of that impression under the victim's feet. If we are going to mark it down as suicide, we need to have at least some sort of evidence to help support the theory. If you could then have them check both the rope and the bark it's rubbing against for any sign that our victim may have been hauled up there by someone else. After that, perhaps you could ask Sally to look up the victim's parents' address. We also need to start looking into the victim's life. That'll be something Gina can do.'

'And you?'

'I suppose I better have a chat to the witness. If he did see his dog running off with a log caught between his teeth, then I think it will be safe for us to assume the scene is as it would appear.'

- CHAPTER FOUR -

F OLLOWING VICKY'S DIRECTION to the carpark where the injured witness was taken, Tanner found himself walking along a completely different footpath to the one he'd arrived on, one that seemed virtually identical.

Reaching the end to find himself standing in front of another plywood barrier, he fumbled with a similar pedestrian access door before emerging out from the woods into what was promising to be yet another scorching hot day.

With his eyes squinting against the glare, he saw a green overall-clad paramedic climb into the driver's seat of an ambulance parked in the carpark on the other side of the road. When it began trundling forward, he quickly crossed to hurry over, raising an arm above his head as he did.

Seeing the driver curse some sort of obscenity at him as the ambulance came to an ungainly halt, Tanner skirted around to the driver's side door.

'Sorry about that,' he began, as the window slid slowly down. 'I don't suppose you have someone in the back with a broken leg?'

'Which is why we're taking him to hospital,' came the driver's sardonic response.

'Would it be possible for me to have a very quick word with him before you do?'

'I'm sorry, but...who are you again?'

'Detective Chief Inspector Tanner, Norfolk Police,' he replied, digging out his formal ID.

'Can't it wait?'

'Well, it could, but I believe he has information that could help determine the nature of a young man's death.'

'You mean...the person found hanging by his neck?'

'That's the one.'

'Wasn't the cause of death somewhat obvious?'

'Not as obvious as you might think.'

The driver took a moment to glare at Tanner with a look of disdainful reproach before shaking his head. 'Very well, but make it quick. Perhaps unsurprisingly, the patient is in some considerable pain.'

Allowing the driver to step down, Tanner followed him around to the vehicle's rear.

'Melicia, my dear,' the man called out, levering open one of the doors, 'I have an undercover policeman wishing to interview our patient.'

'I'm not "undercover",' Tanner retorted. 'I'm simply wearing a suit instead of a uniform.'

'By the looks of it,' began the familiar sound of a woman's voice from inside, 'it's the same one you were wearing the last time I saw you.'

Tanner gazed into the ambulance with a look of curious uncertainty. Standing next to the makeshift bed, her arms locked over her chest, was the paramedic who'd treated him the last time he'd been within such close proximity to the back of an ambulance. 'Oh, hello!' he said, in a cheerful tone. 'Imagine meeting you here!'

'I was thinking something similar myself,' she replied. 'How's that arm of yours?'

'Still attached to the shoulder, thankfully.'

'And what about that girlfriend? Did she ever get

around to saying yes?'

Tanner raised an inquisitive eyebrow. 'You heard that, did you?'

'Sorry,' she replied, offering him a coy smile. 'I couldn't help myself.'

'No. Me neither.'

As they were talking, the driver was staring at them as if watching a tennis match. 'You two know each other, do you?' he eventually asked.

'The Chief Inspector here was one of my more reluctant patients.'

'I only ran off once!'

'So,' she continued, 'when's the big day?'

'Saturday, at least I hope it is. That's one of the reasons why I need to talk to your patient.'

Tanner saw the man lying beside her lift his head off the mattress to stare with obvious pain at him.

'Don't tell me he's your best man?' the paramedic queried, with just the hint of a smirk.

Tanner answered with an unamused smile. 'Is it all right if I have a very quick word?'

'I'm sorry,' he heard the injured man say, 'but can't I go straight to hospital? I've already given a statement to the police.'

'I won't be a moment,' Tanner replied, his eyes remaining focussed on the paramedic.

'OK,' she eventually capitulated, 'but please be quick. I can't set the leg here, so he really does need to go to hospital.'

'Will do,' Tanner smiled, climbing up to switch places with her.

'Sorry about this,' he apologised to the injured man, replacing his smile with a sympathetic frown, 'but I won't be long.'

'Then get on with it, please. I really am in a lot of pain.'

'I'm not surprised!' Tanner continued, his eyes drifting down to the poor man's leg. 'How did you break it?'

'Is that really what you wanted to ask?'

'No, sorry. Your name was again?'

The patient let out a disgruntled huff. 'Hall. Frank Hall.'

'DCI Tanner, Norfolk Police,' Tanner announced, briefly showing his ID. 'I've been told you found the body?'

'My dog did. Then he ran off. For reasons that should be obvious, I was unable to chase after him.'

'So, you don't know where the dog is?'

'I haven't got a bloody clue! Now, is that all, or do I need to fill out a missing dog report?'

'Could you describe the scene for me...when your dog found the body?'

'For what possible reason?'

'It would help if you could.'

'Help how? It's obvious enough how the man died, isn't it?'

'For example, was he dead when you found him?'

'Definitely!'

'How can you be so sure?'

'Because Charlie was trying to eat his foot, something the poor man didn't seem to mind too much.'

'So, when you arrived at the scene, your dog, Charlie, was already attacking the victim's foot?'

'Correct.'

'I assume you tried to stop him?'

'Of course I did! But once he has his mind set on something, it's exceptionally difficult to dissuade him. Besides, he was in a peculiar mood, and I didn't want to push it.'

'May I ask what sort of dog he is?'

'He's a Rottweiler. He's normally as good as gold,' Frank continued, his tone becoming immediately defensive, 'but something had clearly upset him.'

'Probably the fact that he'd just found the body of a man hanging in the woods,' Tanner mused. 'Did you see him run off?'

'I did.'

'I don't suppose you saw if he had anything in his mouth?'

'For example?'

'Something he may have picked up from the ground.'

'What, like a shoe?'

'Something larger, perhaps?

'Not that I saw, but he ran back behind the tree before disappearing into the woods, so he may have done.'

'And you don't have any idea where he is now?'

'He's probably still out there chasing bloody squirrels. I've told my wife what happened. She said she'd head down to look for him. No doubt he'll show up at some point. He's certainly difficult enough to miss.'

- CHAPTER FIVE -

ONFIRMING THAT HE'D already given Cooper his name and address, and warning him that he may also need to provide them with his fingerprints and a DNA sample, Tanner left the injured man to continue with his journey.

As he watched the ambulance turn out of the carpark, his eyes were drawn to yet another row of yellow diggers, again lined up on the other side of the road. It was then that he saw a heated discussion taking place on the pavement beside them: two giant burley workmen shouting at three skinny teenagers, a small attractive young woman flanked by two equally attractive young men, all three dressed as if they were on their way to a nineteen-seventies themed music festival.

The moment he saw the woman jab a disgruntled finger at one of the workmen, only for him to shove her backwards, he leapt across the road to intervene.

'What the hell's going on here?' he yelled, coming to a halt beside them.

'Who the fuck are you?' demanded the workman who'd pushed the woman, his bronzed forearms bristling with faded tattoos.

'DCI Tanner, Norfolk Police,' Tanner replied, showing him the ID he'd yet to put away.

'Then you can tell these tree-hugging hippies to clear off!'

Tanner took a moment to glance vacantly around. 'Sorry, but which "tree-hugging hippies" are those?'

'I think he's referring to us,' the petite young woman replied. 'Although, we're not hippies, we're members of Nature First, and we don't hug trees. We stop brainless morons like the two Neanderthals you see standing in front of you from cutting them down for no other reason than to build hundreds of shoebox-sized flats, none of which anyone can really afford, leading to more cars, more traffic, more pollution, but less of the one thing we actually need. Oxygen!'

'As I said,' the workman smirked, tucking his hands into the pockets of his flimsy fluorescent jacket, 'nothing but a bunch of tree-hugging hippies.'

'I'm also a final year law student,' the young woman continued, 'which means I know my rights. It also means I know when I've been assaulted.'

'You're the one who nearly poked my bloody eye out! I gave you a little shove, out of self-defence. It's not my fault you nearly fell over,' he laughed.

'That's utter bullocks!' the young woman spat.

'Besides,' the workman continued, 'we've already been given permission from the council to start clearing this site, so there's not a whole lot you can do about it.'

'The planning application is still in the consultation phase.'

'That's not what my boss said.'

'If you're referring to Mr Simon Balinger, that greedy capitalist retard, you can tell him to shove his luxury housing development up his arse, the same place all the shit he keeps spouting comes out of.'

'You can tell 'im yourself, if you like. He'll be 'ere in a minute. And when he does arrive, I reckon he'll be asking the chief inspector here to arrest you for trespassing, being that this is his land, and everything.'

'This is a public pavement, you brainless gimp.'

'Mr Balinger owns half of Norfolk, you stuck-up bitch!'

'All right, that's enough!' yelled Tanner, levering himself between the bickering pair to level his eyes at the workman. 'I've already told one of your chums that you won't be able to start today, whether you have permission from the council or not.'

'Yeah? And why's that?'

'Because a body's been found in the middle of the place you seem so keen to start bulldozing your way through. Until we've completed our investigation, you're just going to have to wait.'

'Doesn't bother us,' the man shrugged, smirking around at his mate. 'We gets paid by the hour, whatever we do. But my boss ain't gonna be happy. I knows that much.'

'Who is this man, anyway?' Tanner asked, casting a questioning glance around at the group.'

'Mr Balinger,' the workman replied.

'And he owns half of Norfolk, does he?' Tanner scoffed.

'As I said. He'll be 'ere in a minute, so you'll be able to ask 'im yourself.'

'Yes, well,' Tanner replied, glancing up and down the road at the dozens-upon-dozens of cars crawling slowly past, 'unlike you, I don't have time to just hang about waiting for some guy to show up.'

'Suit yourself,' the man huffed.

'Thank you, I will,' Tanner replied, turning to leave. 'But before I go, when he does eventually arrive, if you could tell him what I told you – about the body being found – I'd be grateful. And if he still decides to put you and your colleagues to work, you can add from me that I'll be arresting him, and the rest of you for that matter, for obstruction of justice.'

- CHAPTER SIX -

NAVIGATING HIS WAY back through the woods, Tanner returned to the scene to find Dr Johnstone directing two uniformed officers with the macabre task of lowering the victim's body to the ground, using the same rope he'd previously been suspended by.

With neither Vicky nor Cooper in sight, he waited for the delicate task to be undertaken before catching the medical examiner's eye. 'Did you find anything else?'

'Not yet,' he replied, instructing the awaiting forensics team to begin carefully removing the noose.

'What about the item used to support the body?'

'You'll have to ask your colleagues. I've been a little preoccupied.'

Tanner glanced furtively about. 'I don't suppose you know where they are, by any chance?'

'Not a clue, sorry,' he replied, wandering away with an ambivalent shrug.

Hearing someone come crashing through the undergrowth behind him, Tanner turned to see Vicky, fighting her way through a tangle of branches and ferns.

'Did you find anything?' he called out.

'Anything...as in?'

'The piece of wood? The one I thought we were supposed to be looking for?'

'Sorry. I wasn't aware I was supposed to be looking for anything at all.'

'Then what were you doing?'

'Er...call of nature,' she replied, blushing slightly. 'Sorry.'

Tanner rolled his eyes. 'Did you at least manage to make a cast of the impression?'

'I was told to wait until they'd taken the body down.'

'What about the rope?'

'We checked.'

'And...?'

'There were no signs of the rope rubbing up against the bark, so it doesn't seem likely that he was hauled up.'

Tanner began tapping a pensive finger against his chin. 'OK, so all we need is whatever he used to stand on.'

'What did the witness say?'

'Only that his dog found the body.'

'Nothing about seeing it run off with a lump of wood caught between its teeth?'

'He was only able to confirm that it ran off, not if it had anything in its mouth when it did. According to him, the tree was blocking his view. He also said that the dog is still missing, which is a concern in itself.'

'Any particular reason why?'

'It's a Rottweiler.'

'Oh, right,' Vicky replied, her eyes suddenly darting nervously around at the surrounding trees.

'According to his owner, he was in a peculiar mood as well.'

'Great!'

'So I suppose we should keep an eye out for both him and the lump of wood he hopefully took with him,' Tanner continued, following Vicky's fitful gaze.

'Yes, I suppose we should.'

A sudden snap from deep within the undergrowth had them both jumping around with a start.

'What was that?' Tanner whispered.

'How should I know?'

Falling silent, they both stared towards where they thought the sound had come from.

'I think it may be wise to get a dog handling team out here,' muttered Vicky, from the corner of her mouth. 'We may not have a psychotic serial killer on the loose, but a deranged Rottweiler could potentially present an even more hazardous scenario. Especially one who's recently acquired the taste of human flesh.'

Tanner glanced around to find her looking as if she was waiting for the gun to go off at the start of a two-hundred meter relay race. Realising he'd adopted a remarkably similar stance himself, he drew in a breath to stand up straight. 'It's a Rottweiler, Detective Inspector, not a Werewolf.'

'I wasn't aware there was much of a difference,' Vicky replied, 'Besides, do you have any idea how many people are killed by dogs in the UK each year?'

'I can't say that I do. Do you?'

'Well, no, but I bet it's more than one.'

'So, two then?'

A grim silence followed as they each took it in turns to stare at each other.

'I'll get a dog unit over here,' Tanner capitulated, reaching for his phone. 'Any idea where Cooper is?'

'The last time I saw him, he was leaning over that rather large chasm in the ground. With any luck, he lost his balance and fell in.'

'I doubt if it's wide enough.'

'Then he's probably still searching for that piece of wood, unless he found it, of course, caught between the jaws of the missing hound. With any luck, he's trying to pry it from its mouth as we speak.'

'I'm not sure he's that proactive. Anyway, if you see him, can you tell him to meet me at the carpark?'

'Which one?'

'The one everyone else seems to have gone to,' he continued, leaving her to begin ambling away.

'If that's where you're heading,' she called after him, 'then I think you'll find it's the other way.'

'I'm going to drive my car around. I also have some construction workers I need to keep an eye on, which reminds me,' he added, stopping to stare back at her. 'If you see a fleet of diggers bulldozing their way through the woods, do me a favour, will you?'

'What's that?'

'Stop them!'

'And just how am I supposed to do that?'

Tanner shrugged. 'You can try telling them that there's a deranged hound on the loose, one who's only very recently acquired the taste of human flesh. If that doesn't work, feel free to arrest them, or maybe you can tie yourself to a tree. Either way, we can't let them through. Not before our forensic bods have finished examining the scene.'

- CHAPTER SEVEN -

A S TANNER ENDEAVOURED to retrace his steps back to where he'd left his car, his mind was struggling to shake off the image of the dog that had discovered the body, in particular its bared teeth, the ones he could imagine glistening with the victim's blood, as it stalked him through the eerie silence of the surrounding woods.

Telling himself not to be so stupid, he shoved his hands deep into his old sailing jacket's pockets to try to make a more concerted effort to control his unusually over-active imagination. But the harder he tried *not* to think about it, the more he seemed unable to, leaving him staring fitfully about whenever he saw so much as a leaf twitch.

The snap of a branch directly behind him had him spinning around to stare dementedly back.

With nothing obvious in sight, he held his breath, listening intently as his heart pounded inside his heaving chest. 'Hello?' he called, cold sweat breaking out over his face and neck. 'Is anyone there?'

Remaining as still as a mouse, he continued to listen, only to see a large squirrel leap from the top of a tree.

'Jesus Christ!' he mumbled to himself, drawing in a faltering breath. 'What the hell is wrong with me?'

Shaking his head with self-condemnation, he turned to continue his journey, only to realise he'd somehow managed to stray off the path he thought he'd been following, and was now surrounded by shrubs and trees, closing in around him from every possible angle.

'How the hell did that happen?' he asked himself, staring wildly about in search of the path he'd somehow managed to lose.

Becoming increasingly disoriented, he spun around in a full circle, trying to work out which way he should have been going, when came the fleeting glimpse of a pretty young woman's face, watching him from behind a nearby tree.

Snatching his head back to where he thought he'd seen her, he stopped to stare. But there was nobody there, only an oval-shaped hole in the trunk of a silver birch tree.

'Am I losing my mind?' he questioned, blinking hard to stare again. He'd definitely seen a woman's face, and not just any woman, either. He could have sworn it was Jenny, the woman he'd fallen madly in love with when he'd first moved up to Norfolk, only to lose just a few weeks before they were due to be married.

Desperate to keep his mind focussed on the task at hand, to find his way back to his car, he gazed up towards the sky, wondering if he'd be able to at least work out which direction he needed to go in relation to the steadily rising sun. But that would only work if he knew if his car was north, south, east, or west of his current position, and unfortunately, he didn't have a clue.

The laughter of a girl, dancing in the air, had him whipping his head around to see the same woman's face again, this time flickering away between two distant trees. Telling himself it wasn't Jenny, no matter how much it may have looked like her, he took cold comfort in the fact that at least she wasn't a figment of his seemingly over-stretched imagination.

Thinking that whoever it was, she'd hopefully be able to direct him back to his car, he called out, 'Hey! Hold up!' only to see her pale beautiful face disappear again.

Stumbling after her, he called out once more, this time to be rewarded by the glimpse of her flowing dark hair, trailing behind her like billowing smoke.

Losing sight of her once more, he was on the verge of giving up when he saw a cottage up ahead, with cream coloured walls and a neatly thatched grey roof. Assuming it to be where the girl lived, he fought his way through the last of the tangled twigs to find himself stumbling out onto a freshly cut lawn surrounded by an abundance of blossoming flowers.

When he heard the same voice drift lazily towards him from one of the cottage's open lattice windows, he crept over the grass to stop outside and listen.

Bluebell Wood, a haunting sight,
Where darkness reigns throughout the night.
Stay close, my child, hold on tight,
Through Bluebell Wood, we tread with fright.

As the song begin to ebb slowly away, he leaned his head closer to the open window to peer cautiously through. Inside was a cosy, dimly lit kitchen with a series of pots and pans hanging from a rack above a clutter-free island. Noticing one of them rock gently to and fro, as if someone had only just hung it there, he called out again. 'Hello? Is anyone home?'

Remaining still, he listened to the sound of his voice reverberating through the cottage, as if it was nothing but an empty hollowed-out cave.

Forced to assume that whoever he'd heard had moved through to another room, he left the open window to look for another.

Then the voice came again, singing the same sad, but serenely beautiful song.

The slam of a door, ringing out from the front, had him leaping into a run.

Skirting around the cottage walls, he found himself scrabbling to a halt on a garden path, at the end of which was a pristine white picket fence. As a gate set within the fence began to swing gently closed, he sprinted to the end, leaping out onto the lane beyond to look desperately about.

But once again, there was nobody there.

Struggling to believe that whoever he'd heard could have disappeared so quickly, he turned back to the cottage to begin searching the windows for even the vaguest signs of life. But with the windows all firmly closed, and nothing more to be heard from anyone either inside or out, he was forced to assume that the place was empty.

'At least I've found a road,' he said to himself, just as something brushed against his leg.

Jumping with a start, he stared down to see the sleek black tail of a cat, curling itself around his calf. When a pair of sharp green eyes appeared from the other side, he crouched down to extend the back of his hand. 'Hello cat,' he said, allowing it to dab its nose against his extended fingers. 'Your owner seems to have abandoned us both.'

As the cat continued to loop itself around his legs, he stood back up to take in the lane again. 'I don't suppose there's any chance you know which way my car is?'

Hearing the cat meow, he glanced down to find it blinking unknowingly up at him.

'I'll take that as a no,' he replied, offering the animal an affable smile. 'Anyway, I'd better be off. If you want to go inside, I think you'll find the back window's been left open. Oh, and there's a dog loose in the woods, although you should be alright. Apparently, it's only interested in humans, their feet in particular.'

- CHAPTER EIGHT -

W ITH A PECULIAR, sickly-sweet taste lingering inside his mouth, Tanner reached the end of the lane to find himself standing beside a road only a few feet from where he'd left his XJS.

Giving himself a congratulatory pat on the back, he navigated his way past the thankfully still stationary diggers, then between two lines of slow moving cars, to eventually reach the other side, only for his head to start spinning like a top.

With a growing sense of nausea, he continued on to his car. There he took a steadying moment before tugging open the door.

Hoping to God that there wasn't something seriously wrong with him, he took a series of long deep breaths before levering himself down into the Jag's plush cream leather seat.

With both windows wound fully down, he remained there for a moment, his mind focussed on his breathing. Only when he felt his head had cleared sufficiently to be able to drive did he start the engine.

Grateful to be feeling better, he slotted the car into gear to head sedately out, joining the slow moving traffic to begin his search for the other carpark, the one that everyone seemed to have been directed to, everyone with the exception of him.

Ten minutes later, he rounded a corner to find the carpark he'd been looking for, the one where he'd interviewed the witness with the broken leg.

Spending a few minutes finding a suitable parking space, he opened the door to climb slowly out, only to come face-to-face with a tall skinny man, his greasy black hair tied loosely behind his head.

'Any comment for the Norfolk Herald?' the man demanded, shoving some sort of handheld recording device into his face.

'About what?' Tanner asked, turning away to close the door.

'About the body found hanging in Bluebell Wood?'

'How the...?' Tanner muttered, spinning around to find the reporter grinning at him. 'Never mind,' he sighed, shoving past both him and his recording device.

'Someone said you thought he may have been murdered?' the reporter called after him.

Tanner stopped dead in his tracks to pivot around. 'Who the hell told you that?'

'I'm sorry, Chief Inspector, but I can't reveal my sources.'

'I can't reveal my sources?' Tanner laughed, with mocking reproach. 'Anyone would think you'd just unearthed a story that was about to shake the walls of Parliament.'

'Sorry, was that a yes?'

'Was what a yes?'

'That you think he was murdered?'

'Listen, I don't know where you get your information from, Mr...?'

'Fletcher. Sidney Fletcher. But my friends call me Sid.'

'And you *have* friends, do you?'

The man smiled silently back.

'Anyway, Mr Fletcher, I'd very much appreciate it if you could have the decency to keep whatever you've been told to yourself, at least until we've had a chance to let the poor man's family know.'

'Does that mean you know who he is?'

Tanner shook his head to walk wearily away, only to see another person marching over the carpark towards him, a middle-aged man with a dark malevolent scowl creasing his orange, suntanned forehead.

'Are you the person who's supposed to be in charge?' the man demanded, removing his hands from his pockets to clench into white-knuckled fists.

'May I help you in some way?'

The man came stomping to a halt, his face just inches from Tanner's.

'My name's Simon Balinger. I assume you've heard of me?'

'Sorry, but is there some particular reason why I should have?'

'Probably because I'm reported as being the richest man in the whole of Norfolk!'

'Not by the Norfolk Herald, I hope,' Tanner replied, doing his best to keep a straight face.

'I understand you've been going around telling my men that they can't start work today because some idiot has decided to kill themselves in the middle of Bluebell Wood, an area of prime real estate, one that I just happen to own.'

'You mean, you own the whole thing?' Tanner questioned, gazing with derisive astonishment at the tops of the trees. 'Wow! That really is very impressive. Congratulations!'

'I don't want your congratulations, Mr...'

'Detective Chief Inspector Tanner,' Tanner replied. 'Perhaps you've heard of me?'

'Why the hell should I have heard of you?'

'I suppose that depends on how much time you've spent inside?'

'If "inside" you mean prison, surprisingly enough, I've never had the opportunity.'

'Oh, right. Sorry. A little bird told me that you were moving your bulldozers in without bothering to wait for the necessary planning permission, so I assumed that such illegal conduct was just your way of doing business.'

'May I ask which little bird that was?'

'Unfortunately, I'm not at liberty to say.'

'Well, you can tell whoever it was that I *do* have the necessary planning permission, and that I have had since Monday.'

'Do you have the paperwork on you, by any chance? It's just that she seemed adamant that it was still going through the public consultancy phase.'

Balinger's eyes darted between Tanner's. 'A *she, was it?*'

Tanner mentally kicked himself for having given away the law student's gender. 'Is that your attempt at changing the subject?' he countered, taking consolation in the fact that he'd still left half the population for him to consider.

'Not at all. I have the paperwork right here,' Balinger said, offering Tanner a conniving smile as he pulled out an official-looking document from the depths of his coat. 'As you can see,' he continued, unfolding it to show him the local council's crest emblazoned in the top corner, and an elaborate signature at the bottom, 'it's been signed by Councillor Jeremy Southcott, no less.'

Tanner briefly examined its contents. 'May I have a copy?'

'You can have this one, if you like?'

Tanner shook his head to dig out one of his business cards. 'Something on email would be fine. The address is at the bottom.'

'I'll have my secretary send one over when I get back to my office.'

'Which is where, may I ask?'

'I'll have her include that in the email, together with the rest of my contact details.'

'Much appreciated, but unfortunately, none of this means you'll be able to start work today.'

Balinger took a belligerent moment to fix Tanner's eyes. 'Do you have any idea when we *will* be able to?'

'Unfortunately, it's too early to say. If we're able to conclude that the method of his death is how it would appear, then maybe tomorrow.'

'Is there any reason for you to think otherwise?'

'No reason in particular,' Tanner replied, his mind harking back to the assumed missing piece of wood, and the dog he was fast concluding must have taken it. 'Out of curiosity, does the planning permission extend to the cottage?'

Balinger stared over at him with a look of curious bemusement. 'Yes, of course! Why? Don't tell me a body's been found there as well.'

'No, but...don't you think it would be wise to wait for the people living there to move out first?'

'Forgive me, Chief Inspector, but what on earth are you talking about?'

'The people living there,' Tanner repeated, 'or at least the one I saw. Wouldn't it be advisable to make sure that they're safely relocated *before* moving the bulldozers in?'

'Unless you're referring to some homeless drunk, I think you'll find the place has long been empty.'

'I can assure you that the young woman I saw was neither homeless nor drunk.'

'Then she's probably one of those bloody tree-hugging activists.'

'To be honest, she looked more like the daughter of some particularly house-proud parents.'

'I'm sorry, Chief Inspector, you've completely lost me.'

'The house, where I saw her,' Tanner continued, becoming as confused as the man standing in front of him. 'I've rarely seen such a fine example of an English country cottage.'

'Er...I think you may need to check yourself in for some psychological counselling. The cottage you're referring to burnt down over five years ago. To the best of my knowledge, nobody has lived there since, nor would they want to.'

- CHAPTER NINE -

B EGINNING TO WONDER if he really was losing his mind, Tanner cast his eyes absently around the carpark, trying to remember what he was doing there, and perhaps more importantly, what he was supposed to be doing next.

Spying Cooper out of the corner of his eye, laughing with someone just out of view, he was reminded that he'd asked Vicky to tell him to meet him there. Hoping, somewhat optimistically, that he'd been able to find the piece of evidence that would enable the incident to be written up as suicide, Tanner bounded over, only to find the person Cooper was joking with was the reporter from the Norfolk Herald, the very same one that he'd been trying so hard to ignore only a few minutes earlier.

'Sorry to interrupt,' he began, clearing his throat.

The sound of Tanner's voice had Cooper spinning around, a look of surprised guilt stamped all over his face. 'Er...no problem, boss. Sid and I were just chatting.'

'So I can see,' Tanner continued, taking in the two of them. 'I don't suppose you'd be willing to share the joke?'

'I'd better leave you to it,' mumbled Fletcher, shaking Cooper's hand. 'We must catch up properly next time,' he added, before slinking quietly away.

'Do you mind telling me what that was all about?'

Tanner demanded, the moment the reporter was out of earshot.

'What *what* was all about?'

'You do know who that was, don't you?'

'Of Course. Sid Fletcher. We went to school together.'

'Did you know that he now works as a reporter for the Norfolk Herald?'

'Well, yes, but we weren't talking about anything work related.'

'Then what *were* you talking about?'

'Er...I'm sorry, but if you don't mind me asking, what's that got to do with you?'

'In case you'd forgotten, Cooper, you're a detective inspector working for Norfolk CID, and that you're currently investigating a possible murder.'

'I thought we'd concluded that it was suicide?'

'Did you find what you were supposed to be looking for?'

'You mean; a piece of wood, left somewhere in the middle of one?'

'I take it that means you didn't?'

'Sadly, no.'

'Did you even try?'

'As much as I felt it was necessary to, although I'm fairly sure I've got better things to do, other than to go crawling around on my hands and knees, looking for some random piece of wood, one that I had zero chance of ever finding.'

'Like staring gormlessly up at a hanging corpse with your hands shoved down into your pockets, or explaining the ins-and-outs of our current on-going investigation to your brand new best friend, a reporter from the Norfolk Herald?'

'It can hardly be described as an "on-going investigation". I mean, anyone with half a brain knows the guy killed himself.'

'And what if he didn't?'

Cooper shrugged. 'Whether he did or didn't, finding the piece of wood he used to support himself with is hardly going to prove it either way.'

'I think you're missing the point.'

'Am I?'

Tanner took a moment to draw in a calming breath. 'Can you at least promise not to disclose any information about the investigation to anyone working for the media, even if that person does happen to be one of your old school chums?'

'I'm not a complete moron!'

With Tanner thinking the exact opposite, he turned away to see Townsend's modest Vauxhall Corsa turning into the carpark's entrance.

Curious to know why he'd driven over, and more than happy to leave Cooper to whatever it was that he *wasn't* doing, he ambled over to wait beside the space Townsend was already reversing into.

'What are you doing here?' he eventually asked, in an affable tone, as Townsend climbed slowly out.

'Cooper called me, asking if I could help him to find some missing evidence. Something about a needle in a haystack?'

'It was probably more like a piece of hay in a haystack,' Tanner muttered.

'Huh?'

'Never mind. So, what are you doing now?'

'Er...I thought I just said.'

'I think Cooper's busy enough helping himself,' Tanner replied, staring over the carpark to where Cooper could now be seen chatting to an attractive female police officer.

'Does that mean he found it?'

'It means he couldn't be arsed to start looking.'

'I'm happy to have a go, if you think it would help?'

'Unfortunately, in this particular instance, I think Cooper is probably right. Even if we were able to find it, I'm not entirely sure it would make much of a difference.'

'What was it he was supposed to be looking for?'

'Whatever it was the victim used to stand on before hanging himself.'

'Am I safe to assume that there is some doubt that he did?'

'Well, yes, but only because whatever he used wasn't there when we arrived, but that could be down to the dog who found him. Anyway, it doesn't alter the fact that I now have the delightful task of telling the boy's parents that their son's body has been found hanging in the middle of Bluebell Wood.'

A grim silence followed as Tanner glanced vacantly about, half-hoping to see someone looking to speak to him. But nobody was.

With Townsend standing quietly beside him, he dug out his phone to check for messages. But the only one he had was an email from Sally, giving him the name and address of the victim's parents. 'How's that girlfriend of yours?'

'Which one?'

'What do you mean, which one?'

Townsend folded his arms to lean pensively back against his car. 'I'm thinking about asking Gina out.'

Tanner put his phone away to stare at Townsend instead. 'But – what about Sally?'

'We broke up.'

'Oh, right. I'm sorry to hear that. You seemed to be getting on really well.'

'We were.'

'So – what happened.'

'We had an argument.'

'Yes, and...?'

'And...we broke up.'

'Because you had an argument?'

'Why else?'

'Er...because you'd come to realise that, over the course of your relationship, you had a number of irreconcilable differences that made it impossible for you to remain together.'

'She was my girlfriend, not my wife!'

'Even so, you don't break up with someone just because you have an argument. If that was the case, nobody would make it past their wedding night.'

'As I said, she was just my girlfriend.'

Reminding himself that he was Townsend's boss, not his dad, Tanner closed his mouth, only to re-open it again a moment later. 'I thought Gina had a boyfriend. Actually, from what Vicky told me, I thought she was engaged.'

'They're not engaged,' came Townsend's taciturn response.

'But she does have a boyfriend, though?'

Townsend fell into a brooding silence.

'May I ask what the argument was about?' Tanner cautiously asked, mindful of the boundaries marking their own relationship.

'I can't remember.'

'Really?'

Townsend let out a petulant sigh. 'She wanted to go shopping, to help find me a new suit, but the rugby was on. England versus the All Blacks.'

'Er...I think you'll find that most women would rather go shopping than to watch the rugby, even if it is England versus the All Blacks.'

'I s'pose,' shrugged Townsend. 'I told her I couldn't afford a new suit anyway.'

'Is that your way of asking for a pay rise?'

'Why, can I have one?'

'Fat chance!'

'Gee, thanks.'

'No problem.'

Smiling briefly at each other, Tanner joined Townsend in leaning back against the car. 'Whoever you end up being with,' he eventually continued, 'you'll soon come to the realisation that one of the main ingredients to a successful relationship is compromise. No two people are ever-so much alike that they always want the same things. Certainly not at the same times.'

Townsend shrugged again.

'Anyway, that's enough of all that. How about helping me with some good old fashioned police work?'

'What did you have in mind?'

'As I mentioned before, I need to inform the victim's parents about what's happened to their son.'

'If it's all the same to you, I think I'd rather stay here with Cooper.'

'I take it you've never had the joyful task of breaking the news to someone that one of their children has been found dead.'

'Thankfully not! Nor would I ever want to!'

'You will have to at some point. Unfortunately, it's part of the job, and now's a good as time as any to have a go.'

'Not seriously?'

'OK, perhaps not today. But there's no harm in you coming along, if for no other reason than to see just how badly a seasoned professional does it.'

- CHAPTER TEN -

REACHING THE FRONT door of a small, semi-detached house at the end of a quiet cul-de-sac on the outskirts of Stalham, Tanner rang the doorbell to stand back beside Townsend. 'OK, now, the boy's parents' names are Peter and Margaret Brogan.'

'Got it,' Townsend replied, nervously adjusting his tie.

With the sound of movement from inside the house, Tanner turned to face him. 'Now, remember what I said back at the carpark. No matter who opens the door, we're about to tell them that their son has been found hanging by his neck in the middle of Bluebell Wood, so under absolutely no circumstances are you to be anything other than the model of respectful remorse.'

'Understood!'

'Even if it's the wife who answers the door, and she turns out to be some famous celebrity who's in the middle of doing some sort of risqué fashion shoot for Playboy.'

'As I said, I understand.'

'I'm only saying this because of what happened last time,' Tanner muttered, listening to the rattle of the door's security chain.

'Can we just get on with it?'

'And don't forget to let me do all the talking.'

'Yes, I know!'

As the door was pulled open, Tanner let out a sigh of relief as a very normal-looking middle-aged woman's face appeared cautiously out from the other side. 'Mrs Margaret Brogan?' he enquired, pulling out his formal ID.

'Yes?'

'DCI Tanner, and my colleague, DC Townsend, Norfolk Police.'

'Oh, right,' she replied, her eyes darting between them with nervous apprehension. 'There's nothing wrong, I hope?'

'Is your husband in?'

'He isn't. Why?'

'Do you know when he'll be back?'

'Er...in about three months.'

'Oh, I see,' Tanner replied, glancing with awkward curiosity at Townsend. 'Does that mean he's currently in – in...?'

'He's in Dubai!' the woman stated, glaring out at Tanner with a look of abject horror. 'He's a structural engineer! He's working on a new-build project out there!'

'Of course he is. Forgive me. Is it alright if we step inside for a moment?'

Mrs Brogan planted her hands down on her hips to take up a defiant stance. 'I'd rather know what it was about, first.'

'I'm afraid we have news regarding your son.'

'He's not in any trouble, I hope?'

'If we could come inside?'

'Whatever it is that you *think* he's done, Inspector, I'd appreciate it if you could stop beating about the bush and tell me.'

Tanner glanced fitfully back at Townsend before returning his attention to the woman. 'At approximately eight o'clock this morning, the body of a young man was found in Bluebell Wood. With the deepest regret, it's our unfortunate belief that it is your son, Samuel Brogan.'

The woman's eyes shifted blankly between the two detectives. 'I'm sorry,' she eventually said, slowly shaking her head, 'but – you must be mistaken. Samuel is at college. He should be back any minute now, if you don't believe me.'

'I'm afraid your son's driving licence was found inside his wallet. We've yet to make a formal identification, but the likeness of the photograph is enough for us to be confident that it is him.'

As the colour began to drain from her otherwise emotionless face, Tanner waited for her to blink before continuing. 'Would it be possible to tell us when you saw him last?'

Glancing down at her watch, she gazed expectantly over Tanner's shoulder. 'Last night, before he went to bed, but I did hear him get up this morning.'

'And what time was that?'

'Just before six.'

'In the morning?' Tanner queried, surprised by the hour.

Still staring anxiously over at the cul-de-sac's entrance, Mrs Brogan nodded her head. 'He's doing his 'A' Levels in Norwich. It takes him nearly an hour to get in every day, which is why he has to get up so early.'

'And you say he should be back any minute now?'

'That's correct.'

'He's not late?'

The woman's bottom lip quivered for the briefest of moments before lifting her chin. 'Perhaps, but only a little.'

Tanner glanced surreptitiously around at

Townsend. 'Would it be possible to ask about your son's state of mind?'

'I beg your pardon?' she demanded, her face flecking with colour.

'Nothing's been upsetting him recently?'

'Not recently, no.'

'But something has in the past?'

Mrs Brogan partially opened her mouth before her eyes sank slowly to the ground. 'He had a difficult childhood,' she eventually replied, 'but he's alright now.'

'May I ask in what way?'

Another hesitant pause followed. 'His parents abandoned him when he was just a baby.'

A confused frown dented Tanner's brow. 'But – I thought you were his...?'

'We're his *adoptive* parents,' she replied, lifting her head with a proud look in her eyes. 'The surname always changes during such a process, as per the adoption certificate.'

'Yes, of course. May I ask what his surname was before?'

'Pickford, originally.'

Tanner glanced again at Townsend to thankfully see him taking notes.

'But you should probably know that we're not his first foster parents,' the woman continued.

Tanner briefly raised an eyebrow.

'There was another, before us,' she added.

'How long was he with them for?'

'Until he was fourteen.'

'What happened then?'

'He left them to live with us,' came her curt response.

'Was there any particular reason why?'

The woman shook her head, as if remembering

something she would have preferred to have forgotten. 'They weren't very nice to him, that's why.'

'May I ask in what way?'

'No, you may not. Besides, it was all a very long time ago.'

'But something *did* happen. Something that may have had a negative impact on his current state of mind?'

'Forgive me, but what, may I ask, has any of this got to do with you turning up unannounced on our doorstep?'

'I'm very sorry to have to say this, Mrs Brogan, but it's our current belief that your son may have taken his own life.'

'And that's another reason why whoever it is you've found *isn't* my son! After a number of very difficult years, Sammy has finally found happiness in his life. I subsequently find it quite impossible to believe that he'd choose *now* to be the time to do something as horrific as that.'

'Yes, of course. But, for the sake of argument, what if something had happened to him more recently. Something that perhaps you weren't aware of?'

'He'd have told me if anything had.'

'Are you sure about that?'

'Absolutely!'

'Maybe something at college?'

'He's an A star student, with an offer to read Computer Programming at Cambridge.'

'Then exam pressure, perhaps?'

'He's never had a single problem passing exams, at least not since he started living with us.'

'What about girls?'

'What about them?'

'Has he been involved in a relationship recently?'

'He has,' she nodded, 'but its only had a positive

impact.'

'Does this person have a name?'

'Tara. Tara Lowe.'

'I don't suppose you know where she lives, by any chance?'

'Somewhere along Rectory Road. I don't know where, exactly, but as I said before, he'll be home soon, at which point you'll be able to ask him yourself.'

Offering her an apologetic smile, Tanner glanced down at his watch. 'Unfortunately, we need to be getting on, but here, let me give you my business card.'

'What would I want your business card for?' she questioned, taking it anyway.

'If you could give me a call when he does show up?' he smiled.

'If I must.'

About to leave, Tanner turned hesitantly back. 'Oh, just one more thing. I don't suppose you know of anyone who may have wished Samuel harm, at all?'

'What?'

'He didn't owe anyone any money, or anything?'

Mrs Brogan fixed Tanner's eyes with a demented look of furious rage. 'First you come here to tell me that my son was so unhappy with his life here with us that he killed himself. Now you're trying to tell me that he was murdered. I suggest you *do* leave, Mr Tanner, before I come down to the station myself to report the two of you for harassing me!'

- CHAPTER ELEVEN -

W ITH THE DOOR being slammed closed whilst they were still standing in front of it, Townsend leaned his head slowly in towards Tanner's. 'That went well,' he eventually said, doing his best not to laugh.

'I thought so,' Tanner replied, pivoting around to lead them back to his car.

'I assume you're still of the opinion that someone may have had a hand in her son's death?'

'Yes, but only because the victim didn't sound like he was mentally imbalanced enough to have taken his own life.'

'That's according to his mum, though?'

'Maybe so, but from my own experience, teenage suicide victims tend not to be quite so motivated. Most spend the days leading up to the moment they decide to end it all by doing nothing more productive than watching endless hours of daytime television. It would certainly be unusual for them to be getting up at six o'clock every morning to go to college, knowing that they had a place waiting for them at Cambridge University.'

'But only if he got the required grades.'

Tanner shrugged. 'It didn't sound like that was going to be much of a problem.'

'Maybe he wasn't doing as well as she thought he was?'

'Perhaps.'

'Or maybe it was someone else, and her son *is* currently making his way back from college? She certainly seemed fairly convinced that it *wasn't* him.'

'Yes, but can you blame her? Imagine if you were called to the front door of your house to hear the news that one of your children had just been found dead?'

'Thankfully, that wouldn't be possible. For a start, I don't have children, and secondly...'

'You live in a flat,' sighed Tanner.

'Correct!'

'I used the word "imagine" on purpose, Townsend. You do still have the ability to call upon that most precious gift only the human species is known to possess?'

'Of course,' he smirked. 'Even more so now that I'm single.'

Tanner glanced surreptitiously over at him before rolling his eyes to look quickly away.

'Anyway,' he heard Townsend continue, 'as I said, what if it wasn't him?'

'You're proposing that I've just gone and told the wrong person that her son is dead?'

'It can't have been the first time.'

'The photograph on his driver's licence was too close a resemblance for it not to have been him.'

'That doesn't mean it was, though.'

'Well, no, but...'

'So...wasn't it a little presumptuous of you to go around telling her that her son is dead, when we're not one-hundred percent sure that it was even him?'

Cupping his hand under the Jag's chrome door handle, Tanner lifted his eyes to meet the young detective constable's contemptuous gaze. 'I think you're allowing yourself to fall into the same psychological trap that the victim's mother did.'

'What's that?'

'That if someone doesn't want to believe something, then it's easy enough to convince themselves that it isn't true, no matter what the evidence is that they're presented with. And I can assure you, being told that either your son or daughter is dead is *definitely* something you wouldn't want to believe. Anyway, we'll soon find out, either way. Meanwhile, whilst waiting to hear if her son *does* come back from college, we may as well see if we can have a chat with that girlfriend of his.'

'Does that mean I can come with you?'

'I'm not sure that I have much of a choice, being that we left your car back at the carpark. However,' he continued, turning to fix his eyes, 'if she turns out to be an attractive young lady, and it becomes obvious that you're unable to control your hormones, I'll be telling you to wait in the car.'

'Don't worry. I'll be fine. Even if she does turn out to be drop-dead gorgeous, I'd only be looking to take down her particulars.'

'Right, that's it. I'm taking you back to the carpark. I'm sure Cooper can't wait to have an in-depth chat to you about last night's football match.'

'No, please, don't!'

'Then you'll have to promise to be on your best behaviour.'

'Scout's honour!'

Tanner narrowed his eyes at him.

'Yes – I promise!'

'OK, good.'

'But what if she wants to take down *my* particulars?'

'Don't worry, she won't.'

'She might!' he grinned.

'Then I suggest we cross that bridge when we come

to it. Meanwhile, we'd better see if we can find her address.'

- CHAPTER TWELVE -

HAVING FOUND THE victim's girlfriend's address, Tanner was soon turning into the driveway of a far more impressive property, with high, red-bricked walls and a sloping, slate-grey roof.

'Looks like they've got some money,' Townsend observed, sitting up in the passenger seat to gawp at it through the windscreen.

'I wouldn't get your hopes up,' Tanner replied, following his subordinate's gaze.

'About what?'

'That the victim's girlfriend is rich, or at least that her parents are.'

'What makes you think they aren't?'

'It's a rental.'

'What is?'

'The house.'

Townsend stared over at him. 'Why do you think it's a rental?'

'Er...I think the rather large "Let By" sign was a bit of a giveaway. The one we drove past on the way in?'

'Oh, right,' Townsend replied, glancing behind them. 'I didn't see it.'

'That's probably because you didn't look, Townsend, at least not with your eyes.'

'It doesn't mean they're not rich, though.'

'If it wasn't for the car, I'd probably agree with

you.'

Seeing Townsend stare blindly about, Tanner directed his attention to a dark green Vauxhall Astra, parked under one of the large overhanging trees, one that had at least three flat tyres and didn't look like it had been washed in years.

'Maybe they're just not into their cars?'

'Maybe,' Tanner mused, parking his own alongside it. 'Anyway, remember what I said,' he continued, turning off the engine.

'Yes, I know. To stand next to you like a brainless moron whilst you do all the talking.'

'Correct!' Tanner stated, climbing cheerfully out.

Waiting for Townsend, he took a moment to cast his eyes over the seemingly abandoned car, thinking to himself that it was a shame to just leave it there to rot. He then turned his attention to the house, in particular the moss covering its walls, its grimy double-glazed windows, and the broken guttering that could be seen hanging from the edge of the roof.

Hearing Townsend behind him, he led the way up to the grandiose wooden front door to peel off a piece of flaking varnish. About to press the faded plastic bell, the sound of a car had them glancing around.

Turning into the drive was an ancient beige-coloured Mini, with an attractive young lady peering out at them from behind its over-sized steering wheel.

With the car grinding to a halt in front of them, Tanner gave Townsend a cautionary look before stepping briskly over. By the time he'd fished out his ID, he found himself staring into the large brown eyes of an attractive young woman, one who he instantly recognised.

'What are you doing here?' the woman demanded, hauling a cumbersome carpet bag up onto her shoulder. 'Please don't tell me you've come to arrest me?'

'You live here, do you?' Tanner responded, as surprised to see her as she was to see him.

'Not really. I just stopped by to see if they had anything worth stealing.'

'I take it you two know each other?' Townsend interjected, his eyes dancing grudgingly between them.

'We met earlier today,' said Tanner, his attention remaining on the woman. 'I'm sorry, but I don't seem able to remember your name.'

'That's probably because you didn't bother to ask.'

'And that was probably because I was too busy trying to stop you from beating up some poor, honest, law-abiding workman.'

'I was the one who was about to be beaten up!'

'It didn't look that way from where I was standing.'

'Anyway,' she continued, tilting her head at him, 'you haven't answered my question.'

'Sorry, what question was that?'

'Have you come here to arrest me?'

'What on earth for?'

'I've no idea. I suppose I just assumed that Mr "I'm the Richest Man in the Whole of Norfolk" had made some sort of complaint against me.'

'You mean, Mr Balinger?'

'That's the one.'

'Not that I'm aware of.'

'Then why are you here?'

Tanner glanced around at Townsend before taking up a more professional stance. 'Am I correct in thinking that your name is Tara Lowe?'

The young woman's eyes narrowed with cautionary suspicion.

'I'm only asking your name?'

'OK, yes, that's me. Why do you want to know?'

'You wouldn't happen to know a young man called Samuel Brogan, by any chance?'

'Sammy? Of course! Why? Is he OK?'

'We've just been speaking to his mother. She mentioned your name to us.'

'Oh…right. I'm not sure why she would have done that.'

'She seemed to think that the two of you were some sort of an item.'

The young woman's eyes flickered briefly at Townsend. 'She told you Sammy is my boyfriend?'

'She did.'

'Well, I've no idea why she thought that. Don't get me wrong. He's nice enough, just a little too young for me.'

'But you are friends, though?'

'Well, yes, but nothing more.'

'May I ask when you saw him last?'

'At the weekend. We went to a protest march in London together, along with some of my other friends.'

'May I ask how he was?'

'How he was?' she repeated.

'His state of mind. Did he seem OK to you?'

'What's happened?' she demanded, the skin around her mouth tightening.

'Regretfully,' Tanner began, holding her eyes, 'the body of someone meeting Samuel's description was found in the early hours of the morning.'

'You mean he's…he's…?'

'From the evidence found at the scene, it would appear that he took his own life.'

Tanner waited in muted silence for her to say something in response, but she didn't say anything at all. She just continued staring at him. 'Do you know if anything had happened to him recently that may have led him to do such a thing?'

As her eyes began filling up with tears, Tara finally blinked. 'No – at least – nothing specific.'

'But...you don't seem too surprised that he did?'

'We all knew he'd been struggling.'

'With anything in particular?'

'College, mainly.'

Tanner looked again at Townsend. 'But...his mother seemed to think he'd been doing really well, and that he was all set to go to Cambridge.'

'He only applied to Cambridge because his parents wanted him to, his mother in particular. They both seemed to have expectations for him to become some sort of computer programmer.'

'Didn't he want to be?'

'God no! He wanted to be a poet.'

'A *poet?*' Tanner repeated, unable to hide his incredulity.

'Or maybe an actor. Certainly not someone who had to sit behind a bloody computer all day. He's far too creative for that.'

'Did his parents know?'

'I've no idea. He said he'd told them, but I was never convinced he actually had.'

'And you think that would have been reason enough for him to take his own life?'

Tara's eyes drifted to the ground. 'Do you know anything about what happened to him, when he was young?'

'Only that he was put up for foster care when he was a baby. Also, that something unpleasant happened under the charge of his first foster parents. His mother seemed reluctant to tell us exactly what.'

'Then I probably shouldn't, either.'

'If it would help us to understand his state of mind, then we'd appreciate it if you could.'

Tara lifted her eyes. 'I'm not surprised his mum didn't tell you. It really isn't very nice.'

'Go on.'

'I don't know the details. All I know is that he was physically abused.'

'By his original foster parents?'

Tara shook her head. 'Not by them, although that would have been bad enough.'

'If not them, then who?' Tanner asked, struggling to understand what she was trying to say.

Her eyes drifted into Tanner's before darting quickly away. 'I don't know if it's true or not, although I can't imagine why anyone would make such a thing up, but according to what I found out on the internet, his original foster parents...' She stopped mid-sentence with a look of uncomfortable disgust.

Tanner's heart went out to her. 'You don't have to tell us if you don't want to.'

'It's OK,' she replied. 'I was always telling Sammy that he needed to talk more about what happened to him as part of the healing process. I'd be a hypocrite if I couldn't do the same myself.'

Tanner waited in silence for her to continue.

'From what I understand, they used to rent him out,' she eventually said.

'Jesus Christ!'

'They were eventually caught, but not before Sammy had been through five years of living hell.'

Tanner stared silently over at Townsend to see his pen hovering hesitantly over his notebook, as if unwilling to write down what the woman had said.

'May I ask how he...how he...?' came Tara's softy spoken voice, as if drifting towards them from some distant shore.

'Is it important?' he heard himself ask.

'No, I suppose it isn't.'

Seeing the despondent look on her face, Tanner took a reflective moment to try and decide if he should tell her or not. 'He hanged himself,' he eventually said, 'from a tree in the middle of Bluebell Wood.'

'Bluebell Wood?' Tara repeated, catching his eye with a questioning frown.

'Is the location relevant?'

'No, at least... You do know that we've been trying to stop that development for months.'

'I gathered as much from our first encounter.'

'But – did you know Sammy had been helping us?'

Tanner shifted his stance. 'May I ask in what capacity?'

'I – I shouldn't say.'

'Oh, I really think you should.'

Tara began fidgeting with her fingers. 'Are you sure about Sammy – about what he did to himself?'

'We're about as sure as we can be.'

'It's just that – I don't want to get him in any trouble, or anything.'

'Under the circumstances, I think that would be difficult.'

'I – I really shouldn't be saying this.'

'I wasn't aware you had said anything. At least not yet.'

'We, as in my friends and I, we were wondering if there might have been something dodgy going on between the local council and that Balinger guy.'

'What made you think there was?'

'His reputation. That, and because it was fairly obvious that the application's approval process was being deliberately fast-tracked. That was when Sammy offered his services to us.'

'And what "services" were those, may I ask?' Tanner questioned, with growing curiosity.

Tara glanced surreptitiously over her shoulder, as if half-expecting to see someone standing behind her with a recording device. 'It was what he considered himself to be best at. It was also the reason why he'd managed to get himself three "A stars" for his mocks, without doing a single hour of revision. It was also why he had an offer from Cambridge.'

'Because of his computer programming skills?'

'Sort of.'

'I think what she's trying to say,' interjected Townsend, taking the opportunity to catch Tara's eye, 'was that he was a computer hacker.'

'Is that true?' Tanner demanded.

'He called it his "little hobby",' Tara nodded.

'So, you asked him to hack into the local council's computer system, to see if there was anything suspicious going on?'

'Not exactly.'

'What do you mean, not exactly?'

'He offered to.'

'And you agreed?'

'Well, we didn't say he should. But then again, I'm not sure we said he shouldn't, either,' she replied, offering Tanner a devious smile.

'You do know that computer hacking is illegal, don't you?'

'Is it?'

'As is aiding and abetting.'

'What are you going to do, arrest me and half my friends for omitting to tell a teenage computer hacker that he probably shouldn't take a look inside the local council's mainframe computer system, when he'd already said he would?'

Tanner held Tara's eyes with a disapproving scowl.

'Anyway, don't you want to know what he found?'

'I'm not sure it matters,' Tanner said, glancing

away with a look of supercilious indifference. 'Whatever it was, it can't be used as evidence.'

'I take it that's a no, then?'

'You can tell *me*, if you like,' said Townsend, offering her a smile that was as affable as it was flirtatious.

'He discovered that Mr Balinger had paid the councillor in charge of new build applications the hefty sum of one-hundred thousand pounds.'

'And he found that out by hacking into the local council's mainframe computer, did he?' queried Tanner, re-engaging himself in the conversation.

'That was actually from taking a look inside Mr Balinger's personal bank account.'

'You must be joking!'

'I said he was good.'

Shaking his head, Tanner stopped for a moment to consider the implications of what she'd told them. 'Do you think Balinger knew that he'd had his bank account hacked into?'

'I'd be surprised if he didn't.'

'How come?'

'Because Sammy was stupid enough to send him an email, telling him he had. Also, what he'd found, including evidence in the form of a screen grab of the transaction in question.'

'I must admit, I'd have to agree with you. That *was* stupid.'

'He also said he'd be sending the same screen grab to you – the police – if he didn't withdraw his application for the Bluebell Wood development.'

'Jesus Christ! Had he completely lost his mind?'

'Very possibly. As I said before, he was pretty screwed up.'

'The question is,' Tanner continued, gazing wistfully off into the distance, 'was he screwed up enough to take his own life?'

'I don't know,' Tara responded, 'but if he did, I'm not sure why he'd have chosen to do so in the middle of Bluebell Wood. Knowing how private he was, I'd have thought it more likely that he'd have done so in the seclusion of his own home.'

'Choosing somewhere away from home is surprisingly normal, being that most suicide victims don't wish to be found by their parents.'

'Or maybe Balinger was responsible,' Tara continued, 'and the location was chosen for a very specific reason.'

'And what reason could that have been?'

'To send the rest of us a message – to stop interfering with his illegally acquired building development plans.'

- CHAPTER THIRTEEN -

NOT ARRIVING HOME until gone eight o'clock that evening, Tanner nudged open the front door of his riverside bungalow to hear Christine's voice, singing out to him amidst the chaotic clatter of an unidentifiable number of pots and pans.

'I'm in the kitchen!'

'Yes, I know,' he mumbled to himself, ditching his keys on the hallway table to make his way through to the main living area.

'Hungry?' she asked, examining the contents of the fridge.

'Starving!'

'Are you happy with what you had yesterday?'

'Er...what did I have yesterday?'

Lugging out a bowl, its contents covered with clingfilm, she took a moment to glare over at him with a look of incredulous contempt. 'You mean, you can't remember?'

'Er...' he began, regretting having basically admitted as much. 'I remember I liked it!' he exclaimed, extending to her an amenable smile.

'It was your favourite, if that helps.'

'Yes, of course! Shepherd's Pie!'

'No, it wasn't!'

'I could have sworn it was,' Tanner replied, with a look of befuddled confusion.

'It was Cottage Pie,' Christine corrected.

'Oh, right. Sorry, but what was the difference again?'

'I told you last night.'

'Er...'

Christine shook her head. 'One's made with lamb, the other beef.'

'And Shepherd's Pie is the one made with beef?'

'Why would Shepherd's Pie be the one made with beef?'

'Um...because it's a well-known fact that shepherds love eating hamburgers, which are made predominantly of beef?'

'Or, alternatively,' said Christine, in a chastising tone, 'Shepherds look after sheep, which is why Shepherd's Pie is made with lamb.'

'So...why is Cottage Pie named after a small house, one that's more often than not found lurking within the depths of the picturesque British countryside?'

'Do you want it or not?' she demanded, one hand holding the plate, the other the microwave door's handle.

'Yes please!'

'OK, but on one condition.'

'What's that?'

'That you make some sort of a concerted effort to remember the difference between a Cottage Pie and a Shepherd's Pie. I can't have my friends over to listen to you make such an embarrassing faux pas. They'll all think you're a complete moron.'

'And they don't already?'

Keeping her mouth firmly closed, Christine opened the door to shove the plate inside.

'Good to know,' Tanner said quietly to himself, propping himself up against the breakfast bar to pour himself a rum. 'Speaking of cottages, I saw a particularly nice one today, or at least I thought I did.'

'What do you mean, you thought you did?'

'It was in the middle of Bluebell Wood.'

About to attack the washing up, Christine looked at him with a bemused expression. 'There isn't a cottage in the middle of Bluebell Wood!'

'That's what someone else told me, only a few minutes after I'd seen it, which is why I was left questioning if I had, or it was merely a figment of my over-worked imagination.'

'You haven't started drinking at work, I hope?'

'Not yet,' he replied, downing the glass's contents.

'Anyway, what were you doing in the middle of Bluebell Wood?'

Tanner poured himself another glass before drifting over to the sofa, his eyes hunting for the TV's remote. 'A body was found there this morning.'

'Oh, right,' came Christine's somewhat apprehensive response. 'I hope that doesn't mean...?'

Tanner knew what she was thinking; about their wedding on Saturday, and the honeymoon they'd planned afterwards. 'At the moment, we're considering it to be suicide.'

'But...you're not sure?'

Finding the remote, Tanner turned on the TV to begin searching the channels for the news. 'One minute I am, the next minute I hear something that has me thinking otherwise.'

'Are you able to go into detail?'

Finding the channel he was looking for, he muted the sound to look back at her. 'The victim was a young man. He was found hanging by his neck by a guy out walking his dog.'

'I'm sorry to hear that,' came Christine's remorseful response. 'Do you know who he is?'

Tanner nodded. 'I had the delightful task of telling

the victim's mother.'

'How did that go?'

'Better than I was expecting, but only because she refused to believe me.'

'That's quite normal.'

'Agreed! But what wasn't quite so normal was that whatever the victim used to support himself with was missing, and looks likely to remain so.'

'How come?'

'Our current thinking is that the dog who found him made off with it.'

'But you still think there's a chance he was killed?'

'The boy's mother was adamant that he was a particularly well balanced individual, who was doing exceptionally well at college, and had an offer to study Computer Programming at Cambridge. However, one of his friends said the exact opposite; that he was desperate *not* to go to Cambridge to study Computer Programming, and wanted to be a poet instead.'

'A *poet?*'

'That was my response.'

'I'm beginning to see your problem.'

'Unfortunately, there's more. The girl who his mother thought he was going out with turned out to be a final year law student, who wasn't going out with him at all. What she *was* doing was holding a protest outside Bluebell Wood, which is about to be bulldozed over to be replaced by what sounds likely to be a rather large housing development. She's also a member of the environmental activist group, Nature First, and guess what?'

'The young man found hanging in the woods was also a member?'

'Not only that, but he had a sideline in hacking into people's computers. According to her, he volunteered to take a closer look at the property developer's personal bank account. There, he found evidence that he'd paid one-hundred thousand pounds to the councillor responsible for new build development proposals. The boy then stupidly decided to email the property developer, detailing what he'd found, along with an ultimatum that if he didn't withdraw his plans, he'd be sending the same information to us.

'So anyway,' Tanner continued, taking a breath, 'although, on the surface, it does look every bit like suicide, there are an increasing number of reasons for me to think otherwise.'

There was a lull in the conversation as Christine finished doing the washing up to begin drying her hands. 'What are you going to do?'

'Have another word with the building developer, I suppose, although I'm not sure what I'm going to say. I mean, I can't mention anything about what our recently deceased computer hacker allegedly found. For a start, I haven't seen the proof he'd supposedly unearthed. Even if I had, the fact that it had been obtained by such an overtly illegal method would mean I'd be unable to use it as evidence against him.

'Forensics hasn't come up with anything to suggest that someone else may have had a hand in the boy's death?'

'Not yet.'

'Do you think they're likely to?'

'I've no idea. What I don't want to do is to tell everyone that we've decided that it is a suicide, only to find out ten days later that it wasn't at all, especially when it was discovered that I was doing nothing more about it than to lie idly beside a private swimming pool on the coast of Spain. I can imagine what the papers would say. "Norfolk's brand new DCI sweeps murder under the rug in order to go on holiday." I'm not sure my career would be able to recover from that.

And with a baby on the way, early retirement isn't an option.'

'Did you tell any of that to the press – that you think the victim may have been murdered?'

'God no!'

'Then why are they running the story on the news?'

'What!' Tanner exclaimed, spinning around to the TV Christine was directing his attention towards, where an attractive female reporter could be seen talking to the camera, the headline, "Local College Student found Murdered", running underneath. 'You must be fucking joking,' he spluttered, fumbling for the remote to turn the volume up.

'...*the police are continuing their search of the area where, once again, the body of local college student Samuel Brogan was found in the early hours of the morning in what has been officially described as "suspicious" circumstances. As yet, no suspects have been identified and no arrests have been made. This is Tina Martin from 24 / 7 News, standing on site at the already controversial Bluebell Wood New Home Development.*'

Turning the TV off in raging disgust, the room was left to fill with an uncomfortable silence.

'I assume you didn't tell them any of that?' asked Christine, gazing over at him with a look of motherly concern.

'Obviously not,' he replied, his jaw tightening, 'but I've got a fairly good idea who did.'

- CHAPTER FOURTEEN -

Thursday, 11ᵗʰ June

AFTER STOPPING AT a petrol station to fill up the seemingly bottomless pit that was his Jaguar XJS's fuel tank, as well as to pick up the latest copy of the dreaded Norfolk Herald, Tanner pushed his way through the doors into the main office to start earnestly scanning the room.

Unable to find the person his mind had been consumed by since watching the news the evening before, he marched over to where Vicky was sitting.

Finding her staring at the front page of the Norfolk Herald's website whilst sipping gently at a steaming mug of coffee, he cleared his throat. 'Morning, Vicky!'

'Oh!' she replied, nearly spilling her coffee as her head jolted up in surprise. 'Sorry, boss. I didn't see you there.'

'I don't suppose you've seen Cooper, by any chance?'

'I'm, er, not sure he's in yet. Why, do you think it was him?'

'Assuming you mean if I think he's the person responsible for telling the world's press not only the identity of who we believe to be the victim, but also that we're proceeding on the basis that he was murdered – I *know* it was!'

'Dare I ask how?'

'Because I caught him talking to the guy who wrote the article you're currently staring at, barely ten minutes after the poor boy's body was hauled down.'

'Ah.'

'Apparently, they were best friends at school.'

'Right.'

'Anyway,' Tanner continued, 'has anything happened since last night?'

'Apart from the story breaking, and the news vans already piling up outside, Superintendent Forrester called.'

'Shit!' he cursed. With so much going on, he'd completely forgotten about him. 'Did he say anything?'

'Only for you to call him.'

'Nothing from Johnstone, or forensics?'

'Not yet, but it's still early, unlike Cooper, that is,' Vicky added, pointing a finger over to the office doors, and the bleary-eyed, unshaven man who could be seen staggering his way through.

'OK, thanks,' Tanner muttered, wondering to himself if the fact that he'd blabbed to the press about a current investigation was enough to charge him with gross misconduct, so enabling him to be dismissed without notice. 'Let me know the minute you hear anything from either Johnstone or forensics. I'm just going to have a chat with our Mr Cooper.'

- CHAPTER FIFTEEN -

'I DON'T SUPPOSE I could have a very quick word?' asked Tanner, watching Cooper tug his chair out from under his desk.

'Can't I at least grab a coffee first?' the dishevelled detective inspector questioned, digging his fingers into his already blood-shot eyes.

'It won't take long.'

'If this is about that story on the news last night, it wasn't me!'

'Can we discuss this in my office?'

'I'd rather talk about it out here, if it's all the same to you.'

Tanner let out an exasperated sigh. 'Look,' he began, keeping his voice as low as possible as his eyes circumnavigated the office. 'I saw you talking to that Norfolk Herald reporter yesterday.'

'Yes, I know.'

'And by the time I got home, the story that our suicide victim had been murdered was already running on the news. They'd even managed to find out his name!'

'At which point you automatically assumed that it was me who told them?'

'Wasn't it?'

'I already told you it wasn't.'

'Then I'm asking you again.'

'I'm sorry, but if you don't believe me, then there's

not a whole lot I can do about it. I'm not sure that there's a lot *you* can do about it, either!'

'I can dismiss you for gross misconduct, that's what I can do about it!' Tanner spat, through grinding teeth.

Cooper levelled his eyes at him with a provocative grimace. 'Go on then. I dare you!'

Meeting his gaze with brooding hostility, Tanner was about to do just that when he saw Cooper take a breath to open his mouth.

'Tell you what. Instead of asking me, why don't you ask the person responsible for the story?'

'There's no point,' Tanner replied. 'I already know what he'd say.'

'And what's that?'

'What they always do. That he can't reveal his sources.'

'If you tell him it's my job that's on the line, then I think you'll find that he will. Even if he's still unwilling to, then he'd at least be able to confirm that it wasn't me.'

'But he's bound to, though, being that you're best friends, and everything.'

'We're not "best friends".'

As a solitary desk phone burbled quietly in the background, Tanner wracked his brain, desperate to think up a new angle to help make his detective inspector confess. 'Can you at least tell me if he asked you about the victim, if we thought he'd been murdered?'

'I thought we were proceeding on the basis that he'd killed himself?'

'Don't try and change the subject.'

'Then I suggest you stop trying to cross-examine me in the middle of the bloody office!'

Cooper's harshly whispered comment had Tanner

glancing about to find everyone staring awkwardly down at their desks. Realising he'd been speaking far louder than he'd ever intended to, he drew in a calming breath. 'This would have been a lot easier if we'd been having this discussion inside my office.'

'Easier for you, maybe,' Cooper smirked back in response.

'Look, did you tell the reporter or not?'

'I've already told you I didn't. And if you have me kicked out of the Force for no other reason than an unproven conversation between me and a local reporter, one I just happen to know from school, you better know that I'll be suing you – personally – for unfair dismissal!'

Tanner spent a seething moment drilling his eyes dementedly down into Cooper's when he heard Vicky, clearing her throat behind him. 'Yes, Vicky, what is it?'

'Sorry to bother you, boss, but a call's come in.'

'Can't you deal with it? I seem to be a little busy at the moment.'

'Well, I can, of course, but I thought you'd want to know about it first.'

Tanner tore his eyes off Cooper's to face her.

'I'm afraid another body's been found, in a house just outside Norwich.'

'Shit!' Tanner cursed, loudly enough for the entire office to hear.

'And I'm afraid that this time,' Vicky continued, 'it doesn't sound like anything other than murder.'

- CHAPTER SIXTEEN -

L ESS THAN AN hour later, Tanner found himself standing outside the open doorway of a cramped, poorly lit study, every corner of which seemed to be piled high with books.

Placing a foot inside, he leaned his head forward to see a double pedestalled writing desk, shoved up against a narrow set of metal framed patio doors. Another step forward had his eyes resting on the crown of an elderly man's balding head, leaning back against a threadbare office chair.

'Ah, DCI Tanner,' came the all too familiar sound of Dr Johnstone's voice, glancing up from where he was crouched beside the body. 'Long time no see.'

'Er...I saw you yesterday, less than twenty-four hours ago.'

'That's longer than normal. At least it is for us. If we're not careful, people will talk.'

'Speaking of yesterday,' Tanner continued, deliberately ignoring the medical examiner's glib remarks, 'I don't suppose you have any news?'

'Had I not been called out here, I probably would have.'

'So, you still don't know if it was suicide?'

'I've yet to find anything that says otherwise.'

'And his identity?'

'No official confirmation, but I'm still waiting to hear back from his dentist.'

Tanner let out an impatient sigh. 'And what about here?'

Lifting himself up, Johnstone pushed his black-rimmed glasses up the bridge of his nose to take in the body. 'Well, it's an elderly man, one who appears to be dead.'

'I don't suppose you could elaborate a little more?'

'I've been told his name is George Baxendale, at least this is his house, I'd say he's somewhere between seventy and eighty years old, and his death was most likely to have been from a heart attack, something I'd estimate to have occurred between nine to twelve hours ago.'

'Oh, right,' began Tanner, feeling both relieved and confused. 'I was told his death *wasn't* from natural causes.'

'Sorry, it wasn't.'

'It wasn't what?'

'From natural causes.'

'But you just said he had a heart attack.'

'I said he most likely died from a heart attack. I didn't mention anything about what caused it.'

'And what was that?'

'See for yourself,' Johnstone chirped, backing away from the body to beckon Tanner over.

Taking his place, Tanner could immediately see what he'd been referring to. Running from one side of the victim's throat to the other was a curving crescent shaped rent, smiling back at him like a dementedly grinning clown. 'You're saying that *didn't* kill him?' he demanded, unable to take his eyes off the gaping wound, and the blackening congealed blood that surrounded it.

'From what I've been able to establish so far, the man had the heart attack a few moments before his throat was cut. Whether his assailant was aware that he was already dead, I've no idea.'

'Can you tell me anything else?'

Johnstone folded his arms to rest a stubby finger against his flabby, clean-shaven chin. 'I'd say the victim was sitting where he is now when he was attacked, the assailant was probably right handed, at least the knife was held in the right hand, and the knife used was incredibly sharp.'

'I don't suppose there's any indication if the attacker was a man or a woman?'

'Impossible to say, but judging by the angle of the cut, it was either a very tall woman or an above average height man.'

'Anything else?'

'Only that I think whoever did this had done it before, or they'd at least had training.'

'For any particular reason?'

'Usually the cut would go from one side to the other. In this case, the knife was inserted behind the trachea and pulled out, making death far more certain.'

'You're saying it was a professional job?'

Johnstone's head swayed from side-to-side. 'Either that, or the assailant was professionally trained, maybe through a stint in the Army, or perhaps more likely, Special Forces.'

- CHAPTER SEVENTEEN -

L EAVING JOHNSTONE TO continue with his work, Tanner nudged his way past an overall-clad forensics officer to find Townsend speaking to a stout, grey haired woman in the hallway.

Glancing up from his notebook with a look of relief, the young detective constable quickly made the introductions. 'Detective Chief Inspector Tanner, this is Heather Baxendale. She's the person who called the police.'

'Are you in charge here?' the lady demanded, taking a long deliberate moment to look him up and down.

'Apparently so,' Tanner replied, unused to being studied with quite such pernicious interest.

'Well?'

'Well, we'll – er – be needing to ask you a few questions. No doubt my colleague, here, has already started.'

'I meant about George!'

'Oh, sorry. Yes, of course. This must be a very difficult time for you.'

'I wouldn't describe it as difficult, Mr Tanner. I think overwhelmingly upsetting would be a more accurate phrase.'

'I take it he's your husband?' Tanner enquired, struggling to believe that she was either overwhelmed or upset.

'My husband? How can he have possibly been my husband?'

Tanner exchanged a confused glance with Townsend. 'You mean, the man in the study *isn't* your husband?'

'I'm not married, so I'm really not sure how he could have been.'

'My apologies, but – isn't the man in the study Mr Baxendale?'

'Of course he is.'

'And your name is Mrs Baxendale?'

'*Ms* Baxendale, thank you very much!'

'Oh, I see. So he's your...?'

'He's my brother, you idiot!'

'Right, yes, of course,' Tanner replied, wiping his forehead to exchange a surreptitious grimace with Townsend. 'I don't suppose you've ever spent any time in the Army, by any chance?' he continued, returning to look at her with a suppressed smirk.

'The Army?'

'Special Forces, perhaps?'

'What are you talking about?'

'Sorry, nothing,' he apologised, straightening his face. 'Is it safe for me to assume that you found your brother?'

'I don't know who else would have.'

'Nobody else lives here?'

'Who else would live here?'

Tanner drew in a deep, calming breath. Rarely had he questioned someone quite so cantankerously belligerent. 'May I ask when that was?'

'When what was?'

'When you found him?'

'This morning, of course, just before I telephoned you.'

'And when did you see him last, before that?'

'Last night, before I went to bed.'

'Which was when?'

'At eleven o'clock.'

'And where was he?'

'In his study, where he always was.'

'You didn't happen to see or hear anyone else between then and when you found him?'

'Not a soul, and I'm a light sleeper as well.'

'Did you check to see if all the windows and doors were locked?'

'Before I went to bed, and immediately after I called you.'

'And...?'

'Everything was as it should be.'

'There were no signs of a forced entry?'

'As I said,' she replied, shaking her head.

'Would it have been possible for your brother to have had a visitor? Someone he knew, perhaps?'

'It's possible, I suppose.'

'But not very likely?'

'Not at eleven o'clock at night. Not at any time, really.'

'I take it he didn't get out much?'

'Hardly ever. He did all his communication via email. He didn't even like to use the phone.'

'If someone had come round, do you think you would have heard?'

'If they'd used either the doorbell or the knocker, then I definitely would have done. They both make the most horrendous noise.'

Tanner took a moment to collect his thoughts. 'May I ask what your brother did for a living?'

'He used to lecture Modern and Contemporary History at Norwich University.'

'I take it he's retired?'

'Hardly! Since stepping down he's written over half-a-dozen books.'

'Anything I know?'

'I suppose that depends if you like books about Eastern Europe and the Cold War.'

'Er, I'm not sure that's really my thing,' came Tanner's honest response.

'Then I doubt you would have done, but he'd made quite a name for himself, at least in academic circles. He was just about to publish his latest book when he...' The woman looked suddenly away, the loose skin around her square jaw trembling. 'He was particularly proud of it, as well, being that it was centred around Norfolk. I also think he secretly knew it would be his last. Unfortunately, he wasn't getting any younger.'

With it becoming obvious that the news of her brother's death was finally beginning to sink in, Tanner nodded at Townsend before pulling out one of his business cards. 'Thank you for your time, Ms. Baxendale. If there's anything we can do to help, or if you remember something that you think might be relevant, please don't hesitate to give me a call.'

Taking the card, she stared down at it. 'For a start,' she eventually said, wiping away at an escaping tear, 'you can tell me how long you're going to be here for?'

'I'm, er, not exactly sure. I can ask our forensics team, if you like?'

'And what are you going to do about that man I was telling your colleague about?' she continued, lifting her head to look at Townsend.

'Sorry, but what man was this?' Tanner enquired, following her gaze.

'Mrs...I mean, Ms. Baxendale was telling me about a man who came to visit him a couple of days ago,' Townsend replied, deflecting the question back to the woman.

'I was in the kitchen, making dinner, when I heard my brother arguing with someone in his study. By the time I came out to see if everything was alright, his visitor was already showing himself out.'

'Does that mean you didn't see him?'

'Oh, I saw him, alright! As clear as day!'

'Are you able to describe him for me?'

'I already have!' she replied, directing his attention to his colleague.

'Oh, er, yes, of course,' Townsend spluttered, quickly turning back a page in his notes. 'Apparently, he was tall, with a long thin face, and closely cropped grey hair.'

'You didn't mention his uncaring eyes and overbearing countenance,' Ms. Baxendale added.

'Sorry,' Townsend apologised, quickly adding to his notes.

'And that he was clean shaven, and was wearing a navy suit with a matching tie.'

'I'll add that as well.'

'And that his shoes had been polished to the point where you could just about see your face in them.'

'Had you seen him here before?' Tanner queried, giving Townsend a chance to catch up with his notes.

'Not to my knowledge.'

'I don't suppose you caught his name?'

'I didn't.'

'Did you hear what they were talking about?'

'I was trying not to. I don't like to eavesdrop on my brother's private conversations. The only thing I thought I heard was something about bluebells.'

Tanner stopped where he was to stare over at her. 'It couldn't have been Bluebell Wood, by any chance?'

'Well, it *could* have been,' she replied, her eyes drifting away, 'but as I said, I was making dinner at the time. It was only when I stopped to listen by the kitchen door that I could hear anything at all.'

- CHAPTER EIGHTEEN -

'I ASSUME YOU'RE thinking what I'm thinking?' said Townsend, keeping his voice low as he followed Tanner down the hallway towards the front door.

'Thankfully, I doubt I'll ever know what you're thinking,' mused Tanner, in a similarly hushed tone.

'The man who came to visit Professor Baxendale,' Townsend continued, 'that you think he was the person who killed him?'

'You mean, because of the military connection?'

'Er...sorry. What military connection was that?'

Passing through the open door, Tanner nodded briefly at the uniformed constable standing outside to begin crunching his way over the small rectangular driveway. As he stopped at its low brick walled entrance, he turned back to the detached Victorian house behind him to see Townsend was still standing in the middle of the drive, flicking through his notes with a confused expression.

'The shoes!' Tanner called over to him, shaking his head. 'Only the specially trained military man Dr Johnstone alluded to would have had his shoes polished to the point where you could see your face in them. Certainly in this day and age,' he added, glancing down at his own with reticent shame.

'Oh, right,' came Townsend's reply, stepping over to join him. 'I didn't know Dr Johnstone had said anything about a military connection.'

'Sorry. I forgot you weren't there.'

'I assume you agree with me, then?'

'Obviously,' Tanner replied, 'but we could do with a little more in the way of evidence. Certainly more so than the somewhat vague testimony of the victim's sister, saying that she thought she'd overheard their visitor having some sort of disagreement with her brother, two days before finding him dead.'

'That shouldn't be difficult. If she's telling the truth, then the man's DNA will be all over the crime scene.'

'Which in itself could be problematic.'

'How so?'

'Because, if whoever Ms Baxendale said she saw admits to having been in her brother's study two days before he was found dead, then his solicitor will simply give that as the reason for his client's DNA being found at the scene. That's if we're able to work out who he is. Any DNA found will only help us to identify him if he's already on our system, and he'll need a prior conviction for that to be the case. Even if we are able to locate him, he's likely to have contrived some sort of alibi by then, making it even harder for us to prove. On top of that would be the question of motive. Why would a presumably retired military man, possibly ex-Special Forces, enter the house of an elderly local historian in the dead of the night with the seemingly deliberate intention of murdering him?'

'Something to do with Bluebell Wood?'

'That's if the word bluebell was even used. If you remember, the victim's sister told us that she could barely hear anything at all, not until she was standing by the kitchen door, by which time the suspect was already showing himself out. If that was true, how was she able to hear the word bluebell. More to the point, why only that one single word? I'm fairly sure that when most people find themselves listening in on someone else's conversation, they're able to pick up more than one.'

'You think his sister killed him, and she's trying to pin the blame on some random, imaginary visitor?'

'Apart from the method used, it would certainly be more in keeping with those normally found guilty of murder: someone from the victim's immediate family. She could have chosen the word bluebell after having seen yesterday's news, to try to steer us towards a motive that doesn't exist.'

'And what motive would she have had?'

Tanner offered Townsend an ambivalent shrug. 'I would have thought having to put up with your brother, day-in, day-out, for the entirety of your life, would have been enough to send anyone reaching for the nearest knife, which reminds me. I want the entire property searched for a possible weapon, but I suggest we start in the kitchen.'

'Is it really very likely that she'd have cut her brother's throat, only to pop the knife back into the same drawer she found it, at least not before running it through the dishwasher first?'

'Not *very* likely, no, but it is still possible. Certainly not something we want to be found to have overlooked in three months' time.'

'And if we don't find anything?'

'Then extend the search to the neighbouring streets and gardens. I know it's a longshot, but if we can find the weapon used, it's possible we'd be able to find some tracc of the assailant's DNA. We also need to see if we can dig up any more witnesses. Then we need to take a look at the victim's sister, at least to see if she has any prior convictions.'

Hearing his phone ring, he signalled Townsend to

instigate the search as he dug it out. 'Tanner speaking!'

'Hi boss, it's Vicky.'

'Yes, Vicky. What've you got?'

'Nothing to do with the alleged suicide victim, I'm afraid.'

Tanner's heart stopped in his mouth. 'Please don't tell me another body's been found?'

'Nothing like that.'

'Then what is it?'

'There's been a reported break-in, sometime last night. I just wanted to ask if it was OK for me to deal with it?'

'Residential?'

'No, office. A local publisher, to be exact.'

With his mind harking back to the conversation with the murdered victim's sister, Tanner glanced around for Townsend, only to find he'd already gone. 'What are they called?' he asked, trying to remember if she'd told them the name of the company her brother had used. 'The publishing company?'

'Morgan & Naylor. Why? Is it important?'

'I'm not sure,' he replied.

Seeing Townsend emerge from the house, he clicked his fingers at him to help attract his attention.

'Can I go or not?' came Vicky's curt request.

'Hold on a sec,' he replied, turning the phone away from his mouth.

Beckoning the young DC over, he whispered, 'Did the victim's sister tell us who his brother's publisher was?'

Townsend came to a halt to dig out his notebook. 'I don't *think* so.'

'Hello?' came the demanding sound of Vicky's voice. 'Are you still there?'

Tanner turned the phone back around as

Townsend rifled through his notes. 'Yes, I'm still here.'

'So, what's the verdict? Can I go?'

Tanner paused as Townsend looked up to shake his head. 'She didn't say. At least, if she did, then I didn't make a note of it.'

'Do you know if she's still around?'

'I don't know where else she would have gone.'

'Hi, Vicky,' Tanner continued, returning to the call. 'Sorry about that. I think it's probably best if I go instead.'

'Oh, right,' came her despondent response. 'You do know that I'm capable of doing more than just sitting around all day answering the bloody phone!'

'Yes, of course.'

'Then why can't I go?'

'Because the break-in might be linked to the victim we've found here, sitting in his study with his throat cut.'

'Uh-huh,' she replied, without sounding the least bit convinced.

'Tell you what, how about I meet you there?'

'OK, fine! But if you don't start giving me a little more responsibility soon, I'll be looking for a more intellectually demanding job, like stacking shelves down at the local supermarket.'

- CHAPTER NINETEEN -

N UDGING HIS XJS onto the kerb opposite the publisher's office that had reportedly been broken into, Tanner stepped out to see Vicky was already there, chatting amicably with a uniformed constable whilst gazing up at the front of the building.

'What have we got?' he called out, stepping over the road to join them.

'Looks like they gained entry through the third floor window,' she replied, directing his attention up to the window in question.

Shielding his eyes from the sun, Tanner stepped back to try and get a better view. 'How the hell did they get all the way up there?' he asked, unable to see anything but a seemingly unassailable red brick wall.

'We assumed with some sort of a ladder,' the constable replied.

'It would've needed to have been one hell of a ladder! Are you sure that's how they got in?'

'Apparently, the window was left open overnight,' he continued.

'There was no other sign of a forced entry?'

'Not that they've found. They think it may have been someone pretending to be a window cleaner, or maybe even a fireman.'

Tanner brought his head down to narrow his eyes at him. 'PC Woodbridge, isn't it?'

'Yes, boss!' Woodbridge replied, pulling himself up to attention.

'Do they have any idea what time they think this happened?'

'Sometime last night. The last person left at around six o'clock, so at some stage between then and when the first person arrived for work at half-past eight this morning.'

'I see. So why on earth do they think it was someone pretending to be a window cleaner?'

'Or a fireman.'

'I'm not sure it matters which. Ascending the front of a building in the middle of Stalham High Street, with either a hand-held squeegee or an industrial-sized hosepipe, would surely have been more suspicious than someone carrying a large black bag with the word "SWAG" written on it in capital letters.'

'I suppose so, boss.'

'Don't call me boss.'

'Sorry, boss.'

Tanner shook his head to cast his eyes over at the smoked glass entrance doors. 'I take it you've been inside?'

'Only into the reception.'

'OK, so who told you that the window had been left open, and the outlandish theory about the window-cleaning fireman?'

'It was the receptionist, boss.'

'Ah, I see. Attractive, was she?'

Woodbridge's face flecked with colour. 'I – I suppose she could be described as such.'

'So, in other words, we don't know if the third floor window *was* left open, if someone used a ladder instead of a hot air balloon, if they were dressed up as a fireman or a pantomime horse, or if in fact the place was even broken into at all?'

'The place was robbed, alright!' he stated. 'The mess inside is proof of that.'

'Which you've seen with your own eyes?'

'Well, no, but...'

'The receptionist told you it was, so you naturally believed her.'

Remaining sullenly silent, Woodbridge's eyes fixed themselves onto a point just beyond Tanner's right ear.

'Rule one of effective police work, Woodbridge: don't just take someone's word for whatever it is that they're trying to make you believe.'

'Yes, boss.'

'And rule number two. Stop calling me boss all the bloody time!'

- CHAPTER TWENTY -

NTRODUCING THEMSELVES TO the company's receptionist, a chatty young woman who was far more attractive than the PC outside had led them to believe, Tanner and Vicky followed her into a lift that was barely large enough to fit them all in, one that squeaked and rattled in the most alarming way, all the way up to the second floor.

When it eventually juddered to a halt, she led them down a short narrow hallway, at the end of which was a door with the name, RICHARD NAYLOR, CEO, etched onto a polished bronze plaque.

'Mr Naylor,' the receptionist said, knocking gently as she nudged it open to reveal a large wooden desk, behind which sat a grey haired old man wearing an ill-fitting navy blue suit. 'There are some more policemen here to see you.'

'*And women,*' whispered Vicky, under her breath.

'Thanks Katie,' the man replied, smiling up at her from beneath a pair of rectangular reading glasses. 'I'll take it from here.'

'Detective Chief Inspector Tanner, and Detective Inspector Gilbert, Norfolk Police,' Tanner announced, stepping to one side to let the young woman out. 'We understand you've had a break-in?'

'The first one in over fifty years!' he confirmed, pushing himself up to begin hobbling over.

'I take it you're one of the founders?'

'Sadly, the last remaining one. My business partner, Mr Morgan, passed away around about this time last year.'

'I'm sorry to hear that.'

'He had a good innings, and we all have to go at some point.'

'Yes, I suppose we do.'

'Shall I show you up to where we think he came in?'

'Er...does it involve having to get back into that lift of yours?'

'Unfortunately, I'm afraid it does,' he laughed, 'but don't worry. It only breaks down on Thursdays.'

'Oh, right.' Tanner replied, sending Vicky a look of mock consternation. 'I thought it *was* Thursday?'

'So it is!' he responded, leading them out. 'Oh well. I suppose we'll just have to risk it. You can take the stairs, if you like. Unfortunately, with my ankles, knees, hips, and back, I don't have much of a choice.'

'The lift's fine,' Tanner acquiesced, stopping nervously beside its closed steel doors. 'Besides, if it does breakdown, at least the emergency services are already here.'

'Not the fire brigade, though, and we'd probably need them.'

'True. Although, according to your receptionist, one of them may have already been here.'

'Really? The last I heard it was a disgruntled window cleaner.'

Smiling as the doors creaked open, Tanner waited for Vicky and the old man to step inside before taking a breath to follow them through. 'Do you know if anything of any value was taken?' he asked, watching the steel doors rumble closed with a look of anxious trepidation.

'Nothing we've been able to identify,' Naylor replied, as the lift jolted in the most disarming fashion before grinding slowly upwards. 'To be honest, I can't imagine what they were hoping to find. Apart from a little petty cash, there's nothing here that's of any value. I mean, we publish books. Not very exciting ones, either. The best they'd have been able to hope for would have been a box of signed first editions from one of our better-selling authors. Saying that, we don't even keep books here, at least not in any quantity. Everything goes straight from our printers out to our distributors.'

Once again, the lift jolted alarmingly under their feet before coming to an eventual halt.

Relieved to see the doors screech themselves open, Tanner waited until they were safely out before asking the question that had been dominating his mind since being told about the break-in. 'I don't suppose you happen to know a local historian by the name of Baxendale, by any chance?'

'Baxendale?' Naylor repeated.

'Professor George Baxendale, to be precise?'

'The name does ring a bell,' he replied, leading them along a dimly lit hallway, out into a quiet open-plan office, where a dozen or so desks could be seen scattered about. 'I'm not sure from where, though.'

'He wouldn't be one of your clients?'

Coming to a halt beside a chair in which sat a particularly flustered-looking woman wearing a lime green dress and an abundance of jewellery, busily searching through a series of files and documents, Naylor turned to look sagaciously at Tanner. 'I know all our active clients. I suppose he could have published with us at some point. We've certainly been in business long enough. May I ask what it's in connection with?'

'Don't worry,' Tanner replied, doing his best to hide his disappointment. 'It's just another line of enquiry we're following.'

With a lull in their conversation, the woman in the chair cleared her throat. 'Sorry to bother you, Mr Naylor,' she began, catching the old man's watery grey eyes, 'but I don't seem to be able to find Clive Chapman's manuscript.'

'Oh...really?'

'I've looked everywhere!'

'Well, it must be here somewhere. I can't imagine anyone would have taken it. When did you see it last?'

'It was here, on my desk. I was about to start reading it through when I realised it wasn't where I'd left it.'

'Then someone must have moved it.'

'I've already asked. Nobody's seen it.'

'The cleaners, perhaps?'

'I don't see why they would have. They certainly wouldn't have thrown it away.'

'May I ask what's missing, exactly?' Tanner queried, with professional interest.

'It's one of our more prolific authors' latest offerings. Nothing of any particular importance. The original copy is on the computer.'

A cloud of angst-ridden horror passed over the old man's eyes.

'It *is* on the computer?' he suddenly asked, his eyes latching onto the rosy-cheeked woman's.

'Of course!' she replied, reaching for the desktop's mouse. 'At least, it *should* be.'

A moment of silent anticipation followed as they waited for her to begin opening and closing various computer files.

'Yes, here it is!' she eventually announced. 'All safe and sound.'

Tanner leaned forward to stare at the convoluted title of the document being displayed. 'It's not a romantic comedy, I take it?'

'Not exactly!' Naylor laughed. 'It's an historical account of the rather minor role Norfolk played in the Cold War, at least that's what he said it was about.'

Tanner stood back up to offer him a look of questioning consternation. 'Are you sure it wasn't written by Professor Baxendale?'

'I don't see how it could have been. The author's name is clearly displayed under the title.'

Once again, the woman behind the desk cleared her throat. 'I'm sorry, Mr Naylor, but that's not exactly true.'

'What's not exactly true?'

'About the author's name. If you remember, he uses a nom de plume. His real name is Professor Baxendale, as the gentlemen correctly said.'

Naylor lifted his eyes to the ceiling. 'Well, there you are. I did tell you the name rang a bell.'

'I don't suppose you've read it, by any chance?' Tanner enquired, catching the man's smiling eyes.

'I can't say that I have.'

'Has anyone here, do you know?' Tanner continued, directing the question at the woman.

'As I said,' she replied. 'I was about to start going through it this morning.'

Naylor turned to face Tanner. 'Do you really think someone would have gone to all the trouble of breaking into our offices for no other reason than to steal the manuscript of what is likely to be a rather dry account of Norfolk's involvement in the Cold War?'

'As unlikely as it may seem; yes, I do,' he replied, 'but only because its author was found dead this morning, and that it looks likely that he'd been murdered.'

'What!' Naylor exclaimed, gawping at Tanner with

perplexed incredulity.

'Which leads me to think that there must be something inside that book that someone doesn't want the world at large to know about.'

'But – as I said,' Naylor continued, 'it's just a...'

'...rather dry account of Norfolk's involvement in the Cold War,' Tanner finished, on his behalf, 'one that nobody here seems to have read, which does seem a little odd, given the fact that you're about to publish it.'

'Well – yes, but I'm afraid that's quite normal. At least it is with authors we've been working with for a while.'

'As nobody here seems particularly keen to, would you mind if we had a look?'

'You want to read it?'

'Only because its contents may have some bearing on what happened to its author.'

'Right, yes, of course,' came Naylor's flustered response. 'I suppose we can print you out another copy,' he continued, his eyes falling to the woman sitting beside him.

'I don't suppose you could email it to us instead?' Tanner enquired.

'I'm sorry, but we can't do that. Company policy, I'm afraid.'

'You're not seriously worried that it will get into the wrong hands, when someone has already broken into your offices to steal it?'

'No, Chief Inspector. I'm worried that someone will publish it before we have a chance to.'

'But – why would they want to do that?'

'Frankly, I don't care why some would, or wouldn't. You're talking about our livelihood. It's a hard copy, or no copy at all!'

Vicky entered the conversation with a placating

smile. 'Perhaps you'd be willing to meet us halfway?'

Naylor took a moment to take her in. 'And how, may I ask, would you propose we did that?'

'By providing us with a copy on a memory stick?'

'Well...I suppose we *could* bend the rules a little,' he smiled, 'just this once, mind. But only on the condition that you promise not to download its contents onto another computer. And under absolutely no circumstances is it to be sent anywhere via email.'

Tanner raised an eyebrow at him. 'Aren't you being unnecessarily cautious, given the manuscript in question would appear to have limited value?'

'That's the best I can do, I'm afraid. Take it or leave it!'

- CHAPTER TWENTY ONE -

WITH A USB flash drive held firmly in his hand, Tanner purposely avoided the lift to lead Vicky down the stairs and out through reception. When he reached the pavement outside, he turned to face her with a mischievous grin. 'Here you go!' he announced, holding it out for her.

Vicky stared down at the flash drive as if she were being offered a poisoned chalice. 'You don't seriously expect me to read it, I hope?'

'I thought you enjoyed a good book?'

'Well, yes, I do...but...'

'There you go, then!'

'As I was about to say, unfortunately, an historical account of Norfolk's involvement in the Cold War isn't really my thing, no matter how thrilling it's advertised as being.'

'I'm sure it can't be *that* bad. You might even learn something.'

'To "just say no", something my mother taught me in relation to sex, drugs, and accepting sweets from strangers at bus stops.'

'I can't imagine it will do you any harm.'

'Apart from making my brain melt with boredom. Why don't you give it to Henderson? With a degree from Oxford, a riveting read about the Cold War sounds like it would be right up his alley. I'd even be happy to shove it there myself.'

'Tell you what, I'll meet you halfway.'

'You mean, *you'll* shove it there, whilst I do something more useful, like some actual work?'

'I was thinking more along the lines of you giving it to him, with the instructions to read it on my behalf.'

'Fine!' she replied, snatching it from his extended hand.

'And make sure he keeps his eyes open for anything that may relate to the investigation, no matter how small.'

'Do you really think he's capable of doing that?'

'Probably not, but unfortunately, he's the only person we have who's ever likely to read it.'

Hearing his phone ring from within the depths of his threadbare sailing jacket, he dug it out to answer. 'Tanner speaking!'

'Hello, boss,' came the familiar sound of someone's voice from the other end of the line. 'It's – er – Henderson?'

'Ah – Henderson!' Tanner exclaimed. 'Vicky and I were only just this second talking about you.'

'Oh, er...'

'Don't worry. It was nothing bad. She's actually got a present for you.'

Vicky sent Tanner an acrimonious glare.

Without a single word coming from the other end of the line, Tanner pulled the phone away from his ear to see if the battery had died. 'Hello?' he asked, realising it hadn't. 'Are you still there?'

'Yes, boss. I'm still here.'

'Oh, good. Anyway, it's nothing special. Just a book for you to read.'

'Right.'

'Some flowers and chocolates, as well.'

Seeing Vicky go bright red with either blinding

rage or acute embarrassment, he realised he'd probably gone a little too far. 'Actually, I don't think the flowers are for you. The chocolates, neither. Sorry about that.'

Unsure as to who he was apologising to, the young detective or Vicky, he grimaced a smile at her before turning away. 'So anyway, what've you got?'

'Sorry?'

'In relation to your call, Henderson, not if you've managed to pick up some God-awful sexually transmitted disease.'

With again nothing coming from the other end of the line, Tanner drew in an impatient breath. 'You *did* phone me just now?'

'Yes – sorry – of course,' Henderson eventually responded. 'A call's come in from one of the constables over at Bluebell Wood.'

'Go on,' Tanner prompted, with wary trepidation.

'A group of environmental activists have chained themselves to the diggers parked outside.'

'Is that all,' he replied, exhaling with relief. 'I don't suppose there's been any news from forensics?'

'About what?'

'About whether or not they've finished at the scene where the victim's body was found?'

'Not that I've heard. As far as I know, they're still there.'

'OK, then I don't see the problem.'

'Er...sorry, boss, but what problem was that?'

Tanner turned to shake his head at Vicky, 'That the activists have chained themselves to the diggers?' he continued. 'Remember?'

'Yes, of course. It's just that the press have turned up, and apparently things are beginning to get a little out of hand.'

'Very well,' he huffed. 'Tell whoever's there that I'll

be down shortly.'

'Yes, boss. Right away!'

Ending the call, Tanner found Vicky still glowering at him. 'Your boyfriend is on good form,' he said, offering her a sheepish smirk.

'He's *not* my boyfriend, and I wish you'd stop trying to make him think that he is.'

'What on earth did I say that would have encouraged him to think such a thing?'

'You mean, apart from the book, the flowers, and the chocolates?'

'I thought I told him that the flowers and chocolates *weren't* from you?'

'But only after you told him that they were.'

'You're right. Sorry about that. It won't happen again.'

'It better not,' she muttered, under her breath.

'Anyway, I'd better be off. Protestors to placate. Disgruntled workmen as well, by the sounds of it.'

'What do you want me to do?'

'I'm not sure, but whatever it is, I suggest you don't run off to the nearest corner shop to buy Henderson any flowers or chocolates. I think that would definitely send him the wrong message.'

'I was talking about work, not your childish efforts to wind me up.'

'Work, right, of course. Well, for a start, we need the names, addresses, fingerprints, and DNA samples of everyone who's stepped foot inside the publisher's office in the last – say – two weeks; cleaners included.'

'Great. I simply can't wait.'

'Then we need to tell Mr Naylor that he'll have to find somewhere else for them all to work for a while.'

'He's going to love that.'

'Probably not, but if our manuscript thief does

happen to be the same person who murdered Professor Baxendale, then we need to give forensics every opportunity to find some sort of evidence that he was actually there.'

- CHAPTER TWENTY TWO -

T ANNER ARRIVED AT the carpark marking the main entrance to Bluebell Wood to find at least a dozen protestors chanting passionately on one side of the adjoining road, whilst a roughly equal number of burly workmen glared cantankerously at them from the other. Meanwhile, both parties were being filmed and photographed by a group of salivating journalists, jostling for position besides two lines of near-stationary cars, all doing their professional best to capture the events as they unfolded.

Forced to mount the kerb to avoid them all, Tanner squeezed his XJS through the carpark's entrance to step wearily out, only for it to immediately start pouring down with rain.

Sending a malevolent curse up to the heavens above, he pulled his sailing coat's hood over his head to see a nearby uniformed constable, observing the proceedings with a dispassionate eye.

'Nice day for it,' Tanner remarked, taking a position next to him.

'Only if you're a duck,' came the constable's emotionless response.

'Hudson, isn't it?'

'It's Judson, boss, but close enough.'

'Sorry, Judson,' he apologised, following the constable's unwavering gaze. 'I see the rain hasn't dampened their spirits. I'd have thought they'd have called it a day by now.'

'They're probably waiting for lunch.'

'I don't suppose anyone's tried telling them to go home?'

'Not yet, but only because they seem to be having too much fun.'

'Fair enough. Maybe give them another half-an-hour?'

'Right you are, boss.'

With water dripping from the end of his nose, Tanner glanced curiously about. 'I don't suppose you've seen an orange faced middle-aged man going by the name of Balinger, wearing a sheepskin coat, by any chance?'

'I think so,' the constable replied, craning his neck. 'Yes, there!' he added, pointing to a man huddled underneath a giant-sized golfing umbrella, having an animated discussion with a heavily tattooed workman.

'That's him, thank you. Oh, and keep up the good work.'

'Will do, boss.'

Leaving the constable to continue monitoring the situation, Tanner trudged his way through the now near torrential rain to where Balinger was standing. 'Sorry to interrupt,' he began, smiling first at the workman, then at the building developer. 'I was wondering if I could have a quick word?'

'Ah, Detective Inspector Tanner!' Balinger exclaimed, turning to face him. 'I was wondering if you were going to show up.'

'It's Detective *Chief* Inspector Tanner, actually,' he smiled, 'but let's not fall-out over it.'

'We will be falling out if you don't do something about those damned protestors of yours.'

'And what, specifically, would you like me to do about them?'

'You can arrest them, for a start.'

'Sorry, but what for?'

'For preventing my men from gaining access to my land.'

'I thought I'd already told you that you won't be able to start until our forensics team have finished.'

'You said they'd be done by today.'

'Had it been anything other than a suspected murder, then they probably would have.'

'Murder?'

'Suspected,' Tanner repeated.

'The last time we met, you told me it was suicide.'

'As I said, the jury's still out, which reminds me,' he added, fixing Balinger's eyes. 'I wanted to ask if you knew the victim?'

'Who? The guy found hanging by his neck in the middle of Bluebell Wood? Why on earth would I know him?'

'You do at least know his name, though?'

'Sorry, not a clue.'

'But you just said you didn't know him. You'd only be able to make such a claim if you at least knew who he was.'

'I suppose you'd better tell me his name, then,' Balinger huffed, with fractured impatience.

As the rain rattled relentlessly off the man's umbrella, Tanner took a long deliberate moment to dig out his notebook.

'Please, take your time,' Balinger muttered. 'I mean, it's not as if I've got anything better to do.'

'The victim's name is Samuel Brogan,' Tanner eventually said.

Balinger shrugged with indifference.

'Does that mean you don't know him?'

'I've already said as much. Finding out his name has made no difference.'

'He was an 'A' Level student, if that helps?'

'Not really.'

'One of his subjects was Computer Programming.'

'Uh-huh.'

'Something he seemed to be rather good at.'

'This is all fascinating, Chief Inspector, really it is. However, as much as I'd love to listen to you narrate the entirety of his life to me, there are one or two other matters that need my attention.'

'He had some interesting hobbies as well.'

'Then why didn't you say? Please, tell me more!'

'For starters, he was an environmentalist, like your friends over there.'

'Sorry, I was actually being sarcastic just then. What I actually meant was, shut up and leave me alone.'

'Believe it or not, he was a member of that very group.'

'Would it help if I said please?'

'I haven't told you the best bit yet,' Tanner continued, unable to prevent a smile from spreading out over his face.

'I can't wait!'

'Apparently, his real talent lay in computer hacking.'

Balinger opened his mouth, only to slowly close it again.

'Do I have your attention now, Mr Balinger?' Tanner enquired, meeting the man's faltering gaze.

'In relation to what?'

'The young man's body we found in Bluebell Wood, and the area of land which you've somehow managed to secure planning permission to build on.'

With Balinger remaining uncharacteristically

silent, Tanner was happy to continue. 'Regretfully, I'm unable to use the evidence he'd allegedly found against you – one hundred thousand pounds transferred to the councillor responsible for overseeing planning applications – but only because of the illegal method by which it was obtained. But don't worry. It won't prevent us from launching our own inquiry, enabling us to gain access to the financial accounts in question. Should we then reach the conclusion that Samuel Brogan *was* murdered, that would naturally make you our prime suspect, if for no other reason than because of what else we've discovered. That he was attempting to blackmail you.'

'You're not seriously suggesting I murdered him?'

'At this stage, we're only considering it to be a possibility. However, it may be worth your while to remain silent for a while, just in case we do, at least until you've had a chance to discuss the situation with a half-decent law firm, preferably one with a better-than-average track record of criminal defence.'

- CHAPTER TWENTY THREE -

WITH THE RAIN rattling off the roof of his XJS like a kettle drum, Tanner arrived back at the station some twenty minutes later to park as close to the entrance as possible. There he waited for a moment, hoping for a break in the rain. But if anything, the deluge was only becoming more intense.

Wishing he'd had the good sense to keep an umbrella in the car, he stepped quickly out to make a run for the entrance door, only to have to wait for a uniformed officer to come barging out the other way. By the time he made his way inside, the lower half of his trousers were sticking to his legs in the most uncomfortable fashion.

Peeling off his hood to wipe at his face, he glanced up to see the duty sergeant, waving at him from behind the security screen. Assuming he was endeavouring to garner his attention, and wasn't just saying hello, he stamped his feet on the doormat to make his way over.

'Afternoon, boss!' the duty sergeant said. 'Nice day for it!'

'Is it?' he replied, with an unamused grimace.

'I just thought you should know that Superintendent Forrester called.'

'Shit!' he cursed, under his breath. Once again, he'd completely forgotten about him.

'He said that if you don't return his calls, he's going to be forced to pay us a visit in person.'

Tanner pulled out his phone to see that he'd somehow managed to miss no less than three calls, two of which were from his superior officer.

Desperate for a coffee, and for some time to be alone, he dialled Forrester's number, only to realise the duty sergeant was still staring at him with an expectant look. 'Was there something else?' he queried, hearing the number click through to voicemail.

'There's someone here to see you as well, boss.'

Ending the call without leaving a message, Tanner followed where the duty sergeant was pointing, to a stick-thin elderly gentleman sitting on one of the plastic chairs, dressed in a khaki wax cotton jacket and a pair of muddy Wellington boots. Noting with wry amusement the cap on his head, one sold primarily to tourists with the word CAPTAIN emblazoned above its peak, he turned back to ask, 'I don't suppose he has a name?'

'Mr Campbell.'

'Did he say what it was about?'

'Only that he wanted to speak to you.'

Tanner let out an irritated sigh. 'Very well, but next time, if you could ask what it's about first, that way I can decide if I really have to speak to them, or if I can palm them off onto someone else.'

'Right you are, boss.'

Grinding his teeth, Tanner trudged his way over to the awaiting man to find him staring vacantly at the floor. 'Mr Campbell?' he enquired, coming to a halt directly in front of him.

Looking up with a start, the man climbed awkwardly to his feet. 'That's right, but please, call me Colin.'

'Not Captain?' Tanner smiled, lifting his gaze to take in the man's nautical-themed cap.

'Oh, the hat!' he exclaimed, whipping it off his shaved grey head with a sheepish smirk. 'Sorry! It's a silly retirement present. I normally only wear it when I'm pottering about onboard my boat.'

Resisting the urge to ask what sort of boat he had, Tanner held out his formal ID. 'DCI Tanner. How may I help?'

Campbell glanced anxiously about. 'I don't suppose there's somewhere a little more *private* we can talk?'

'It would help if I knew what it was about first?'

'It's in relation to Samuel Brogan.'

With Tanner still staring at him with a look of silent expectation, Campbell leaned his head in towards him. 'I'm his father,' he whispered. 'His biological one.'

- CHAPTER TWENTY FOUR -

LEADING CAMPBELL INTO one of the interview rooms, Tanner was quick to offer him a seat. 'Can I get you anything to drink? A coffee, perhaps?'

'Nothing for me, thank you.'

Tanner waited for the man to sink cautiously down into the chair before pulling one out for himself. 'So, Mr Campbell...?' he prompted.

'Right, yes. Well...I suppose I just thought I'd better introduce myself,' he began, wringing his cap between his hands like a sponge. 'Also, to see if you needed anything from me.'

Tanner sat back in his chair. 'Nothing that springs to mind, but it's certainly good of you to come in.'

'You don't need me to identify the body, or anything?'

'That would probably depend on when you saw him last?'

'Not since he was a baby, I'm afraid.'

Resisting the temptation to look at his watch, Tanner folded his arms over his chest. 'Then I'm not exactly sure how you'd be able to.'

'No. Of course. Sorry. That was stupid of me. If I'm being totally honest, I suppose the main reason I'm here is to try to unburden some of my guilt.'

'And just what exactly are you feeling guilty about, Mr Campbell?'

'For abandoning him when he was only three months old.'

Tanner raised an eyebrow. 'Given the fact that he was in the middle of doing his 'A' Levels, I'd have thought you'd have come to terms with that by now.'

'I'm not sure that's something a parent can ever really get over, at least not fully.'

'May I ask why you did?'

Campbell let out a juddering sigh. 'Looking back, I wish I hadn't. Especially with what's happened, and everything.'

'But you did, though.'

'Sammy was the result of an affair,' he eventually said. 'Taking responsibility would have meant having to tell my wife. If I had, she would have left me. We couldn't have children of our own, you see, something she always insinuated was my fault. Knowing I'd had a child with someone else would have been unacceptable for her. Rightly so, I may add.'

'Are you still married?'

'I am officially, I suppose.'

'Officially?'

'She passed away a few years ago.'

'I'm sorry to hear that.'

Campbell's eyes drifted down to the table.

'And your son?' Tanner continued. 'Did you stay in contact with him?'

'I'm afraid I didn't.'

'I assume you knew that his mother gave him up for adoption?'

He nodded quietly in response. 'With the money I was sending her, I'd hoped she wouldn't have to, but I wasn't surprised to hear that she did.'

'Did you know what happened to him afterwards?'

'Other than being adopted?' Campbell asked, with a confused frown.

Forced to assume that the man knew nothing about what his son had been through at the hands of his first set of foster parents, the darker side of Tanner's nature toyed with the idea of telling him, for no other reason than to help deepen the man's sense of guilt. 'Nothing important,' he eventually said, surrendering to his better nature. 'May I ask how you knew that it was your son, given that his surname had changed?'

'From the newspapers. I can't remember which, but one of them mentioned his mother's name.'

'Did you also hear that we're questioning the cause of death – that it may not have been by his own hand?'

'I did,' he nodded, still staring at the table, 'which was another reason why I came to see you. I wanted to ask if there was any truth to it?' he continued, glancing up. 'If he might have been...?'

'I suppose that would help to alleviate some more of that guilt of yours, if you thought someone had?' Tanner questioned, becoming increasingly angry that the real reason he'd come in was to hopefully find out that his son *had* been murdered. That way he wouldn't have to spend the rest of his life knowing that abandoning him as a baby had set off a chain of events that ultimately led to the poor boy hanging himself.

Seeing Campbell's eyes return to his hands, and the cap being mangled between them, Tanner's mind turned again to what had happened when Samuel had first been adopted. With the sudden urge to intensify his torment, he opened his mouth to tell him, when there was a knock at the door.

'Sorry to bother you, boss,' came the wavering voice of DC Henderson.

'No problem,' Tanner replied, glancing over at Campbell before turning to face him. 'I think we were just about done here. What's up?'

'It's that flash drive. The one with that book on it. I don't seem to be able to read it.'

'Cold War historical fiction not your thing?'

'It's not that, it's the file. It's been password protected.'

Tanner shook his head with frustrated disbelief. 'Couldn't you have told me this a little sooner? I was hoping you'd have read it by now.'

'Vicky only gave it to me an hour a go.'

'And may I ask what you've been doing since then?'

Henderson shifted his weight from one foot to the other. 'I've been attempting to open it, boss.'

'But you just told me it was password protected?'

'I was trying to work out what the password was.'

'For an hour?'

Tanner heard Campbell clear his throat behind him.

Having managed to forget he was there, he lurched around to see him stand quietly up.

'If it's OK with you, I think I should probably be on my way.'

'Of course, yes, that's fine,' Tanner replied, climbing to his feet.

'I'm only sorry to have taken up so much of your time.'

'No need to apologise. The detective constable here will show you out. Won't you, Henderson?'

'Er...yes, of course,' came his somewhat hesitant response. 'Then should I call the publisher, to ask for the password?'

'I would have liked you to have done that an hour ago,' Tanner muttered, taking a calming breath. 'Do you have the zip drive with you?'

'I do,' he replied, tugging it out from his trouser pocket.

'Then you may as well give it to me,' Tanner said, taking it from him. 'It's probably best if I look at it, anyway.'

'I don't mind reading it. It won't take me long. I just need the password.'

'Then you'd better give the publisher a call. Whilst you're at it, you may as well ask them for another zip drive.'

'Can't we just make a copy of this one?'

'For some reason, they're rather keen for us not to,' Tanner replied, glancing down at his watch to see that it was already gone six o'clock. 'Anyway, they'll probably be closed by now. It will just have to wait till tomorrow.'

- CHAPTER TWENTY FIVE -

EAVING HENDERSON TO lead Campbell out to reception, Tanner headed back to his office to find Vicky, scrawling him out a message on his desk. 'Anything I can help you with?'

'Oh, you're still here!' she exclaimed, glancing up.

'What do you mean, I'm still here? I'm always bloody here!'

'Sorry, boss. I couldn't find you, so I assumed you'd left for the day.'

'Fat chance.'

'I had a call from forensics,' she continued, screwing up the note. 'They've finished at Bluebell Wood.'

'OK, good.'

'Should I let the property developer know?'

'I assume the protestors are still down there?'

'The last I heard they were.'

'And his men?'

'I doubt it, given the hour.'

'Maybe you can find out? If they are, then I think it's probably best if we keep the fact that we have no legal right to stop them bulldozing their way through the wood to ourselves, at least for now.'

'And if they've gone?'

'Then you can tell our officers to call it a day.'

'Right you are, boss,' she replied, heading out.

'Before you go, I don't suppose forensics have sent

their report through?'

'Not that I've seen. Dr Johnstone has, though.'

Tanner scooted around the desk to pull out his chair. 'Have you had a chance to look at it?'

'Only briefly.'

'And?' he continued, opening his email.

'His conclusion was that the victim died from strangulation, caused by the rope found around his neck. There was nothing to suggest that anyone else had a hand.'

'So, it *was* suicide, then?'

'That's what he's concluded.'

'What about Professor Baxendale?'

'Nothing from either forensics or Dr Johnstone.'

'I don't suppose the knife's been found?'

'Everything's been collected from inside the house. We still have officers looking for anything outside.'

'Witnesses?'

'So far, only the professor's sister.'

'And what's the verdict on her?'

'She doesn't have any prior convictions. I can start running a background check, if you like?'

'Can't someone else do it?'

'Well, I could ask Henderson?'

'How about Townsend, instead?'

'He's already gone.'

'Sally?'

'Who do you think he went with?'

Tanner rolled his eyes. 'What about Cooper?'

'I suppose that depends on if you want it done before Christmas.'

'OK. Maybe you'd better make a start. But please don't feel you need to stay all night. I'm only going to take a quick look through Johnstone's report before heading home myself.'

'Right you are, boss.'

Hearing the door close, he leant forward to open Johnstone's email, and his attached report. The moment he realised it was over twenty pages long, he pushed himself away from his desk with an irritated sigh.

Returning a minute later with a much needed coffee, he began speed reading his way through. It was only when he reached the toxicology section that his eyes snagged on something that his mind hadn't even registered until he was already halfway through the next page.

Scrolling up again, he re-read the list of chemicals found in the victim's bloodstream, stopping where it said, "Unknown: ng/mL 25" listed at the very end.

His eyes skipped down to the following paragraph, expecting to find more details. But no further mention of it was made.

Rubbing his eyes, he dug out his phone to call Dr Johnstone's mobile. When it clicked through to voicemail, he left a brief message, asking him to call him back before hanging up.

'What's the point of having mobile phones if nobody ever bothers to answer them,' he moaned, quietly to himself.

Ditching the phone on the desk, he continued ploughing through the report, stopping only at the section relating to the cause of death. There he found himself studying the method used, what Johnstone described as a "short drop", leaving the victim suspended by his neck for between ten and twenty minutes before eventually succumbing.

Imagining what it must have been like to die in such a horrific manner, he continued on to the end, and the eventual conclusion Vicky had already relayed.

Closing the report, he went back to his inbox. With

nothing else there of any importance, he glanced at the time before reaching for his phone again.

'Hey, darling,' he began, a few seconds later. 'It's me.'

'Hi ya,' came Christine's cheerful voice.

'I just thought I'd let you know that I'm about to leave.'

'Not for good, I hope!'

'The office,' Tanner laughed, 'heading for home.'

'Oh, right. That's a relief. For a minute there I thought you were going to abandon me with an unborn child and a half-empty church.'

Her comment had Tanner's mind harking back to the suicide victim's father, the guilt he'd been carrying all those years for abandoning his infant son, and the reason why he'd come in to see him; to endeavour to alleviate himself of some of it.

Finding himself becoming angry all over again, his mind turned back to the suicide victim, and the unimaginable abuse he'd suffered under the care of his foster parents, the very people who were supposed to have been looking after him. 'Anyway,' he continued, clearing his mind, 'traffic depending, I should be home in about twenty minutes.'

'OK, see you then.'

About to hang up, he heard Christine's voice calling him back.

'Sorry, I forgot to ask. I don't suppose you can pick up some milk on the way?'

'Of course. No problem.'

'And could you also see if you can find me an aubergine?'

'Remind me what one of those is again?'

'You know; that large purple marrow-like thing, the one that looks like a giant...'

'Yes, thank you!' he quickly interrupted, 'I

remember. What I fail to understand is where you expect me to find one that's on my way home?'

'The corner shop at the end of our road should have them.'

'Really?'

'Well, they should. They did the last time I looked.'

'And if they don't?'

'Then I suppose I can make do without.'

'OK, I'll see what I can find. See you soon.'

- CHAPTER TWENTY SIX -

W ITH A LITRE of milk, and the requested aubergine, both bulging at the bottom of a blue plastic bag, Tanner stepped out of his local corner shop to cross the unlit country lane towards his car. Delighted to find that it had finally stopped raining, he was about to unlock the doors when he saw something move from within the pitch-black shadows behind him.

'Oi mate! D'ya know wot time it is?' came a man's low muffled voice.

Tanner's heart leapt instinctively into his throat. There was no way the person had been waiting there simply to ask a passing stranger the time. 'It's – er – about nine o'clock,' came his cautious response, discreetly returning his Jag's keys to his pocket as he turned slowly around.

Emerging from the darkness came a man dressed in black, the hood of a raincoat pulled over his head.

'Thanks. Now give us your fuck'n wallet!'

'Seriously?' he asked, surprised to find himself more angry than afraid. 'Do you have any idea who I am?'

'I don't give a shit who you are. Give us your fuck'n wallet!'

'Er...no,' Tanner replied, in a matter-of-fact tone of voice.

His would-be assailant hesitated for a moment

before the glint of a blade appeared by his side. 'If you don't, then I'm gonna to cut ya.'

Tanner's teeth locked together with mounting rage. Rarely had he experienced a moment in his life when he could so clearly tell the difference between right and wrong, and he was most definitely in the right! 'Listen, you little shit. If you don't fuck off and leave me alone, I'll have you arrested.'

'Oh yeah?' the man laughed, glancing wildly about. 'By who?'

Tanner wrestled out his formal ID to hold out in front of him. 'By me, you muppet-brained moron!'

The would-be assailant hesitated for a moment. 'You ain't no policeman,' he eventually said.

'No, you're right. I'm not just *any* policeman. I'm Detective Chief Inspector Tanner, or can't you read?'

'And I'm Brad Pitt,' came the man's sardonic response, lifting the knife to hold out in front of him. 'And yes, mate, I can read. Now, give us your wallet! Your phone, as well!'

'Good luck with that.'

The man took a half-step forward. 'I'm warning you.'

'And I'm warning you!'

In the blink of an eye, the knife flashed through the air, sweeping towards Tanner's still outstretched hand.

Feeling the sting of its blade, he flinched his hand back, dropping his ID as he did.

With the certain knowledge that he had less than a second before the blade came arcing back, he charged head-first at his assailant.

Throwing every ounce of his weight against the man's chest, he drove him into the shadows, slamming him hard into the thick gnarly trunk of an overhanging tree.

The sound of the knife, clattering to the pavement, only helped to urge him on.

Determined to force him to the ground to then somehow grab his handcuffs from his car, he brought his arms down to encircle his legs. As he did, his attacker twisted his body around, jamming a knee hard into Tanner's ribs.

With the air knocked out of his lungs, Tanner slumped to the ground.

Barely able to breathe, he tried to pick himself up, only to be shoved violently back, his head cracking against something solid behind him.

As a blinding white pain exploded inside his skull, he tried once again to climb to his feet. But the moment he did, his head spun to the point where he couldn't tell up from down, sending him spiralling forward, the side of his face smacking hard into the still wet concrete path.

- CHAPTER TWENTY SEVEN -

'I SINCERELY HOPE your fiancée doesn't know about us meeting like this all the time?' came the sound of a woman's voice from some unknown place above Tanner's head.

'Where am I?' he asked, opening his eyes to find a strangely familiar female paramedic, staring down at him with a vaguely amused expression.

'Apparently, it's your favourite place in the whole wide world!' the woman continued.

'You mean, a queue outside Tesco?'

'Even better. It's an ambulance. Not just any ambulance, either. It's the very same one you've been in the back of at least twice before. Three times if you count yesterday, when you were doing your best to stop that poor man from going to hospital.'

Remembering who she was, Tanner closed his eyes. 'Patricia, isn't it?'

'It's Melicia, actually, but that's closer than most people get.'

'It sounds like you make a habit of meeting strangers in the back of your ambulance.'

'I think it's more a question of strange men meeting *me* in the back of my ambulance; like you, for example.'

'I'm not strange!'

'You are a *bit* strange.'

'In what way?'

'Considering the number of times you seem to end up here, you never appear to be all that keen to stay. Like the last time, for example.'

'That was only because I had somewhere else I needed to be.'

'And that's not the case today?'

'As far as I know, the only place I should be is at home.'

'I don't need to lock the door, then?'

'Not on my account.'

'And you don't mind being taken to A&E?'

'Why do I need to be taken to A&E?'

'Your head's going to need stitches, I'm afraid.'

'Is that really necessary?'

'You've got a nasty cut on top of your head,' she continued, leaning forward to try to examine it. 'If we can't close the wound, then it will take too long to heal, increasing the risk of infection.'

'And just how long is all that going to take?'

Melicia shrugged. 'That'll probably depend on how busy A&E is.'

A loud thump on one of the rear doors had her spinning around to open it.

'I don't suppose you've got a certain Detective Chief Inspector Tanner inside there somewhere?' came the all too familiar voice of DI Vicky Gilbert. 'He's about yay-high, dark hair, and has a general air of irritability about him.'

'Looks like there's someone here to see you,' Melicia announced.

Tanner lifted his head to see the detective inspector's lightly freckled face emerge into view. 'Hello Vicky!'

'Evening, boss! The news is that you've hurt your head.'

'Some idiot decided to mug me.'

'So I've been told. Didn't you tell him who you are?'

'Of course I did!'

'I take it they didn't believe you?'

'I suppose not.'

'Did they take anything?'

'Aren't you going to ask if I'm OK?'

Vicky shrugged. 'Are you?'

'Just about,' he replied, pushing himself up to begin searching the pockets of his crumpled suit.

'The bastard!' he spat, a moment later. 'He took my wallet – and my phone!'

Seeing Vicky pull out her notebook, he checked to see if he still had his. 'I don't believe this. He's taken my notebook as well. And my ID!'

When he realised his car keys were also missing, he stared over at her with a frantic expression. 'Please God – tell me my car's still there?'

Vicky nodded with a smile. 'That was how I knew it was you.'

'Well, that's something, I suppose.'

'We also managed to find these,' she continued, holding up a set of keys. 'Yours, I presume?'

Tanner sent her a relieved smile.

'They were left on the pavement. There was this shopping bag there as well,' she added, holding it up. 'It contains some milk, and what would appear to be a large purple vegetable.'

'Aubergine,' commented Tanner.

'Actually, my name's Vicky.'

'Very funny.'

'Anyway, I'll leave them all down here for you,' she continued, dropping the keys into the bag to place on the ambulance's floor.

'Thank you. Christine will be thrilled, which reminds me. I don't suppose you could give her a call, to let her know that I'm going to be late?'

'You don't want to call her yourself?'

'I don't have a phone, remember?'

'Oh yes, I forgot,' she laughed. 'Do you want me to tell her what happened?'

'You probably should, if for no other reason than she'll need to cancel my credit cards.'

Speaking of which,' Vicky continued, pulling out her notebook, 'are you able to give me a description?'

'Of my credit cards?'

'The person who mugged you.'

Tanner shook his head. 'Of course, sorry, although I don't think I'm going to be of much use. It was dark, obviously, and there are very few streetlights around here. He also had a hood over his head.'

'A hood, or a hoodie?'

Tanner took himself back to the scene. 'It was the hood of a raincoat. Black, I think.'

'Gloves?'

'Yes, at least, I think so. The main thing I remember was that he was carrying a knife.'

Recalling the events as they'd unfolded, he lifted his hand to find it had already been bandaged.

'Anything else?'

'He was taller than me, around six foot. Athletic build.'

'How about his voice?'

'Oh, you know. The normal.'

'Did he have a Norfolk accent?'

Tanner shook his head. 'More like East London.'

'What about age?'

Again, Tanner found himself thinking back. 'I had the impression he was old.'

'Old, as in...?'

'Like the wrong side of forty. He certainly didn't come across as being your average teenager. I don't know why. He just seemed a little too confident, but not in a cocky way, if that makes any sense.'

'OK, that'll do,' said Vicky, finishing with her notes. 'I'll see how we get on. You never know, we might get lucky.'

'If you do find him, I don't suppose you could ask for my phone back? I'd only just bought the damned thing.'

'Will do. Oh, and good luck at A&E. The last I heard it was about a five hour wait.'

'Not seriously?'

Seeing her step down from the ambulance with an impudent smile, he called quickly out. 'Don't forget to call Christine!'

'No probs,' she replied, reaching the ground to peer back inside. 'Anything else before I go?'

Tanner attempted to wrack his brain, only to feel like he was wading through a mud-filled swamp. 'I don't think so. No – wait! I was going to read that book tonight,' he said, once again searching his pockets. 'I've got the flash drive for it somewhere.'

'I thought Henderson was going to read it?'

'Long story.'

'Well, I don't mind giving Christine a call, but I'm buggered if I'm going to stay up half the night reading that insipidly dull account of Norfolk's involvement in the Cold War.'

'Don't worry. I'll skip through it whilst waiting for my head to be stitched up.'

'Won't you need a laptop to do that?'

Tanner again shook his head. 'Yes, of course. I'm not thinking straight. I can't find it, anyway,' he added, still searching his pockets. 'My assailant of the day must have taken it as well.'

'Mr Naylor *will* be pleased,' mused Vicky, 'being that the whole idea of them giving it to us on a flash drive, instead of via email, was to prevent it from getting into the wrong hands. Now, not only have they had a hard copy stolen, but someone's made off with the Word Doc version as well!'

'Then I suppose it's a good job it was password protected.'

'Oh – right. I assume you have it?'

'Have what?'

'The password?'

Remembering he didn't, and that he'd told Henderson to wait until the morning to ask for it, he shook his head, wondering how on earth he thought he was going to read it, with or without a laptop.

'Time to go, I'm afraid,' Melicia announced, presenting a smile to first Tanner, then Vicky.

Tanner watched Vicky step away from the door as the paramedic reached out to close it. 'Let me know if you find him!' he called out.

'Will do.'

'And don't think I'll be skiving off tomorrow because of my head,' he continued.

'I expected nothing less.'

As the door began to swing closed, Vicky stopped it with her hand to lean forward. 'Sorry. Very quickly. Before you do come back to work, may I suggest you give your face a wash?'

'Why? What's wrong with it?'

'Apart from the fact that one half is covered in congealed blood, and that you look like you're on your way to a Halloween party – absolutely nothing.'

- CHAPTER TWENTY EIGHT -

ATCHING A CAB back to where he left his car, it wasn't until gone two in the morning when Tanner eventually crept through the front door of his unlit riverside bungalow.

'Honey, I'm home,' he whispered to himself, placing his keys gently down on the counter before quietly closing the door.

'Hello, stranger!' came Christine's voice, calling out to him from the other end of the pitch-black hallway.

'Jesus Christ!' Tanner exclaimed, jumping in his skin. 'You nearly gave me a heart attack!'

'Oops,' she replied, turning on the light.

'Did Vicky call?'

'She did.'

'Did you cancel my credit cards?'

'New ones are on the way,' she replied, her forehead rippling with concern as she took in the bandage on top of his head. 'Are you OK?'

'Apart from having to wait in A&E for hours on end to eventually have half-a-dozen staples stamped into my skull, I'm fine, thank you.'

'They didn't give you stitches?'

'They said there'd be less chance of infection if it was stapled.'

'Oh, right. I bet that hurt.'

'They injected the area around the cut with local

anaesthetic first, but that was probably more painful than the staples!'

'But you're OK, otherwise?'

'Just about. Anyway, sorry I'm so late.'

'Don't be silly,' she responded, stepping forward to give him a comforting hug.

'I brought gifts!'

'Really?'

'A litre of milk and one rather large aubergine.'

Christine laughed as Tanner presented her with the shopping bag he'd been carting round with him all that time.

'The milk's probably a little warm by now, but it should be OK.'

'More importantly, how's the aubergine?' Christine enquired, peering inside.

'In better condition than the person who bought it. Oh, and sorry about the blood.'

'I was wondering what that was. There's still some on your face,' she added, looking up to examine him more closely.

'The doctor tried scrubbing it off with what felt like sandpaper.'

'Well, he didn't do a very good job. Have you eaten?'

'I was given a bowl of cereal, but that was hours ago.'

'OK, then why don't you have a shower, and I'll make you a quick sandwich.'

'Tell you what. How about making the sandwich first?'

'I take it you're hungry.'

'Starving!' he replied, following her through to the main living area.

'So...are you going to tell me what happened?'

'I thought Vicky already had.'

'Only that you were mugged. She didn't go into detail.'

Tanner nudged himself up onto one of the kitchen stools. 'Well, it was as she said, really. Someone mugged me.'

Christine rolled her eyes as she heaved open the fridge door. 'I think my question was more along the lines of how?'

'Some guy asked for my wallet. Despite making it abundantly clear that I didn't want to give it to him, he took it anyway.'

'Didn't you tell him who you are?'

'Of course!'

'And?'

'He asked for my phone as well.'

'Seriously?'

'Uh-huh. I even showed him my ID.'

'Then he probably didn't believe you.'

'Either that, or he was so desperate to get his hands on a ten-year old wallet containing a single five-pound note and three credit cards, he was prepared to take the risk.'

Christine spun around with a plate held at the end of her arm. 'Here you go. One freshly made aubergine sandwich, drizzled with sour, lukewarm cow's milk.'

Tanner stared down at it as if it had been recently possessed by the Devil. 'Oh, thanks. It looks...er...delicious.'

'I'm winding you up. It's cheese and pickle.'

'Oh, right. Thank God for that. For a minute there I thought I was going to have to eat the entire thing whilst pretending to like it, like I normally do.'

Christine locked her arms over her chest to glare at him. 'You always like my cooking!'

'I'm joking!' he replied, offering her a calming smile.

'Anyway, you'd better eat it before it gets cold.'

Tanner stared back down at it with renewed suspicion. 'I thought you said it was a sandwich?'

'And that was *my* idea of a joke.'

'Oh – right. Good one.'

She waited for a moment for him to take the first bite before asking, 'I don't suppose you're taking the day off tomorrow, by any chance?'

'Why would I be taking the day off tomorrow?' he replied, through a mouthful of food.

'Er...because you've only just come back from A&E having had half-a-dozen staples stamped into your head.'

'Oh, right. Well, I'd love to, but unfortunately, there's just too much going on. Especially if I'm going to make our wedding on Saturday.'

'What do you mean *if* you're going to make our wedding on Saturday?'

'Sorry. Let me rephrase that. I meant, as I *will* be attending our wedding on Saturday, I'm definitely going to have to go to work tomorrow.'

'And our honeymoon?'

Tanner offered her a non-committal shrug. 'We'll have to see.'

'We *have* to go away!' she stated. 'It will be our last chance for God knows how long!'

'I know, but with a suicide, and now a murder, it's looking increasingly less likely with every passing day.'

- CHAPTER TWENTY NINE -

Friday, 12ᵗʰ June

REMEMBERING TO DIG out a notebook, together with his old phone and ID, Tanner arrived at work the following day to find that there wasn't a single member of his CID team there. Even Sally Beech, who could normally be found examining her nails whilst chatting on the phone, was nowhere to be seen.

'Where the hell is everyone?' he said out loud, to nobody in particular.

Glancing fitfully about, he shook his head in disbelief to make his way over to his office. 'Anyone would think we hadn't had a suicide, and a murder, all in the same bloody week!'

Half expecting to find at least one of them waiting there for him with a long list of personal complaints, he opened the door to find it empty.

For one brief moment his mind questioned what day it was, and if it was in fact Sunday. But his wedding was on Saturday. He was fairly sure Christine would have mentioned something about it had he somehow managed to miss it.

Pouring himself a coffee, he opened up his inbox to glance miserably down at the two dozen or so emails that had arrived overnight. Girding his loins, he was about to open the first when there was a tentative knock at the door.

'Ah, Sally!' he remarked, glancing up to see her pretty face, peering at him from the other side. 'Good to see that at least one of you is here.'

'Hello, boss,' she said, with a concerned smile. 'I just thought I'd look in to see how you were?'

'Oh, you mean this?' he replied, tilting his head forward to run his fingers over the staples he could feel lined up over the crown of his head. 'Strangely, it hurts more now than it did yesterday.'

'Can I get you some painkillers?'

'No need. I have a drawer full of them,' he replied, pulling open the drawer in question to take out a box, 'but thanks for the reminder.'

'To be honest,' he heard Sally continue, as he wrestled a couple of pills out from their foil-lined plastic holder, 'I was a little surprised to find you here.'

'It would take more than being mugged at knife point to stop *me* from coming into work,' he laughed, knocking the pills into the back of his mouth to wash down with the coffee. 'But I guess that's just the type of guy I am,' he added, glancing up at her with a boyish grin.

'I – er – didn't mean here, as in the office.'

'Oh, right. Sorry, but where else did you think I would be?'

'Where everyone else is.'

'Which is…?'

'At the publishing house. The one that was broken into yesterday. Didn't anyone call, to let you know?'

'They may well have done, but as my assailant took my phone, as well as my wallet, I'm not sure how they could have.'

'Oh, right. Sorry. I didn't know.'

'Don't worry. It's not exactly your fault, unless

you're the person who mugged me, of course.'

Sally stared at him with an expression of confused perplexity. 'But – I wouldn't even know how to!'

'Don't worry, Sally, I was only joking. But if you *would* like to know how, apparently, it's a fairly straightforward process. All you have to do is pick a quiet spot, wait until it gets dark, then ask the first passing stranger for the time before pulling out a knife.'

'Is that what happened?'

'Pretty much.'

Sally paused for a moment, before asking, 'Didn't you tell them who you are?'

With an annoying sense of déjà vu, he opened his mouth to question why everyone kept asking him that, when he changed his mind. 'Apparently, they didn't believe me.'

'Did you show them your ID?'

'Yes, of course,' he sighed, hoping to move the conversation along.

'And they still didn't believe you?'

'Either that, or they didn't care. Anyway, you were saying – about the publishing house?'

'That's right.'

'Well?'

'Well...?' she repeated back to him.

Tanner dug his fingers into his eyes. 'Why's everyone down there instead of investigating the murder of one of their clients?'

'Because of the fire.'

'The fire?'

'Someone set fire to it early this morning. It looks like they've found a body inside, as well.'

- CHAPTER THIRTY -

TANNER SAW THE smoke long before the sign for Stalham, where the publisher was located. It was a thin, grey, dirty plume, lying stark against the white puffy clouds drifting effortlessly over Norfolk's wide open horizon.

When he eventually reached the town, the people he drove past were clumped into groups, all pointing up at the smoke, billowing over their heads like a lethal swarm of killer bees. The closer he came to the publishing house, the more people he found, until reaching the end of the road it was located on to find it blocked by two squad cars.

Unable to see any of his colleagues, he bumped his XJS onto the kerb to climb quickly out. 'I seem to be late for the party,' he announced, addressing the nearest uniformed constable. 'Is it alright if I go through?'

'Of course, boss,' the young man replied, instantly lifting the blue and white tape for him to duck underneath. 'You'll find everyone at the end of the street.'

Thanking him, Tanner scooted his way past various emergency vehicles before finding two hulking great fire engines, each parked immediately outside what was left of Morgan & Naylor Publishing.

Seeing Vicky and Gina by its side, talking to an elderly women behind more blue and white tape, he caught Vicky's eye to head quickly over.

'Morning, boss,' he heard her say, his attention being drawn by the smoke. 'I take it you got my message?'

Drifting to a halt, he turned to look at her. 'Surprisingly, no, I didn't.'

'Oh, right. I did call.'

'Yes, I know. Sally told me. For future reference,' he continued, spying Cooper on the other side of the street, sharing a seemingly hilarious joke with Townsend and Henderson, 'the next time I'm mugged, and the assailant makes off with my phone, it may be worth trying to find some other way of contacting me.'

Vicky's face flecked with colour. 'Oh. Sorry, boss. That was stupid of me.'

'It was a bit, but don't worry. At least I was able to have a lie in.'

'How are you, anyway?'

'Other than a splitting headache,' he replied, lifting a hand to the top of his head, 'I'm OK. So, anyway, what's the story here?'

Vicky dropped her eyes to her open notebook. 'An emergency call was made at half-past seven this morning. It wasn't until gone half-past eight when the firemen on site informed us that a body had been found on the third floor, which was when I called you.'

'Do we know the body's identity?' he asked, glancing about.

'We're still trying to account for everyone.'

Tanner turned to see the reserved expression on her face. 'But you think you know who it is?'

Her lips tightened as she looked up at him. 'From what was left of the credit cards, we're fairly sure it was the CEO, Richard Naylor.'

Tanner took a contemplative moment to listen to the ambient noises surrounding them. 'Have you seen the body?'

'I have,' she replied.

'Is there anything to suggest that his death was anything other than accidental?'

'Dr Johnstone is taking a look now.'

'And where is he?'

'In the back of the ambulance,' she replied, pointing towards it with her pen.

'May I ask why the body was moved?'

'The firemen said that the building's lack of structural integrity left them with no choice.'

'I don't suppose we have any idea what he was doing there at half-past seven in the morning?'

'Not yet.'

'Is there anyone we can ask who may know.'

'I was about to head over to see his wife. I was planning on asking her then.'

'What about the fire itself? Do we know what caused it?'

'Not officially, but the fireman seem fairly convinced it was arson. They found traces of petrol on the reception floor. Their initial thoughts are that it was either poured in through the letterbox, or someone broke inside to do so.'

'I don't suppose they said if they'd be able to tell which one it was?'

'To be honest, I can't say I asked.'

'OK, well, it would certainly be useful to know.'

'Is it important?' Vicky questioned, with just the hint of irritability.

'I suppose that depends on if we want to know if Richard Naylor was murdered or not?' Tanner replied, his eyes drifting thoughtfully over to the building's smouldering remains. 'If the aim of the fire was to try and cover up the fact that he'd been killed, either beforehand, or maybe by somehow trapping him up there, then I'd have thought it was more likely that the petrol was poured directly onto the floor, being that the arsonist would already have been inside. The letterbox alternative suggests that he may not have known anyone was there, leading naturally to the next question.'

'If the fire wasn't started to cover up whatever happened to Mr Naylor, then why was it?' Vicky mused, following Tanner's gaze.

'I'd have thought the answer to that would most likely lie with the stolen manuscript, especially as its author was found yesterday with his throat cut.'

'What about what happened to you last night?'

'What about it?'

'That whoever mugged you wasn't after your wallet, but was really trying to get his hands on the book, or at least the zip drive it was on.'

Tanner looked wistfully away. 'He asked for my wallet, then my phone. He never mentioned anything else.'

'What if he was trying to hide the fact that he was actually after the zip drive? Would he really have asked for it by name?'

Tanner again had to think back. 'I don't *think* so,' came his considered response. 'If he had been, he'd have said something like, "empty your pockets", which he didn't. There's another reason why it doesn't seem very likely. He'd have had to have known I had it.'

'OK, then who did?'

'Only Henderson,' Tanner replied. 'He gave it to me after wasting half the day trying to guess what the password was.'

'Nobody else?'

Tanner thought back to the moment Henderson had given it to him. 'Well, there *was* someone else there, but it couldn't have been him.'

'Couldn't have been who?'

'The suicide victim's father, the one who'd abandoned him after he was born. He came in asking about what happened to his son, primarily to find out if there was a chance he'd been murdered. He was in the interview room when Henderson gave it to me.'

'And why do you think it couldn't have been him?'

'Apart from the fact that I can't think of a single reason why he'd want to steal an unpublished book about Norfolk's role in the Cold War, he wasn't the guy who mugged me. I'd have recognised him if he was.'

'I thought you said you didn't see his face?'

'I didn't need to. The suicide victim's father is a well-spoken stick-thin man, who looks like he'd snap in two in a stiff breeze. He was also about the same height as me. The guy who mugged me was bigger in every way. He also sounded like he'd been brought up in a skip kept round the back of an East London council estate.'

'What if the suicide victim's father paid the man to mug you, with the specific instruction to make sure he got the flash drive?'

Tanner folded his arms with a doubtful frown. 'Firstly, it goes back to the point I made earlier; that my assailant was only interested in my wallet and phone. Secondly, the idea that he was paid to attack me seems a little far-fetched, don't you think?'

'But it *is* possible, though?'

'So's being attacked by a shark whilst sailing up the river Thurne.'

'Er...actually,' Vicky began, 'someone *was* attacked by a shark whilst sailing up the river

Thurne.'

'Not seriously?'

'It turned out to be a baby seal, looking for its mum. But that's not the point. In this day and age, I think it's *very* possible for someone to pay someone else to do such a thing.'

'I'll keep it in mind. Meanwhile,' Tanner continued, seeing Dr Johnstone emerge out from behind the ambulance, his face appearing tired and strained, 'I suppose we'd better have a chat with our medical examiner, who isn't looking particularly well himself.'

- CHAPTER THIRTY ONE -

RAISING A HAND to help attract Dr Johnstone's attention, Tanner elbowed his way between a couple of burly, square-jawed firemen, to lead Vicky over to him.

'Are you alright?' he immediately enquired, taking in the medical examiner's ashen grey complexion, and the red-raw skin encircling the edges of his nose.

Johnstone suddenly lifted his head to violently sneeze, causing everyone around him to take a cautionary backwards step.

'I take it that means you're not,' Tanner mused, holding his breath. The last thing he needed was to catch whatever viral disease Johnstone had managed to pick up.

'Man-flu, I'm afraid.'

'Well, I suppose it's better than woman-flu,' Tanner joked, offering Vicky an amused smirk, only to find her staring back at him with a particularly unamused grimace. 'Anyway,' he continued, clearing his throat, just as Johnstone blew his nose like a crumpled trumpet, 'shouldn't you be in bed?'

'I was, thank you,' Johnstone sniffed, lifting his watery blood-shot eyes to glare at Tanner with a look of hostile accusation.

'Don't look at me! It's not my fault that half of Norfolk's dwindling population seems to end up being murdered every other week. At least, I don't think it is.'

'I suppose you want to know if the charcoaled remains of what is left of the person found in the fire was one of those who'd been murdered?'

'Only if the answer is that he wasn't.'

'Then I'm afraid I can't help you.'

'You mean…he was?'

'No. I meant what I said.'

'And what was that?'

'That I can't help you.'

'Sorry, I'm confused.'

Lifting his head high in the air, Johnstone ever-so slowly opened his mouth.

Thinking he was about to sneeze again, Tanner leaned away.

'I wasn't sneezing,' Johnstone announced. 'I was sighing with annoyed frustration, or at least I was trying to.'

'Oh, right. And there was me about to ask for a plastic bag to be put over your head.'

'The point I was about to make is that I sincerely doubt if I, or anyone else for that matter, will be able to tell you if what is left of the person in the back of the ambulance was murdered or not, being that there's barely enough left of him to say with any certainty that he's even human. I'm not even sure I'm going to be able to tell you what he had for breakfast. The only thing remaining of him even vaguely recognisable is the contents of his wallet.'

'Do you at least know how he was found?'

'By one of the fireman, I assume.'

'Sorry, I meant, if he'd been tied up, maybe to a chair?'

'Well, he didn't arrive on one, if that's what you mean.'

'You can't tell if he'd been tied to anything?'

'Nope.'

'Not even by his hands?'

'Sorry, not a clue. If you don't believe me, you're more than welcome to take a look for yourself.'

Tanner considered the invitation for a moment before shaking his head. 'I think I'll wait for your post-mortem report.'

'Fair enough, but don't expect to get your hands on it anytime soon. I still haven't finished with the last body you left me with, and this bloody cold I've managed to pick up is hardly helping.'

- CHAPTER THIRTY TWO -

'EXCUSE ME,' CAME a deep baritone voice from Tanner's side. 'Are you the police officer in charge here?'

Tanner turned to find himself staring into the impossibly handsome face of a square-jawed fireman, his sapphire blue eyes burning bright against his smoke-blackened face. 'I wouldn't say I was in charge, as such,' he responded, keen to avoid taking on any more responsibility than he felt he'd already been burdened with, 'but I suppose I am the highest ranked officer here.'

'It's just that I was wondering what you wanted us to do now?'

'Er...' Tanner said, his eyes drifting over to what was left of the building as his mind searched for a suitable, preferably intelligent sounding response, '...to keep putting the fire out?' he eventually replied, immediately kicking himself for having said something that must have made him sound like a complete idiot.

The fireman grinned at him with a brilliant white smile. 'I must admit, I was thinking more along the lines of the building. The whole thing could collapse at any minute.'

'Right, I see. What do you – er – *normally* do under such circumstances?'

'Well, for a start,' the firemen began, glancing

sagaciously about, 'all these people need to be a lot further back than they currently are. Emergency personnel as well.'

'Of course.'

'These parked cars need to be moved.'

Tanner reached for his notebook.

'To be honest,' the fireman continued, 'it might be wise to evacuate the entire street, certainly the shops on either side. Then I'd suggest giving a demolition firm a call, together with the building's insurance company.'

'I assume you'll be able to provide us with some sort of a report, before the whole thing is demolished?'

'Well, yes, of course,' he replied, 'although there's not all that much more to say that you don't already know. I'd be very surprised if it wasn't arson. The fire originated in the reception area, the floor of which was covered with some form of flammable material, most likely petrol.'

'You mentioned to my colleague that you think it was either poured in through the letterbox, or someone broke in to do so.'

'You're going to ask me which one it is, aren't you.'

'It would be useful to know.'

'At this stage, I'm only going to be able to make an educated guess.'

'Which is?'

'That it was poured in from the outside, probably through the letterbox, but that's only because we found more petrol – if that *is* what was used – near the entrance than anywhere else.'

'None's been found outside the building, near the front door?'

'Not yet. We'll hopefully be able to provide you with a more definitive answer, but that depends on whether we think the building will remain standing long enough for us to find out. At the moment, I'm not risking the lives of my men until we're a little more confident that it will.'

'Can you tell me anything more about the body that was found?'

'Only what I've already told your colleague,' he replied, offering Vicky a brief but courteous smile.

'You don't have any idea if he'd been left there deliberately?'

'You're asking me if I think the fire was started in an attempt to cover up what happened to him?'

'Was it?'

'My primary job is to extinguish fires, Chief Inspector. Bodies found as a result aren't my responsibility, at least not directly.'

'Can you at least tell me *where* he was found?'

'I've already said. On the third floor.'

'Anywhere in particular?'

'Underneath one of the windows.'

'Could he have been trying to get out?'

'Possibly.'

'Was the window open?'

'The glass was broken, but the frame itself was closed, and there's no way to know if he'd broken it, as there isn't a single window in the entire building that hasn't been shattered by the heat.'

'Would he have been able to open it?'

'How do you mean?'

'Could he have been tied up?'

The fireman shook his head. 'Again, there's no way for us to know.'

'There must have been some indication if he had been?' Tanner continued, becoming increasingly frustrated.

'Have you seen the body?' the fireman shot back in

response.

'Well, no, but...'

'Then I suggest you do. I think you'd then be able to understand why neither myself, nor anyone else for that matter, would be able to offer you a single idea as to what he was doing there, be it trying to open a window for the chance of some fresh air, or staring out of it to enjoy the view.'

'Can you at least tell me if he was found with his arms held behind his back?'

'The twisted stubs of what remained of his arms were found stuck to the sides of his body. Whether they were originally there is impossible to say. If you'd like to form your own opinion on the matter, you're more than welcome to take a look at him for yourself, but I really don't think it will help.'

- CHAPTER THIRTY THREE -

'OTHER THAN THAT it would appear to have been started deliberately,' Vicky began, watching the fireman turn on his heel to leave, 'it doesn't look like we're going to learn a huge amount more from being here.'

'Unfortunately, I'm not even sure we know that!' Tanner responded.

'Er...he seemed fairly confident that it had been started intentionally.'

'All he said was that some sort of flammable material had been found on the reception's floor. For all we know, a cleaner kicked over a can of lighter fluid whilst sparking up a cheeky cigarette.'

'Yes, of course,' Vicky replied, nodding her head with exaggerated vigour. 'That must have been it.'

'Assuming someone did start the fire deliberately,' Tanner continued, ignoring her sarcastic response, 'I'm becoming increasingly convinced that the yet-to-be-published book lies at the heart of it.'

'More like the never-to-be-published book, given the fact that the company that was about to has just had its office burnt to the ground, and that its CEO was stuck on the third floor at the time.'

'Which could well explain why the fire was started in the first place: to make sure it wasn't!'

The tortured sound of twisting metal and crumbling masonry had them both staring around to see a large section of the building's roof collapse in a cloud of dirty-grey dust.

'It would help if there was some CCTV footage of the front of the building at the time in question,' mused Tanner. 'Maybe you could ask Gina to have a look? We could also do with getting our hands on that book. I assume it's stored on a server, somewhere?'

'It should be,' Vicky replied. 'Although, if it was located inside that building, then we could have a problem.'

Tanner's attention drifted over to a crowd of onlookers, held behind a line of blue and white tape. 'Isn't that one of the employees?' he asked, lifting himself onto the balls of his feet.

'Which one?' Vicky asked, attempting to follow his gaze.

'The woman sitting behind the desk when they first realised the manuscript had gone missing.'

'You mean, the one with the makeup, the jewellery, and the incandescently bright lime green dress, the same one she still appears to be wearing?'

'Uh-huh.'

'What about her?'

'I think we should see if we can have a chat. I don't suppose you can remember her name?'

'Not off the top of my head.'

'C'mon!' he suddenly announced, setting off towards her. 'Before she disappears.'

'I'm not sure how she's going to do that,' muttered Vicky, hopping into a run to keep up with him.

Reaching the crowd, Tanner held up a hand to help garner the woman's attention. 'Excuse me!' he called out, as discreetly as he thought was possible. 'I don't suppose we could have a quick word?'

He watched the woman glance furtively over each of her shoulders before looking back at him with a look of fretful consternation.

As everyone in the crowd stared first at him, then at the woman, Tanner ducked under the tape to begin apologetically elbowing his way through. 'I'm sorry,' he eventually said, stopping breathlessly in front of her, 'but aren't you one of Morgan & Naylor's employees.'

'I am,' she replied, her mascara-lined eyes dancing erratically between his, 'but I didn't set fire to the building!'

'Don't worry. I'm not suggesting you did.'

'Then what do you want to talk to me about?'

'Can we go somewhere a little more private?' he asked, glancing about at the group of on-lookers, pressing in around them.

Without waiting for her to reply, he led her through the crowd to a deserted shop front. There, he waited a moment for Vicky to join them whilst rummaging around for his old ID. 'DCI Tanner, Norfolk Police,' he eventually said, hoping she wouldn't notice the discrepancy in the displayed title. 'This, here, is my colleague, DI Gilbert.'

'Right – yes,' the woman replied. 'I remember you – from the other day.'

'Sorry, your name was again?'

'Clare Oxley, but I've already given a statement.'

'Regarding the fire?'

'In relation to the break-in.'

'About which you said…?'

'That I had nothing to do with that, either!'

'Again, Ms. Oxley, we're not saying you did.'

'I should hope not!'

'We were wondering, well, hoping really, that there's still going to be a copy of that stolen manuscript, perhaps stored on a computer somewhere?'

The woman's gaze returned to what remained of the building. 'Do you think that's why someone started the fire?'

'We don't know, but it's certainly a possibility, which is why we're keen to make sure that we can still get our hands on a copy.'

'What happened to the one I gave you?'

'Rather annoyingly, I was mugged last night.'

'Someone took it?' she gasped, putting two and two together surprisingly quickly.

'Along with my wallet, phone, and just about everything else.'

'My gosh! How awful!'

'Yes, quite,' he readily agreed.

'Well, I can download another copy for you, if that would help.'

'You can?'

'Of course! All our files are kept in the Cloud these days, which is rather fortunate, given what's happened, and everything.'

'That would certainly be appreciated,' Tanner replied, presenting her with a relieved smile. 'Thank you!'

'Shall I drop it around on another flash drive?'

'I don't suppose you could email me a copy, instead?'

'I'm sorry, but as I think Mr Naylor explained, it's against company policy to transfer copies of our clients' work via email.'

'I suppose I was hoping you'd be able to make an exception, given the circumstances?'

'Well, I'd have to ask Mr Naylor, of course.'

Tanner glanced around at Vicky. 'With regret,' he continued, turning back, 'I think that might be difficult.'

A look of curious concern flickered over the

woman's eyes. 'I'm sorry, but why's that?'

'A body was found inside what remains of your offices. We've yet to make a formal identification, but at the moment we're proceeding on the basis that it's your CEO.'

'You mean...Mr Naylor?'

Tanner replied with a remorseful nod.

'But...that's not possible. I only saw him yesterday evening. He left the office before I did.'

Tanner offered her a look of apologetic dispassion. 'Then I can only assume he came back at some point, before the fire started.'

The woman lifted her orange suntanned hand to stare down at her large gaudy watch. 'But – it's only just gone ten o'clock!'

'Your point being?'

'Well, Mr Naylor... He's not exactly what one would describe as an early bird. To be honest, these days we're lucky if we see him at all. When he does come in, it's certainly not before lunchtime. I'm fairly sure that if you go over to his house, you'll find him still having his breakfast, that's if he's even started it.'

- CHAPTER THIRTY FOUR -

AFTER THE WOMAN eventually agreed to email them a copy of the book in question, Tanner drove Vicky along Norfolk's winding country lanes, hoping to find out if what she'd said about the publishing director was true.

Parking in front of a surprisingly modest bungalow, tucked discreetly away at the end of an unassuming cul-de-sac, Tanner rang the doorbell to wait impatiently to see who was going to answer the door.

With no immediate response, he rang the bell again before stepping back to examine the windows for any signs of life.

'Are you sure this is the correct address?' he eventually asked Vicky.

'This is the one we've been given,' she responded, reaching inside her handbag for her phone.

The sound of movement from behind the door had Tanner adjusting his tie, as the timid grey face of an elderly woman peered out at them from the other side.

'Mrs Naylor?' he enquired.

'I am, yes. Who is it?'

'It's – er – Detective Chief Inspector Tanner, Norfolk Police,' he replied, once again having to pull out his old ID.

'Oh dear! I do hope we haven't done anything

wrong?'

'Not at all. We were hoping to speak to your husband?'

'I'm sorry, but Richard isn't in right now.'

Tanner exchanged a foreboding glance with Vicky. 'You wouldn't happen to know where he is, by any chance?'

'He's already gone to work, I'm afraid.'

'I must admit, I was kind of hoping he'd still be having his breakfast.'

'Normally, he would be!' she laughed, glancing down at a minuscule watch hanging loosely around her narrow bony wrist.

'Was there any reason why he did go in so early?'

'No reason in particular. He's been struggling to sleep recently – after the office was broken into. I think he just went in to make sure everything was still there.'

Taking a breath, Tanner couldn't help but to stare around at Vicky again.

'Is everything alright?' he heard the woman ask.

'Mrs Naylor,' he continued, searching his mind for the most sympathetic way of explaining to her what had happened. 'I'm afraid there's been a fire.'

'A fire?' she repeated, her watery grey eyes staring back.

'At the office – where your husband works.'

Seeing her lips had already started to quiver, as much as he didn't want to, he knew he had to tell her. 'I'm afraid that the body of a man was found inside. With the deepest regret, it is our belief that it's your husband.'

With the woman's gentle face still staring at him with confused incomprehension, Tanner wished he'd kept his mouth shut. 'We've yet to make a formal identification, of course,' he continued, hoping to somehow be able to take back what he'd already told her, 'being that he was only found a few hours ago, so there's every chance it isn't him. To be honest, at this stage, it could be anyone!'

Tanner watched the woman's jaw tighten as she lifted her chin.

'What did you say your name was again?' she demanded. 'Chief Inspector Tanner, wasn't it?'

'*Detective* Chief Inspector Tanner,' he corrected, with an anxious nod.

'Tell me, Detective Chief Inspector Tanner, why would a high-ranking police officer, such as yourself, come all the way over here to tell me that a body's been found if you aren't at least ninety percent sure that it *is* my husband?'

Unable to maintain eye contact, Tanner shifted awkwardly from one foot to the other. 'Well, I...'

'So, you *do* think it's him, then?'

Tanner pulled in a reticent breath. 'As I said, we can't be sure.'

'Would it help if I was to identify the body?'

Remembering the words of Dr Johnstone, and the fire officer he'd spoken to, Tanner opened his mouth. 'I'm afraid that – with the injuries he's reported to have sustained – I'm not sure if it – I don't think it would be...'

Seeing the woman's legs suddenly give way underneath her, Tanner leapt forward, catching her just in time before her head hit the floor.

'Call an ambulance!' he called back to Vicky, easing the elderly woman gently down until she was lying on the hallway's beige-coloured carpet.

Unable to tell if she was breathing, Tanner took hold of her wrist before placing two fingers against her neck.

'Is she OK?' he heard Vicky whisper.

'I – I don't know.'

'This is Detective Inspector Gilbert,' Vicky said on the phone, her tone strained with urgency. 'We need an ambulance.'

'I can't find a pulse,' Tanner muttered, abandoning her neck to hold an ear against her mouth.

With beads of sweat rippling over his forehead, he tugged up the sleaves of his suit. 'I don't think she's breathing,' he continued, placing his hands on top of her fragile, birdcage-like chest. 'I'm going to try CPR.'

'Do you know how?'

'Not really, but I'm going to have to try something.'

Doing his best to remember what he'd been taught during various first aid courses, he began pressing rhythmically down on her chest.

'How long till the ambulance arrives?' he asked, a few breathless moments later.

'They said about fifteen minutes.'

'Shit,' he cursed, opening her flaccid jaw to force air down into her lungs.

With Vicky looking on in muted silence, he repeated the process three more times before stopping to return his fingers to her neck.

'Anything?'

'I'm – I'm not sure. I don't suppose you've got a torch on you, by any chance?'

'You can use my phone,' she replied, fumbling to turn on its light.

Taking it from her, he peeled back one of the old woman's paper-thin eyelids to shine the light first down, then away. Repeating the process with the other eye, he slowly handed it back to climb unsteadily to his feet.

'Any sign of that ambulance?' he asked, glancing vacantly about.

'Nothing yet,' came Vicky's muted response.

'Well, wherever they are, they're too late,' he sighed. 'To be honest, even if they'd been parked outside when you called them, I'm not sure it would have made any difference.'

- CHAPTER THIRTY FIVE -

WHEN THE AMBULANCE eventually pulled up a few minutes later, Tanner left Vicky with the paramedics to wander back to his car. On the way, he checked his phone for messages. Seeing he'd had two missed calls, both from the main office, he quickly checked his email, hoping to find a copy of the mysterious book.

'Finally!' he exclaimed, finding an email with the attachment he'd been waiting for.

Relieved to be able to open it without the need of a password, he forwarded it onto Henderson to immediately follow it up with a call.

'Henderson, it's Tanner,' he began, the moment the DC's dithering voice came over the line. 'I hope you've been keeping yourself busy?'

'I've – er – been helping Cooper type up his notes.'

'Right. Well, I've just sent you an email. It's that book I asked you to read yesterday.'

'The one with the password?'

'The very same, just without the unnecessary encryption. So, as before, please, but this time it's an absolute priority.'

'Do you mind me asking if there's any particular reason why? It's just that I haven't finished Cooper's notes yet.'

Tanner could already feel his blood pressure beginning to rise. 'OK, well, first up, *I'm* your boss, not bloody Cooper!'

'Yes, boss. Sorry, boss.'

'And secondly, on the off chance that nobody's been keeping you up-to-date, the author of the said book was recently found with his throat cut, the company that was due to publish it was broken into before being burnt to the ground, what was left of the CEO's body was later found on the third floor, the man's poor, sweet, elderly wife just died of a heart attack on hearing the news, and I've got a splitting headache, which perhaps isn't too surprising, being that I spent the best part of last night wandering around A&E having my head stapled together, after some idiot decided to attack me, quite possibly to steal the exact same book I've just emailed to you.'

Hearing nothing from the other end of the line but the sound of muffled rustling, Tanner pulled in a breath before blaring down the line in furious consternation. 'ARE YOU LISTENING TO ME, HENDERSON?'

'Yes, boss. I've downloaded the file and I'm already halfway through the second page.'

'Oh, right,' Tanner replied, in a subdued, guilty tone. 'So, how long do you think it will take?'

'It's only about six-hundred pages, so I should be finished by five.'

'OK, good. Let me know the minute you have. Remember, you need to be on the lookout for anything relating to Bluebell Wood, no matter how small. Also, the names of our suspects. I'll email you a list of them at some point, but can you specifically make sure to keep your eyes open for a mention of that building developer?'

'Simon Balinger, wasn't it?'

'That's the one,' Tanner replied, grateful for having Henderson on board, probably for the first time since he'd offered him the job. 'Actually, you'd better keep your eyes open for anything relating to what's been going on around here recently.'

'I'll make notes as I go.'

Tanner smiled in grateful response. 'I'll leave you to it, then.'

'Oh, sorry, boss, before you go...?'

'Yes, Henderson, what is it?'

'Gina – I – I mean, DC Boothe has been trying to get hold of you.'

'Oh, right,' Tanner replied, raising an eyebrow. 'Any particular part?'

'I'm sorry?'

'Never mind. Is she about?'

'She's at her desk.'

'OK. If you can put me through, that would be useful.'

'Yes, boss. Right away.'

'And don't forget to call me the minute you find anything, no matter how small.'

'Will do!'

- CHAPTER THIRTY SIX -

'THANKS FOR CALLING me back,' came Gina's voice, a moment later.

'No problem. How can I help?'

'I've just finished that research report relating to Samuel Brogan.

'Yes, and...?'

'I was wondering if you wanted the gist of it now, or if I should simply send you the whole thing on email.'

'I'll take the highlighted version now, if that's alright.'

'OK, well, the main thing I thought to be of interest were the names of his first set of foster parents.'

'Which were?'

'Alan and Rebecca Adlington.'

The names rang a vaguely familiar bell inside Tanner's aching head, but for the life of him he couldn't remember from where.

'The Adlington Child Prostitution case?' Gina continued.

'Jesus Christ! That was them?'

'The very same. If you remember, it took over five years for them to be caught, only to be found hanging by their necks when the police turned up to arrest them. The fact that they were ever allowed to be foster parents caused a national outcry.'

'And the foster child in question. That was Samuel

Brogan?'

'For obvious reasons his name was never made public, but yes, I'm afraid it was. There's something else, as well.'

'Go on.'

'The place they were all living at the time. It was a small cottage, right in the middle of Bluebell Wood.'

Tanner's mind instantly took him back to the mysterious girl, and where she'd led him to, the same place he later discovered couldn't possibly have existed, at least not in the pristine condition he could have sworn he'd seen it in. 'There's that name again,' he eventually muttered, shaking his head to try and clear his thoughts.

'Do you think it's relevant?'

'Apart from it being where their sexually abused foster son chose to kill himself, it's also the same place Professor Baxendale's sister said she overheard her brother and his late night visitor discussing.'

'But what can a couple renting out their foster son to the highest bidder have to do with the murder of a history professor and his yet-to-be published book?'

'Or that the company about to publish it was burnt to the ground,' added Tanner, 'whilst its CEO was still inside.'

A moment of contemplative silence followed, eventually broken by Gina's voice. 'Maybe it's just a coincidence?'

'I don't believe in them,' Tanner stated, with curt dismissiveness. 'I don't suppose you found out who led the investigation into the Adlington case?'

'I did,' she replied, in a hesitant tone.

'You're going to say Superintendent Whitaker, aren't you?'

'I'm afraid I am.'

'That's just great! The only person who might have

been able to shed a little more light on the matter was probably involved himself!'

'He's also dead, of course,' added Gina, a little unhelpfully.

'I don't suppose you could see if anyone else was working here at the time?'

'I've already looked.'

'And…?'

'Cooper and Vicky joined the year after.'

'Anyone else?'

'Nobody that still works here.'

'Well, it would certainly be useful to find someone we could talk to about it.'

'I was thinking that maybe Superintendent Forrester might know, being that he's your old boss, and everything?'

'For a start, he's still my boss, and secondly, he started after I did.'

'Then I suppose you could always go straight to the horse's mouth.'

'I wasn't aware that there were any horses involved.'

'I was referring to the perpetrators themselves, or at least one of them.'

'You just told me they hanged themselves?'

'They did, but only as they were about to be arrested. The husband was already dead by the time they were found, but they managed to cut down the wife in time.'

'She's still alive?'

'Just about. She was given ten years for her involvement.'

'Anywhere nice?'

'Broadmoor Hospital.'

Taking a quiet, contemplative moment, Tanner's eyes drifted off into space.

'I can try to make an appointment for you to see her, if you like?'

'I'd rather not have to spend an entire day travelling all the way down to sunny Berkshire, unless I have to, of course. Let's just hope Henderson comes up with something.'

'Henderson?' Gina questioned.

'He's reading Professor Baxendale's book as we speak, at least, I hope he is.'

- CHAPTER THIRTY SEVEN -

HEARING HIS PHONE make an unfamiliar bleeping noise, he pulled it away to see that none other than Forrester was trying to get through.

With the uncomfortable realisation that he'd once again forgotten to return his various calls, a wave of nauseating guilt left him swaying unsteadily on his feet. 'Hold on a sec, Gina,' he said, resting a steadying elbow onto his car's sleek low roof. 'I've got someone else on the line.'

Accepting the incoming call, he pulled himself up straight. 'Forrester, sir. I'm sorry I haven't had the chance to call you back yet.'

'No doubt you've been busy,' he heard his superintendent reply, 'but I am becoming increasingly curious to know how many times I'm going to have to call in the future before I can realistically expect to get a call back?'

'Once again, I apologise. I was going to phone you last night, when I got home,' he lied, 'but then I was mugged, just down the road from where I live.'

'Not seriously?'

'I'm afraid so.'

'Are you alright?'

'Just about. I was told I needed stitches in my head, forcing me to spend half the night in A&E. I'm fairly sure I didn't, but unfortunately, you can't really argue with a paramedic, two nurses, three doctors, a cleaner, and the guy who operates the MRI machine, at least not all at the same time.'

'Why didn't you tell me this before?'

'Probably because the guy who mugged me took my phone.'

'You mean, the one I'm speaking to you on now?'

'This is my old one, sir.'

'I see. So, you *could* have called me, then?'

'As I said before, sir, with so much going on, and with what happened, I simply forgot.'

'I still can't believe someone actually mugged you. Didn't you tell them who you are?'

Tanner rolled his eyes into the back of his head. 'Yes, sir. Several times, in fact. But for some unknown reason, the guy didn't seem to believe me.'

'Did he take anything else?'

'My wallet and ID. My notebook as well.'

'But not your car?'

'Thankfully not.'

'And you're alright?'

'Yes, sir. Thank you for asking.'

'OK, good. So anyway, how about that update I've been asking for, maybe starting with the suicide victim not being one, despite the fact that he was found hanging by his neck?'

'We're fairly confident that it was as it appeared.'

'But the news said his death was being treated as suspicious?'

'There was a brief moment when we were, but only because whatever he used to support himself with was missing, and that we've been unable to find it, which perhaps wasn't too surprising.'

'Why's that?'

'Because we believe he used a log of some description, which was possibly taken by the dog who found the body. And as his body was discovered in the middle of a wood, finding a particular piece inside one did prove to be somewhat challenging.'

'And what about the historian, Professor Baxendale, the man found with his throat cut? I suppose you think he killed himself as well?'

'No, sir. We're definitely treating that as murder.'

'And...?'

'And, er...what, sir?

'Do you have any suspects?'

'Oh, right. Well, we've yet to identify anyone specifically, but a man was seen entering the victim's house to engage in what was apparently a somewhat heated discussion two days before. According to the witness's description, and the method used to cut the victim's throat, it's possible that his attacker was a military man, possibly with special forces training.'

'Who was the witness?'

'The victim's sister.'

'Are you sure it couldn't have been her?'

'We haven't ruled her out, but she doesn't appear to have a strong enough motive. There's also the link to the publishing house, the one that was burnt down after it was broken into. It was the same one that was due to publish the professor's latest book.'

'So I've heard. I don't suppose we have any idea how it started?'

'Petrol, or something similar, had been poured out over the reception floor.'

'And the body found inside?'

'You know about that as well?'

'I do read my own police departments' reports, Tanner!'

'Then why the hell do you keep phoning me up every five minutes demanding bloody updates?' he asked, fortunately only to himself. 'At the moment,

we're proceeding on the basis that it's the publishing house's founder and CEO, Mr Richard Naylor, but we've yet to formally identify the body.'

'What time did the fire start?

'At around half-past seven.'

'Do we know what he was doing there at such an ungodly hour?'

'According to his wife, he just happened to go to work early that day.'

'She didn't know if there was any particular reason why?'

'All she said was that he hadn't been sleeping well, since the office was broken into.'

'Did you ask her if she knew of anyone who may have wished him harm; sending him threatening letters, that sort of thing?'

'Unfortunately not, sir.'

'Then I suggest you go back and ask her.'

'I'm afraid, under the circumstances, that could be a little difficult.'

'And what circumstances are those, may I ask?'

'Because she's dead, sir.'

'What?'

'She passed away, whilst we were talking to her.'

A moment of silence followed, before Forrester's subdued voice came rasping back over the line. 'I'm sorry to hear that.'

'I suspect the news of what happened to her husband was just a little too much for her.'

Tanner heard Forrester draw in a breath.

'OK, so, what happens now?'

'We need to establish a connection between the murder of Professor Baxendale and the fire at the publishing house,' Tanner replied.

'With the lengths someone is clearly going to, to stop the book from being published, I'd have thought that was obvious.'

'Which is why our attention is currently focussed on what was written inside it.'

'Which was?'

'We don't know.'

'Haven't you read it?'

'Not yet. We were given a copy on a flash drive, only to discover that it was password protected. That was before I was mugged, of course.'

'Please don't tell me it was taken as well?'

'Regretfully, yes, it was.'

'And let me guess; with the book's publisher being burnt to the ground, a copy of it no longer exists?'

'The publishing house in question keeps all their computer files in the Cloud.'

'So, you do have a copy, then?'

'Yes, sir.'

'Forgive me for asking, Tanner, but are you deliberately trying to wind me up?'

'Er...not on purpose,' Tanner replied.

'Then why the hell have you just spent the last five minutes telling me that you don't have a copy of the book, when, in fact, you do?'

'I was simply endeavouring to explain the reasons why we've yet to read it, sir.'

'You are winding me up, aren't you?'

'Absolutely not, sir.'

A moment of silence followed as Tanner wondered if the peculiar sound he could hear coming from the other end of the line was his superintendent, grinding his teeth.

'OK,' Forrester eventually continued, 'so, what does the book say?'

'I've no idea, sir. I haven't read it.'

'If you're not extremely careful, Tanner, I'm going to come over there and thump you!'

Tanner resisted the urge to ask him how he'd be able to do that, given the fact that he didn't know where he was. Instead, he endeavoured to take a more serious tone. 'DC Henderson has just started working his way through it. He has a degree from Oxford, or was it Cambridge, I can never remember which. Anyway, he's apparently rather good at that sort of thing.'

'You don't mean to tell me that you've managed to employ someone who can actually read?'

'Yes, sir. At least, he says he can. I think it was even mentioned on his CV.'

'Can you please take this a little more seriously, Tanner?'

'Sorry, sir, I thought I was.'

Another peculiar sound came from the other end of the line.

'So, anyway,' Forrester eventually continued, 'do you have any idea how long it's going to take him to get through it?'

'He said he should be done by five o'clock today.'

'Oh, right. That's not so bad, I suppose. I assume he knows what sort of things he needs to be on the lookout for.'

'Anything relating to the people involved, including the mention of Bluebell Wood.'

'Why Bluebell Wood?'

Tanner shrugged. 'It just seems to be coming up a little too often to be ignored.'

'I was only aware of it being mentioned in relation to where the suicide victim's body was found.'

'That's correct.'

'Which you just told me *isn't* being treated as suspicious.'

'Correct again.'

'Then why is DC Henderson reading a book with

the specific instruction to look out for anything relating to Bluebell Wood, when there would appear to be nothing to connect it to the murder of the book's author, or the fire where the owner of its publisher was found?'

'As I said, sir, the name just seems to keep coming up.'

'But you haven't said in what context?'

Tanner pulled the phone away from his mouth to let out a heavy sigh. He had little interest in spending his precious time and dwindling mental reserves having to explain his reasoning. He also resented the fact that he was being asked to. But at the end of the day, he knew he didn't have much of a choice, being that it was his immediate superior who was asking. 'It was what Professor Baxendale's sister said about the man who came to visit her brother the night before he was murdered,' he eventually continued.

'Which was?'

'That she thought she heard the word "bluebell" being mentioned when they were arguing.'

'Is that it?'

'Well, yes, sir, but it was the *only* word she heard, and being that Bluebell Wood was the location Samuel Brogan chose to hang himself, and that it's an ancient woodland that Simon Balinger has magically acquired planning permission to build what looks likely to be a sizeable housing development, it's just too much of a coincidence to ignore.'

'I'm sorry, but who the hell is Simon Balinger?'

'He's a property developer; the self-proclaimed, "Richest Man in Norfolk".'

'By the sounds of it, the most egotistical one as well.'

'Very possibly,' agreed Tanner. 'We have unconfirmed evidence that the only reason he was able to acquire the aforementioned planning permission was by bribing the local councillor in charge. On top of that, the young man who uncovered the evidence was the same person we found hanging by his neck in the middle of where there will shortly be about five-hundred brand new homes.'

'Once again, Tanner, I thought you said that the suicide victim's death *isn't* being treated as suspicious?'

'It isn't, sir.'

'Well, it sounds to me like it should be, and I'm probably the least suspicious person in the entire British Police Force.'

'We've since discovered that the suicide victim had a number of personal problems. His father abandoned him and his mother when he was only three months old. He then spent five years being farmed out to various paedophiles by his foster parents, which is where I've just found yet another connection to Bluebell Wood.'

'Which is...?'

'They used to live in a cottage, slap-bang in the middle of it.'

There was a momentary pause before Forrester's voice came back over the line. 'OK, I'd have to agree with you, the name does seem to be coming up rather a lot, but not in connection to Professor Baxendale's murder, nor the fire that burnt down the publishing house. And just because Samuel Brogan was the victim of sexual abuse, doesn't automatically mean he wasn't murdered.'

'As I said at the beginning, sir, apart from the unproven motive that Simon Balinger may have had for doing so, there's no material evidence to support the idea that he was.'

'You mean, apart from the missing piece of wood

the young man apparently used to support himself with?'

'Which we still think was most likely taken by the dog who found him. If he *was* murdered, then there's no logical reason for someone to have taken the one thing that would help confirm that he did indeed commit suicide.'

'Unless the murderer knew it had his DNA on it?'

'Well, yes, sir, but as I said, with the item in question being missing, lost inside approximately two-hundred acres of densely packed trees, each one made up of the exact same material, it seems highly unlikely that we'll ever be able to find it. Besides, I'm not exactly short of murder victims at the moment.'

'But you still haven't explained why you're using Bluebell Wood to connect the murder of Professor Baxendale to the fire at the publishing house? Everything relating to it: the boy's suicide, what happened under the care of his foster parents, and your suspicions that a property developer bribed a local government official to secure the planning permission, doesn't appear to have the slightest thing to do with it.'

'If it wasn't for the fact that Professor Baxendale's sister thought she heard the word bluebell being mentioned during an argument between her brother and the man we believe to have killed him, then I'd have to agree with you.'

'To be perfectly honest, Tanner, it sounds to me like you're grasping at straws.'

'I'd rather be grasping at straws than trying to find a piece of hay in a rather large haystack, sir.'

'Sorry, Tanner, but what are you talking about?'

'Nothing, sir. Anyway, I think we'll just have to wait and see if there's any mention of Bluebell Wood in Professor Baxendale's book.'

'Which DC Henderson says he should have finished by five o'clock today?'

'With any luck, sir, yes.'

'OK good, then I look forward to hearing back from you then.'

Tanner cursed under his breath. 'Yes, sir,' he replied, with an undertone of grudging contempt.

'Whilst I'm here, how's Christine doing?'

'She's fine.'

'And the baby?'

'Yet to make an appearance.'

'I assume you're still planning on getting married tomorrow?'

'Unless Christine's changed her mind,' he laughed, a little nervously. 'You are still coming, I take it?'

'I wouldn't miss it for the world, although, I'm not sure how I could, being that you asked me to be your best man, and everything.'

- CHAPTER THIRTY EIGHT -

NDING THE CALL with Forrester, Tanner was left staring along the elongated bonnet of his XJS, unable to shake the feeling of growing apprehension about his rapidly approaching wedding, the one everyone seemed to have to keep reminding him about. It wasn't the wedding, so much. He didn't have a single doubt in his mind about his decision to marry Christine. It was the timing of the whole thing. Exactly how he was going to get through an entire day professing his love for his new wife in front of just about everyone he knew – including his boss – whilst being preoccupied by an increasingly complicated murder investigation, one he still didn't have a single suspect for, was frankly beyond him. What was perhaps more concerning was that if something didn't swing in his favour soon, he didn't have a chance of making their honeymoon, the one he'd already paid an arm-and-a-leg for, the same one he knew Christine was in desperate need of. Even if he *was* somehow able to go, who could he leave in charge in his absence? Not Cooper! Vicky was a more likely candidate, but there was no way she was ready to take on such a huge responsibility, even if it was on a temporary basis.

With the sudden urge to talk to Christine, he dialled their home phone number to start pacing up and down beside his car.

'Hey, honey, it's me,' he said, the moment the call was answered.

'Hi, darling. What's up?'

'Nothing, really. I just wanted to hear your voice.'

'Oh, that's nice. Are you OK? You sound a little down.'

'A little, perhaps. How about you?'

'I'm alright.'

'And the baby?'

'Yet to make an appearance.'

Tanner laughed. 'That's exactly what I just said to Forrester.'

'I assume he's been on your back about the investigation?'

'You could say that. He's also reminded me about our wedding.'

'Did he need to?'

'A little, perhaps.'

'Oh – right.'

'It's just this bloody investigation!'

'Isn't it always?'

'This one more than most. Did you hear there'd been a fire?'

'No! Where? Not at the police station?'

'It was at an office in Stalham. We think it's likely to be linked to the murder of Professor Baxendale, being that it was his publisher's office that was burnt down, and that the body of its owner and CEO was found inside. Worse still, when I relayed the news to the man's wife, she collapsed, and despite my very best efforts, I was unable to revive her.'

There was a momentary pause from the end of the line. 'It sounds like you've had quite a day.'

'It isn't over yet. I've still got a suicide victim who I don't even know *did* kill himself, a murder victim who definitely didn't, the charred remains of a publisher who I've got no idea is a murder victim or not, and the only suspect I have for everything is the self-proclaimed "Richest Man in Norfolk", who most likely didn't murder anyone, being that the only person he had any reason to was the aforementioned suicide victim, a young man who by all accounts had every reason to kill himself, as he spent his childhood being farmed out to a network of local paedophiles.'

Pausing for breath, Tanner re-opened his mouth to ask, 'I don't suppose the name Adlington rings a bell?'

'You mean...the young man found in Bluebell Wood? He was the Adlingtons' foster child?'

'I take it that means you have.'

'Good God! That poor boy! What he must have gone through. It doesn't bear thinking about.'

'You didn't happen to counsel him, by any chance?'

'Not me, no. He was too young. He'd have been seen by a child psychologist.'

'But you do know about it, though?'

'Only what I heard on the news.'

'Did you know they all lived inside that cottage in the middle of Bluebell Wood, the one I mentioned to you the other day.'

'I don't think I did. Do you think it's relevant?'

'Only in that it helps to explain why Samuel Brogan chose that particular location to take his own life, which, in turn, gives us another reason to conclude that *was* what he did.'

'What about the murder of that professor, and the fire? Do you think they could be connected?'

'Forrester doesn't seem to think so.'

'I wasn't asking what Forrester thinks, I was asking what *you* think?'

Tanner took a moment to collect his thoughts. 'The name Bluebell Wood came up when we were interviewing a witness about Professor Baxendale's murder, or at least the word "bluebell" did. She heard it mentioned whilst listening to an argument between the murder victim and a visitor he had two days before he was killed.'

'Then there must be a connection.'

'I'd have thought so, but what it is, I have no idea. I've currently got Henderson speed-reading his way through the professor's yet-to-be-published book, to see if Bluebell Wood gets a mention. If it doesn't, then I don't know what I'm going to do, and with our wedding tomorrow...'

'Don't worry about that. Everything's set. All you have to do is show up.'

'I'm actually more concerned about the honeymoon afterwards. I'm sorry, honey, but unless something turns up, and fast, then I really don't see how I'm going to make it.'

There was a prolonged silence before Christine's voice eventually came back on the line. 'How long will it take for Henderson to read that book?'

'He said he should be done by five o'clock today.'

'Do you have any leads you can chase up between now and then?'

'I really don't,' he admitted, glancing guiltily about, as if checking to make sure a reporter wasn't eavesdropping on his conversation.

'There must be something.'

'As I said before, the only suspect I have is in relation to Samuel Brogan, who most likely wasn't even murdered. He's a property developer by the name of Simon Balinger.'

'What makes him a suspect?'

'As I said, he isn't, being that Samuel Brogan wasn't murdered.'

'But if he was?'

Tanner drew in a frustrated breath. 'It's complicated. It's also unproven.'

'Does it have anything to do with Bluebell Wood?'

'Well, yes, but...'

'And your murder victim was heard discussing the very same place with some mysterious person the night before he was killed?'

'You think Professor Baxendale's visitor could have been the property developer?'

'I don't see why not. I mean, there *is* a connection.'

'Albeit tenuous.'

'Beggars can't be choosers.'

'Are you calling me a beggar?'

'In this particular instance, yes!'

'Fair enough, I suppose.'

'I assume you had a reason for considering him to be the sort of person who *could* have killed someone. If you didn't, then you wouldn't have suspected him of being involved in what happened to Samuel Brogan.'

Tanner said nothing in response.

'Have you at least asked him about it?'

'I can't say I have.'

'Well, there you go. That's one suspect for you to chase. Now, who else do you have?'

Grateful to have Christine to talk to, Tanner pulled out his notebook as he took a moment to think. 'There's the professor's sister. She's the witness I mentioned, the one who said her brother, the professor, had a visitor two days before he was killed. She's also the person who told us that she overheard the word bluebell being mentioned.'

'Could she have been lying – about the visitor?'

'The thought had crossed my mind.'

'I assume you've spoken to her?'

'Only about what happened to her brother.'

193

'Do you know where she was when the fire started?'

'Not yet,' Tanner replied, making notes.

'Maybe you could ask her about Samuel Brogan as well?' Christine continued. 'It's possible that she knows him. You never know, there could even be a connection between all this and the Adlington case.'

'We've already thought about that. I was thinking about trying to find someone to talk to who was involved, but the only person we've been able to identify was the guy heading it up, and he's indisposed, permanently, I may add.'

'I assume you're referring to Superintendent Whitaker?'

'The one and only.'

'There's nobody else?'

'No one we can think of.'

'What about the Adlingtons?'

'The husband hanged himself before they had a chance to arrest him.'

'But not the wife,' Christine commented. 'I remember seeing her being lifted into the back of an ambulance on TV.'

'No, but she's serving a ten year sentence at Broadmoor, all the way down in Berkshire.'

'I think you'll find that she was transferred a few years ago.'

'Oh, right. I don't suppose you know where to?'

'Weybourne Psychiatric Hospital, on the North Norfolk coast.'

'Are you sure?'

'Not one hundred percent, but I can check if you like.'

'Don't worry. With any luck, Henderson will find something in Professor Baxendale's book.'

'I thought you said he won't be finished until five?'

'I did.'

'Then you may as well go and see her.'

'Who? Mrs Adlington?'

'If she's only up in Weybourne, then why not?'

'Er…because I don't particularly wish to have a hot date with some deranged psychopathic nutjob, thank you very much.'

'We all have to do things in life we don't want to.'

'I don't.'

'At least it would give you the opportunity to ask if she knows anything about any of the people involved.'

'Not if she's pumped full of drugs and doesn't know what day of the week it is.'

'You won't know until you go.'

'I think I might just wait until Henderson finishes that book,' he muttered, propping himself up against the side of his car.

'What on earth are you worried about? Do you think she's going to come at you with a knife?'

'I was more worried that she might come at me with her tongue.'

'That's disgusting.'

'I know!'

'For goodness' sake, John. Just go!'

'Alright! Alright!' he replied, shoving himself off the car like a disgruntled teenager. 'I'm going!'

- CHAPTER THIRTY NINE -

ENDING THE CALL with Christine, Tanner turned lazily around to unlock the car, only to find Vicky, staring over its roof at him from the other side. 'Jesus Christ!' he exclaimed, clutching at his chest. 'You scared the absolute shit out of me!'

'Good to see you too, boss.'

'What the hell are you doing standing there, anyway?'

'Er...listening to your private conversation, obviously.'

Tanner narrowed his eyes at her before tugging open the door.

'So, where are we going again?' she continued, cupping her hand under the Jag's polished chrome doorhandle.

'I'm going to see Samuel Brogan's original foster parents, at least one of them.'

'Any particular reason why?'

'It's a long story.'

'OK, that's fine. You can tell me on the way.'

'No. I want you to go and see Professor Baxendale's sister again, to ask her where she was when the fire started.'

'And you trust me to do that on my own, do you?'

'Not really, but with my wedding tomorrow, I'm running out of time.'

'Good to know.'

'Then I want you to pay a visit to our property developer friend.'

'Simon Balinger?'

Tanner nodded in response. 'Ask him the same thing. Also, where he was the night before Professor Baxendale was murdered. If you need me, I'll be on my mobile.'

'Do you mind me asking where you're going?'

'Weybourne Psychiatric Hospital.'

Vicky glanced up at him with a confused expression. 'Why are you going there?'

'I've already told you. To see one of Sammy Brogan's original foster parents. Seriously, Vicky, if you ever expect to be able to lead your own murder investigation, you really will have to try a little harder to keep up.'

- CHAPTER FORTY -

ARRIVING AT WEYBOURNE Psychiatric Hospital to spend a frustrating half-hour being dragged through a variety of stringent security checks, Tanner eventually found himself twiddling his thumbs inside a claustrophobically small white room, devoid of anything but a rectangular table and two chairs, all of which had been screwed down to a tiled floor from which arose the caustic smell of undiluted bleach.

As he wondered just how much longer he was going to have to wait, he went to pull out his phone to check for messages, only to remember that it had been confiscated, together with his watch, shoes, belt, and tie, apparently in case the patient he'd come to see was to overpower him with the sudden urge to try on his various fashion accessories. The actual reason they'd given; that she could potentially use any of the items to hurt either him or herself, possibly both, one before the other, only left him with an anxious sense of extreme vulnerability. He didn't mind being without his belt and tie. He could even cope without a watch and phone. But having to sit inside such an inhospitable room without his shoes on made him feel as if he was stark naked.

The muffled rattle of chains from the other side of the metal door in front of him had him clenching his hands together on top of the table.

Cursing Christine for making him go, he braced himself as the door swung open to reveal first a large female nurse with a miserable looking face, then the woman he'd been waiting so patiently to see.

As he watched the patient being led inside, he took a moment to take in her grey skeletal-like arms, and how her head slumped forward at an acute angle, as if she'd just been cut down from the hangman's noose.

Waiting for her to be sat silently down in the chair opposite, he tilted his head forward to try and see her face. But all he could make out were a hooded pair of eyes, part-hidden by a mop of long straggly grey hair.

'Mrs Adlington?' he gently enquired, clearing his throat before doing so. 'My name's Detective Chief Inspector Tanner. I'm from Norfolk Police. If I may, I'd like to ask you a few questions, particularly in relation to where you used to live, the cottage in the middle of Bluebell Wood? Do you remember?'

An uncomfortable silence fell over the room as he waited for her to nod, smile, or to provide some sort of indication that she'd heard him. But her face didn't seem to move. All she did was to stare vacantly at the top of the table whilst her body rocked slowly back and forth, as if she were sitting on a rocking chair.

'She's just had her afternoon meds,' commented the nurse, standing beside the door. 'To be honest, I doubt you'll get much out of her.'

With the realisation that he'd completely wasted his time, Tanner transferred his attention to the nurse. 'Does she really need to be given quite so much?'

'I suppose that depends on if you want her to gouge out your eyes with her fingernails,' she replied, offering him a chilling smile.

'How long till they wear off?'

'You don't want them to wear off.'

Tanner drew in a breath in an effort to suppress his rising anger. 'I came here with the explicit intention of being able to talk to her about an on-going murder investigation, so yes, I *would* like them to wear off!'

'Then I can only apologise,' the nurse shrugged. 'Someone should have advised you as to her mental condition before you came.'

'Are you saying she's incapable of talking?'

'Not at all. She's actually one of our more vocal patients. It's what she says that I doubt you'd find particularly useful.'

'Which is?'

'Random words. Nothing that would appear to have any meaning. When she's at her most lucid, she does sometimes quote Shakespeare. Other times the Bible. More often than not, she just sits there rattling out a list of numbers.'

'Numbers?'

'Thirty-two. Sixty-four. That sort of thing.'

'Why on earth does she do that?'

'I've no idea.'

'You don't know if they have any meaning?'

'I doubt it.'

'You don't think to make a note of them?'

'One of the doctors might.'

Tanner returned his attention to the seemingly half-comatosed patient. 'Has she always been like this?'

'For as long as I've been here.'

'And how long is that?'

'I started just after she was brought in.'

'She hasn't improved since?'

'In my experience, patients rarely do. They normally only seem to get worse.'

'But I thought they came here to be treated, with the aim of helping them to get better?'

'That may be the intention, but it rarely seems to work. The only change I've seen in Mrs Adlington, for example, is that she started singing a few months ago.'

'Singing?' Tanner repeated.

'If you can call it that,' the nurse added. 'I remember one of the doctors remarking on it at the time that it was a sign she was in a more peaceful state of mind. 'Would you like to sing us one of your little songs, Mrs Adlington?' the nurse enquired, stepping forward to lift her voice in a patronising tone.

Tanner found himself waiting in silent anticipation.

'Looks like she's not in the mood,' the nurse smirked. 'Sorry.'

Letting out a frustrated sigh, Tanner was about to push himself up when he heard a melodic murmuring sound coming from between the patient's pale cracked lips.

'Sounds like it's your lucky day!' the nurse exclaimed, offering Tanner a sneering grimace.

Tanner held up a silencing hand as he leaned forward over the table.

With the nurse huffing with indifference as she leaned back against the wall, Tanner closed his eyes to listen.

Like the sound of a gently building breeze, brushing against the top of a bed of reeds, the patient's voice grew steadily louder.

"Bluebell Wood, a haunting sight,
Where darkness reigns, throughout the night.
Stay close, my child, hold on tight,
Through Bluebell Wood, we tread with fright."

Straining his ears to listen, a cold shiver began

creeping down the length of his spine. There was no doubt about it. It was the same song he'd heard that pretty young woman sing, when he'd stumbled across that cottage in Bluebell Wood, the very same one he'd later been told he couldn't possibly have seen, as it had been burnt to the ground five years before.

- CHAPTER FORTY ONE -

WITH NEITHER A notepad nor a pen, Tanner began repeating the song's words to himself as he left the patient to make his way out. The moment he was reunited with his personal possessions, he grabbed a seat in the hospital's sterile reception area to quickly scrawl them down. Once done, he made his way out to the carpark to put a call through to the office.

'Hi, Gina,' he began, asking for her by name, 'how's everything been going?'

'OK, but no news, I'm afraid.'

'No problem. I've actually got a poem I'd like you to take a look at.'

'If it's to confess your undying love for me, bearing in mind what's happening tomorrow, I think you might be a little too late.'

'Sorry, but what's happening tomorrow?'

'Er...your wedding?'

'Yes, of course,' he replied, shaking his head. 'It's actually for research purposes.'

'What, your wedding?'

'No, the poem!'

'Well that's a relief. I was about to call Christine, to let her know.'

'It's actually more like a song,' Tanner continued. 'Anyway, I've just emailed it to you. Any chance you can plug it into Google, to see if anything comes up?'

'No problem, boss.'

'I don't suppose you've heard anything from Henderson, by any chance?'

'Should I have?'

'I was just wondering how he's getting on with that book.'

'I've no idea. I haven't seen him in ages.'

'He's not at his desk?'

'Not that I can see.'

'Oh, right,' Tanner replied, with a note of concern. 'Can you ask him to call me, the minute you see him?'

'No problem.'

'And don't forget that poem.'

'I'm just taking a look at it now.'

With another call coming through, he ended the conversation to find Vicky, waiting for him on the other line.

'Hello, boss. Where are you?'

'I'm about to leave Weybourne. Why?'

'I was just wondering if you'd be able to pick me up?'

'I thought you were driving over to see Professor Baxendale's sister?'

'I've already done that.'

'Oh, right. So why do you need me to pick you up?'

'Because I came outside to find that my bloody car won't start!'

'I'm sorry to hear that,' he laughed, 'although, it's reassuring to know that I'm not the only one with a car that keeps breaking down.'

'I think, in this particular instance, it might actually be my fault.'

'Why? What did you do?'

'It's not so much what I did, than what I didn't.'

'Which was?'

'Fill it with petrol.'

Climbing into his own car, he laughed again. 'Have you tried calling the AA?'

'Well, I would, of course, but I'm in desperate need of petrol, not a double Vodka with a twist of lemon.'

'I was actually referring to the Automobile Association.'

'Oh, right! No, I haven't called them.'

'Any reason why not?'

'Well, firstly, I'm not a member, and secondly, I thought you might have a spare can in your boot, being that you drive the most uneconomical car on the planet.'

'And that's where you're wrong, my dear.'

'You mean, you don't?'

'No, you're wrong in the sense that I think the original Ford GT40 is the most uneconomical car on the planet. I've got a spare can in the boot. Hold tight, I'll be there in a few minutes.'

- CHAPTER FORTY TWO -

ARKING ON THE pavement, two cars down from Vicky's beaten-up old Peugeot 106, Tanner stepped out to wave at her before scooting around to the boot.

'So, what do you fancy?' he asked, opening it up as she sauntered her way over. 'E10 Unleaded, E5 Super Unleaded, or some good old fashioned under-the-counter 4 Star with extra lead?'

'I don't suppose you've got any diesel?'

'Please, tell me you're joking?'

'Sorry, yes. E10 is fine.'

'That's handy, because that's all I've got,' he smiled, heaving out a small green plastic can. 'That'll be one-hundred and fifty pounds, please.'

'I wanted five litres of petrol, not a party-sized bag of cocaine.'

'I added a hundred and forty for delivery, being that's probably how much my car used to drive over here.'

'I don't suppose you take American Express? It's just that I'm a bit skint at the moment, hence the reason why I'd left filling up to the very last minute.'

'Is this your way of asking for a pay rise?'

'It might be?' she replied, the inflexion in her voice turning it into a question.

'OK, well, I'll think about it. And the petrol's on the house, but only if you tell me that you've spoken to

Professor Baxendale's sister, and that she's openly confessed to murdering her brother and setting fire to the publishing company?'

'Well, I did speak to her.'

'And...?'

'She denied any involvement.'

'That's a shame. Did she say where she was when the fire started?'

'The same place she was when her brother was murdered. In bed, on her own. I also asked her if she knew the property developer, Simon Balinger. She said she didn't.'

'What about the Adlingtons?'

'Only from what she saw on the news at the time.'

'Fair enough. Let's keep her in mind for now, just in case anything comes up that relates back to her. I assume you didn't get to see Balinger?'

'That was my next stop.'

Hearing his phone ring, Tanner pulled it out to answer.

'Hi, boss,' came Gina's voice. 'Is now a good time?'

'It's as good a time as any. What've you got?'

'I've found a reference to that poem you sent me.'

'Anything of interest?' Tanner questioned, putting it on speaker phone for Vicky to hear.

'It's an old children's nursery rhyme, thought to date back to the 17th Century, supposedly about a witch, one who used to live in a cottage in Bluebell Wood.'

'Was it the same one where the Adlingtons lived?'

'The Norfolk Herald seemed to think so.'

'No surprises there.'

'They ran a story about it, after the Adlingtons were caught, about how the cottage had been cursed by the witch in the nursery rhyme. According to them, she was hanged by Matthew Hopkins, the infamous

Witchfinder General, in the exact same place the Adlingtons were found. Do you think any of this is relevant?'

'I don't know,' came Tanner's frustrated response. 'All I do know is that there's a voice inside my head telling me that either the cottage, or Bluebell Wood itself, is lying at the heart of all this. I don't suppose Henderson is back at his desk yet?'

'Sally said he's sitting in his car, and that he's been there for some time.'

'He must be out there, plodding his way through that book.'

'I don't know if it's of interest, but I saw an advert running in the same newspaper for the cottage. It was posted by a local estate agent by the name of Higbert & Hall.'

'Are they still around?'

'They have an office down the road from where my parents live. I can send you their address, if you like?'

'You may as well. Could you also send me the newspaper article?'

'No probs. Anything else?'

'Could you check on Henderson? I need to know how he's getting on with that book.'

'Can I get Sally to ask him?'

'Either / or, thank you,' Tanner replied, ending the call to find Vicky staring at him with a quizzical expression.

'Why is Gina researching a poem about Bluebell Wood?'

'It's complicated.'

'And now you're thinking about going to see an estate agent, to ask about a property that they probably haven't had on their books since the Adlington case?'

'Well, there's not much point talking to anyone

about it at the Norfolk Herald.'

'There's not much point talking to anyone about it at the estate agents, either! I mean, what are you hoping to find out?'

'Something that connects Bluebell Wood to the murder of the history professor.'

'Don't you think you're grasping at straws, a little?'

'That's what Forrester said.'

'I think he may have had a point.'

'Possibly,' Tanner admitted, 'but beggars can't be choosers.'

'So, you're a beggar now, are you?'

'According to Christine I am, and in this particular instance, I think she might be right.'

- CHAPTER FORTY THREE -

AFTER HELPING VICKY pour the contents of his petrol can into her car, Tanner left her to continue on her way to see Simon Balinger, whilst he himself went on what he had to admit was most likely to be a pointless wild goose chase.

Following the directions emailed to him by Gina, he arrived at a small village called Swafield to nudge his car onto the pavement, directly in front of the estate agents in question, only to be met by a number of acrimonious glances from shopper's passing idly by.

Happy to ignore them, he heaved himself out to amble over to the estate agent's window. There, he did what most middle-aged homeowners did when finding themselves outside an estate agent's window, began staring through the glass at the advertised properties, trying to assess how much his own was worth in comparison to those on display.

'Is this your car?' came a loud disgruntled voice, from somewhere behind him.

'It is,' Tanner replied, turning around to find a short, sweaty, red-faced man, dressed in an ill-fitting navy blue suit, glaring at him from beside it, 'but it's not for sale, I'm afraid. Sorry about that.'

'Do you know what a single yellow line means?'

'Er...is it a miniature version of a yellow brick road?'

'It means, you're not allowed to park here between the hours of eight o'clock in the morning and six o'clock at night, as the sign clearly states!'

Tanner glanced up at the sign he was being made aware of before staring quizzically back at the yellow line under discussion. 'That's strange. There was me thinking I was supposed to follow it.'

'It's also against the law to park on the kerb,' the man continued, 'and if you don't move it, I'm calling the police!'

Hearing that, Tanner raised an eyebrow with curious interest. 'I'm fairly sure they've got better things to do.'

'Oh, really! And how, may I ask, would you know that?'

'Because I am one.'

'I beg your pardon?'

'Detective Chief Inspector Tanner, Norfolk Police,' Tanner announced, presenting his old ID. 'I don't suppose you work here, by any chance?' he quickly continued, gesturing over at the estate agents they were standing outside of.

'I – I...' the man began, seemingly unable to drag his eyes from Tanner's ID.

Tanner tucked it discreetly away, forcing the man to look up at him. 'Higbert & Hall. Do you work here?'

'I do, yes. I'm the Senior Negotiator.'

'Then you're just the man I came to see. Do you have a name?'

'Smith. John Smith.'

Tanner eyed him with dubious suspicion. 'And that's your real name, is it?'

'Of course!' the man exclaimed. 'Look, here's my business card,' he added, frantically digging one out of his wallet. 'You can see my driver's licence as well, if you like.'

'That won't be necessary,' commented Tanner, taking the proffered card. 'It just sounds like the sort of name someone would make up, that's all.'

'You can blame my parents for that. They called my sister Jane. I think they were just trying to wind us up.'

Tanner smiled in response. 'May we go inside?'

'If it's about that speeding ticket, I *am* going to pay.'

'It's not about the speeding ticket.'

'Oh. Right.'

May we...?'

'Yes, of course. Sorry.'

Following behind, Tanner stepped into the office to find it devoid of either staff or customers. All he could see were three uncluttered desks surrounded by numerous empty chairs, with a sleek black coffee machine installed in the corner.

'May I get you a coffee?' the man enquired, following Tanner's gaze.

'I wouldn't say no,' he responded. 'Milk, no sugar, if that's OK?'

Looking forward to a half-decent cup of coffee, Tanner perambulated around the deserted office with his hands behind his back, once again perusing the various advertised properties.

'Are you looking for anything in particular?' he heard Smith ask, in a polite, respectful tone.

'Actually, I am,' Tanner replied, taking the coffee being offered. 'An old cottage with a traditional thatched roof.'

'Oh, right. I'm not sure we have any of those. To be honest, they don't come up all that often. When they do, they normally get snapped up pretty quickly.'

'I'm actually interested in a very particular one. It's located in the middle of Bluebell Wood, and is apparently in need of major refurbishment.'

'You mean, the old Adlington property, the one that burnt down about five years ago?'

'That's the one.'

'Well, I'm sorry to disappoint. It did take us a while, but we eventually managed to sell it.'

'To anyone in particular?'

'I'm not at liberty to disclose such details, I'm afraid.'

'Would it help if I were to tell you that my interest is part of a murder investigation?'

Smith paused momentarily before giving his shoulders an apathetic shrug. 'Let me see if I can pull up the file,' he eventually continued, skirting around the nearest desk.

Taking a seat, he pulled the keyboard towards him. 'Adlington...' he mumbled to himself, squinting studiously at the screen. 'Adlington, Adlington, Adlington. Yes, here it is! It was bought by a property development company by the name of SKB Holdings.'

Tanner recalled the name from the advertising he'd seen erected around Bluebell Wood. 'How long ago was that?' he asked, pulling out his notebook.

'That was back in April. Not for much money, either, but by that time we were just glad to get rid of it. I've never known a property so difficult to shift, but I suppose that was hardly surprising, given its history, not to mention all the stories floating around about Bluebell Wood at the time.'

Tanner glanced up from his notebook with a look of vague interest. 'Dare I ask which stories those were?'

'About the witch who was supposedly executed there by the Witchfinder General. Apparently, she was hanged in exactly the same place the Adlingtons were found.'

'I've heard that one before,' Tanner muttered.

'Also, how she put a curse on the entire place,' Smith continued, 'the woods included.'

'No doubt according to the Norfolk Herald,' Tanner commented, in an air of mocking reproach.

'Well, yes, but in this instance, I think they were probably right.'

Tucking his notebook away, Tanner folded his arms to cast his eyes over at the man. 'You honestly believe that Bluebell Wood has been cursed by a seventeenth century witch?'

'When you read about all the things that have happened there over time, it's difficult to believe that it *hasn't* been.'

'And what sort of things are those, may I ask?'

'What the Adlingtons' allowed to happen to that foster child of theirs, for a start!'

'Somehow, I doubt if they were the first couple in the world to allow one of their children to be mistreated, especially when he wasn't their own.'

'That's just it. When they first moved in, they didn't.'

'They didn't, what?'

'Allow their children to be mistreated.'

'I see. And how can you, or anyone else for that matter, possibly know that?'

'Because, when they first moved in, they had a family of their own; two boys and a girl, and according to witnesses at the time, they were all exceptionally happy. But then their children started dying, one by one, each the result of some freak accident. The first fell out of a tree and broke his neck, the second was attacked and killed by a stray dog, and the third one, the youngest, died from hypothermia when she got lost in the woods in the middle of winter, all within six months of having moved in.

Then they took in that boy, and we all know how that ended up.'

'It sounds more like they were left mentally unbalanced by what happened to their own children, as opposed to suffering from some sort of spell cast by a seventeenth century witch.'

'Did you know that Bluebell Wood is the most frequently used location in the whole of Norfolk for people to take their own lives?'

'I didn't know that.'

'And that each and every one of them hanged themselves, the most recent being just this week?'

'Again, I...'

'Also, that it's the most commonly reported location in Norfolk for dog attacks?'

'Well...'

'And more dogs have gone missing there than anywhere else, most never to be seen again, with their owners saying they just seem to go berserk the moment they step inside.'

'All this according to the Norfolk Herald, I presume?'

'Then there's the lack of wildlife.'

'Wildlife?'

'Have you ever been there?'

'I have.' Tanner replied. 'Quite recently, in fact.'

'Then you'll know what I mean.'

'What...about the lack of wildlife?'

'About how quiet it is.'

'Well, yes,' Tanner agreed, thinking back, 'but it is an uninhabited forest in the middle of an already quiet part of England.'

'OK, then let me ask you this. When you were there, did you see any animals?'

'I saw a squirrel,' Tanner replied. 'Does that count?'

'What about birds? I guarantee that during your entire time there, you neither saw nor heard a single one.'

- CHAPTER FORTY FOUR -

UNABLE TO STOP wondering if he *had* heard the sound of birds when he'd been stumbling around Bluebell Wood, or more to the point, if it was even the slightest bit relevant to his current investigation, or anything else for that matter, Tanner left the estate agent's office to immediately check his phone.

With no voice messages, and not a single email, he was about to call Henderson when he changed his mind. The boy would have called if he'd finished the book, or at least he should have done.

Climbing into his car, he checked the clock on the wood veneered dashboard to see that it was half-past four.

I'll give him till five, he thought, before calling Vicky instead.

'Hi, Vicky, it's Tanner.'

'If you're about to ask if I've managed to see Balinger yet,' came her immediate response, 'the answer is no.'

'You haven't run out of petrol again, have you?'

'Not yet. I went round to his office, but he wasn't there, so I spoke to him on his mobile.'

'And...?'

'He asked to meet me in person, rather than talking over the phone.'

'Fair enough, I suppose. I assume you suggested

somewhere busy, like a pub, or a coffee shop?'

'I did, but he suggested somewhere else.'

'Which was where?'

'The Harkenwell Water Treatment Plant.'

Tanner raised a dubious eyebrow. 'I sincerely hope you didn't agree?'

'He said he had a business meeting there, so I thought it would be OK.'

'You do remember that he's the suspect in an ongoing murder investigation, and that your job is to find the person responsible?'

'He only suggested we meet at the entrance. He didn't say anything about going inside.'

'I'm not sure he had to. If he thinks you're onto something, i.e. *him*, and he comes to the conclusion that all he needs to do to make sure you don't tell anyone is to bash you over the head before dropping your body into the nearest two thousand-litre vat, filled to the brim with untreated human excrement, then I'd have thought the entrance to a water treatment plant would be the perfect place.'

'I hardly think that's very likely.'

'Then perhaps you should ask him, preferably before you get there. At the same time, maybe you could find out *why* he has a business meeting at a water treatment plant, of all places.'

'I already did.'

'And what did he say.'

'That he was thinking of buying it.'

'A man with a reputation for talking shit, buying a place designed to purify it,' Tanner mused. 'Makes sense, I suppose.'

'Anyway, I'm sure I'll be fine.'

'Famous last words,' Tanner muttered, starting his engine to nudge his car off the kerb. 'Where was this place again?'

'Near Colby.

'I think I know it. I'm not all that far away. Tell you what, I'll meet you there.'

'Honestly, boss, I'll be fine. Besides, don't you have a wedding to get ready for?'

'According to Christine, all I have to do is show up.'

'And you think she meant that, do you?'

'I *think* so. You are still coming, I take it?'

'I suppose that depends on if I'm about to find myself lying at the bottom of a vat filled with human excrement. Changing the subject, how did you get on with that estate agent?'

'Pretty much as you said.'

'Which was?'

'A complete waste of time. All he said was that the cottage had been on the market for years, before eventually being sold to SKB Holdings, which I suspect is Balinger's company, although that's not exactly news. He'd have had to have bought the place in order to bulldoze his way over it. I can't see how it has anything to do with Professor Baxendale's murder, or the fire at the publishing house.'

'Maybe whoever owned the cottage was refusing to sell?'

'The estate agent said that the last people living there were the Adlingtons.'

'But did they actually own it?'

'That's a very good question,' Tanner replied, kicking himself for having assumed that they were the owners. 'Probably one I should have asked the bloody estate agent.'

'Don't worry, you can always ask them later.'

'I take it you don't want me to turn around?'

'Not if you're already on your way.'

'You mean, you *do* want me to babysit you?'

'Only since you planted the idea into my head that

Balinger has ulterior motives for meeting me at a water treatment plant, other than to give me a guided tour of his latest acquisition. How far away are you?'

'If it's where I think it is, only about five minutes.'

'OK, good. I'm just turning in now.'

'Any sign of him?'

'Not yet, but I am a little early.'

'If he arrives before I get there, I suggest you stay in the car.'

'Roger that!'

'Whilst you're waiting, I have a question for you.'

'If you want to know what I've bought for your wedding present, I'm not telling.'

'It was actually more ornithologically related.'

'Horny-what?'

'About birds.'

'Sorry, boss. I don't know anything about birds.'

'This may seem like a strange question, but when you were at the scene where Samuel Brogan's body was found, did you hear any of them singing?'

'Anything in particular? Something from Adele's latest album, perhaps?'

'Just normal, good old fashioned birdsong?'

'Not that I recall, but then again, I wasn't exactly listening out for it. Is it important?'

Tanner shook his head. 'Not really, at least I don't think it is. It was just something the estate agent said. Anyway, I'm driving into Colby now. I should be with you in a couple of minutes. Three, at the most.'

- CHAPTER FORTY FIVE -

REACHING THE END of a long narrow road, devoid of a single shop, house, or vehicle, Tanner turned into the entrance to the Harkenwell Water Treatment Plant to see Vicky, leaning idly back against her car whilst staring down at her phone.

'I thought I told you to stay inside?' he said, opening his door.

Glancing up, she put her phone away to smile over at him. 'I saw your car a mile off!'

'I see. And how did you know that Balinger doesn't have a jet-black Jaguar XJS, just like mine?'

'*Nobody* has a Jaguar XJS just like yours. It doesn't matter what colour it is.'

Tanner looked back at it with a proud glint in his eye. 'I must admit, you don't see them very often.'

'I'm not sure you *ever* see them, apart from yours, of course.'

'That's probably why I like it so much,' he added, turning back to gaze up at a pair of ten-foot high steel mesh gates, held together by a thick chain and a hefty-looking steel padlock. 'I assume our Mr Balinger has yet to make an appearance?'

Vicky shook her head. 'Looks like the place is closed as well, which makes me wonder how he was expecting to take part in a business meeting here.'

'Maybe he's got the key?'

'Or maybe you were right – that he knew the place would be deserted?'

The sound of an approaching car had them turning around to see a gleaming metallic-gold Land Rover Defender come rumbling down the road towards them, eventually rocking to an ungainly halt besides Tanner's XJS.

'That's quite a car,' Tanner commented, as Simon Balinger stepped carefully out.

'I wish I could say the same about yours,' he replied, staring down his nose at it.

'Don't worry. I didn't mean it as a compliment.'

Balinger's face cracked into a malevolent grin as he buried his hands deep into the pockets of his sheepskin coat. 'Chief Inspector Spanner, wasn't it?'

'Something like that,' Tanner replied, smiling back.

'And this must be your girlfriend?' he asked, looking Vicky up and down with a derisive smirk.

'Detective Inspector Gilbert,' Vicky replied, holding up her ID. 'We spoke on the phone.'

Ignoring her, Balinger stared absently up at the steel mesh security gates. 'I must admit, I was expecting the place to be open.'

'You don't have a key?' Tanner enquired, smelling alcohol on the man's breath.

Balinger glanced down at a glittering gold watch, strapped around his orange sun-bronzed wrist. 'Not yet. I'm supposed to be meeting the property agent. I suppose I am a little early. So anyway, as we're all here, how can I help?'

'We'd like to ask where you were on Wednesday, between the hours of nine o'clock and twelve o'clock at night,' Vicky enquired, swapping her ID for her notebook.

'Couldn't you have asked me that on the phone?'

'I seem to remember trying to, but you were rather keen to meet me here, instead.'

'As I recall, you asked to meet me outside some God-awful pub. Unfortunately, I'm far too busy for that sort of thing. I guess that's what you get when you're a self-confessed workaholic.'

'Don't you mean *alcoholic?*' Tanner enquired, offering the man a spurious smile.

Balinger opened his mouth to glare over at him. 'I had half-a-Guinness during a working lunch, which hardly makes me an alcoholic, Mr Tanner. Nor does it make me a drunk driver. If you really have nothing better to do than to breathalyse me, then I suggest you get on with it.'

'We didn't come here to ask about your drinking habits, Mr Balinger. We came to ask where you were on Wednesday, between nine o'clock and twelve o'clock at night.'

'I've no idea. In bed, probably.'

'How about this morning, at around half-past seven?' questioned Vicky; her pen poised over her notebook.

'Getting ready to go to work?' the man replied, in a rhetorical tone.

'Would anyone be able to vouch for you on either occasion?'

'Whichever lucky woman I happened to be with at the time,' he grinned back in response.

'I assume you'd be able to provide us with the names of these so-called "lucky women"?'

Balinger shook his head in frustration. 'Look, what's all this about, anyway?' he demanded, turning his attention to Tanner.

'I don't suppose you heard that the body of an elderly man by the name of Professor Baxendale was found murdered inside his study on Thursday morning?'

'And you think I killed him, do you?'

'That *is* what we're trying to establish,' Tanner remarked.

'Well, I didn't, probably because I don't have a single idea who he is!'

'How about the fire in Stalham this morning? I don't suppose you heard about that, by any chance?'

'I can't say that I did, but then again, unlike most people, I don't spend half my life watching the news.'

'Is it therefore safe to assume that you didn't know that the body of a Mr Richard Naylor was found burnt to a crisp on the building's third floor?'

Balinger opened his mouth for the briefest of moments before snapping it closed.

'So, you do know something about it, then?'

'I've never heard of the man.'

'I didn't ask if you'd heard of him, Mr Balinger, I asked if you knew anything about the fire.'

'I don't know the man, and I don't know anything about the fire.'

'Do you at least know the name of the business that went up in flames? They're a local publishing firm, if it helps.'

'Why should I have done?'

'Because of your reaction when I mentioned the name of the man found inside.'

'And what reaction was that?'

Hearing his phone ring from the depths of his coat, Tanner held Balinger's contemptuous gaze. 'Bear with me for just a moment,' he eventually said, turning away to answer it.

'Tanner speaking!'

'Hi boss, it's Gina.'

'Yes, Gina, how can I help?'

'You asked me to see if I could find any CCTV

footage taken of the front of the office where that fire was.'

'And did you?'

'Unfortunately not.'

Tanner pulled in a breath in bid to control his rising temper. 'Then why, may I ask, are you calling?'

'Because I was able to find something from the other side of the road instead, from a motion sensor camera used by a local coffee shop. It was triggered by a car pulling up directly outside the publishing house, close to the time we think the fire started.'

'Does it show anyone getting out?'

'It does, but cuts out a moment later.'

'Is it a man or a woman?'

'A tallish man wearing a suit and tie.'

Tanner swivelled his head around until his eyes met with Balinger's. 'Tell me, Gina, what car was he driving?'

'Oh, sorry, I'm not very good with cars.'

'Perhaps you could describe it for me?'

'Er...large, boxy. If I was to hazard a guess, I'd say it was a Range Rover, or something similar. Brown, or maybe gold.'

As his eyes traversed around to the car parked next to his own, a thin smile crept its way over Tanner's mouth. 'Thanks Gina. If you could email me that video, I'd be very grateful.'

Ending the call, he put his phone away to square himself up to Balinger. 'Sorry about that,' he began. 'Where did you say you were this morning again, at around half-past seven?'

Balinger's eyes darted erratically between Tanner's.

'Mr Simon Balinger,' Tanner continued, pulling himself up straight, 'you're under arrest for suspected arson and manslaughter, very possibly murder as well.'

The moment the words left Tanner's mouth, Balinger spun around to leap into a run, only to come skidding to a halt against the ten-foot high steel mesh gates.'

'Where on *earth* do you think you're going?' Tanner enquired, with an exaggerated frown.

Turning slowly around, Balinger's mouth twisted into a vindictive curse. 'Nowhere special,' he eventually muttered.

'That's where you're wrong. You're going somewhere *very* special. It's called Wroxham Police Station. I'll even be happy enough to give you a lift there myself.'

- CHAPTER FORTY SIX -

FOLLOWING VICKY'S CAR into the station, Tanner left a couple of uniformed constables with the task of hauling Balinger out from the back of his Jag to drag him unceremoniously inside for formal processing.

Happy enough to leave them to it, he scouted around the carpark in search of the beaten-up old car he knew Henderson drove, a badly rusted bright red Fiat Uno. Eventually spying it under a tree, he marched over to find its owner leaning back against the headrest with his eyes closed. When he noticed drool leaking out from the side of his half-open mouth, he lifted his eyes to the sky above. 'Un-fucking-believable,' he muttered out loud, before knocking hard against the glass.

Taking a pleasurable moment to watch Henderson jump in his seat to begin blinking about, he motioned for him to wind the window down.

'I'm not keeping you up, am I?' he asked, the moment it began creeping open.

'N-not at all. I was j-just – er...' Henderson stuttered, his face going nearly as red as his car.

'Having a little nap-nap?'

'Just resting my eyes, boss.'

'And are they now fully rested?'

'Very much so, thank you.'

'Dare I ask how it's been going?' Tanner enquired,

glancing down to see a tablet lying on his lap.

'The book! Right! Well, it's hardly the most engaging read, which is probably why I fell a... had to have a quick rest, but I've just about finished.'

'Did you find anything relevant?'

'Hold on. Let me just find my notes.'

Tanner waited impatiently as he watched Henderson begin swiping at the screen.

'OK. Here we go. The name Bluebell Wood was mentioned twice, but only in relation to the Bluebell Wood Military Research Facility.'

'And that's around here, is it?

'It's actually nowhere, boss.'

'What do you mean, it's nowhere?'

'It was closed down in 1991, at the end of the Cold War. It was then demolished to be turned into what is now the Millbank Shopping Centre.'

'And there's no other mention of Bluebell Wood?'

'Not that I could find.'

'How about just the word bluebell?'

Henderson shook his head.

'What about our suspects? Did you find any of their names?'

'I've kept my eyes open for all the ones you emailed to me', he replied, swiping again at the tablet's surface. 'Simon Balinger, the suicide victim, Samuel Brogan, his female environmental activist friend, Tara Lowe, his foster parents, Peter and Margaret Brogan, and the owner of the publishing house, Richard Naylor. I didn't find anything relating to any of them.'

'What about Samuel Brogan's first set of foster parents, the Adlingtons?'

'Not a single mention, I'm afraid.'

Tanner glanced about with fitful frustration. 'I don't suppose there was anything about a witch's curse, by any chance?'

'Er...I didn't know I was supposed to be looking for one, but I'm fairly sure there wasn't. I can read it again, if you like?'

'How about something that someone may have found personally upsetting, or offensive, in any way?'

'Not that I found. The book was very much as it said it would be in the introduction: an historical account of the Cold War, one which was attempting – rather badly I may add – to document the events from Norfolk's perspective.'

'And what *was* Norfolk's perspective?'

'There was hardly anything in it about Norfolk at all, which is why it seemed to fail at its primary objective. The only thing that was even remotely relevant was that the Bluebell Wood research facility was apparently used by MI6 to help train and monitor its overseas operatives.'

Tanner crossed his arms to tap a finger against his stubble-covered chin. 'Maybe that's what someone didn't want anyone reading about,' he mused. 'Government secrets? That sort of thing?'

'Maybe,' Henderson replied, without sounding particularly convinced, 'but if that was the case, I'm not exactly sure what they were worried about. Apart from the rather small section relating to MI6 using the research facility, there's nothing in it that hasn't been documented about a million times before, at least nothing I could find. It wasn't written particularly well, either. To be honest, I've no idea why it was even published.'

'It wasn't!' Tanner stated. 'At least, it hasn't been yet.'

'Anyway, I've only got about a dozen or so more pages to go. Do you want me to carry on?'

'You may as well, but if you could email me the

passages relating to the research facility now, that would be useful.'

- CHAPTER FORTY SEVEN -

TANNER ENTERED THE station to find Vicky, waiting for him in reception.

'Where did *you* get to?' she asked, in an inquisitive tone. 'I thought you were right behind me.'

'I was talking to Henderson, in his car.'

'Oh, right. And what's Henderson doing in his car?'

'Well, he *was* asleep. Prior to that, I think he was reading Professor Baxendale's book.'

'Does that mean he's finished it?'

'Just about.'

'And...?'

'And it would appear to be another dead end. The only mention of Bluebell Wood is in relation to an old military research facility, one that doesn't even exist anymore.'

'What about our suspects?'

'None would appear to have had even so much as a mention.'

'Then why's someone going to so much trouble to stop the book from being published?'

'You've got me! Maybe the British Government thought the professor was about to publish classified military secrets.'

'But the British Government doesn't go around killing people threatening to publish military secrets, at least I don't think they do.'

'The *British* Government doesn't,' Tanner replied, gazing sagaciously off into space.

Vicky stared at him with an ambivalent frown. 'You're thinking this could have something to do with Russia?'

'At least they have a history of assassinating people as a way of silencing them.'

'But...in Norfolk?'

'I'm not sure they care where such people are located.'

'But...in Norfolk?' Vicky repeated, word-for-word, as her expression changed from one of mild misgiving to incredulous disbelief.

'It may be more believable when I tell you what the book said the military research facility had been used for, at least in part.'

'Which was?'

'For training and monitoring MI6 operatives.'

'Well, OK, but even so.'

'I must admit, it doesn't seem very likely. If we were to go down such an improbable line of enquiry, then I suppose it's *possible* that Professor Baxendale was an MI6 agent, and he was threatening to expose military secrets to the other side.'

'By publishing them in a book?'

'Or maybe someone else is, like our very own Mr Balinger, for example.'

'Your suggesting Simon Balinger is a Russian spy?'

'It could explain where he got all his money from.'

'I'm fairly sure he got his money from his parents,' Vicky replied, 'or in the form of a bank loan, like most rich people do.'

'Do we know for a fact that he *didn't* get it from some dubious Russian bank account?'

'We haven't been granted access to his financial records, yet.'

'I'm not sure it matters. Even if he had, it wouldn't prove much.'

'Maybe not, but we still need to see them, if for no other reason than to establish what Samuel Brogan allegedly discovered; that the only reason Balinger was able to get planning permission for the Bluebell Wood development was by bribing a local government official.'

'That's as maybe, but unfortunately, Balinger's dodgy property dealings are of little interest to us.'

'Unless it has something to do with Professor Baxendale's book?'

'I suppose,' Tanner replied, with an ambivalent shrug.

Hearing his phone ping out a notification, he pulled it out to find Henderson's requested email. Keen to take a quick look, he opened it up, only to see the duty sergeant creeping towards him from out of the corner of his eye. 'Yes, Taylor, what is it?' he demanded, glancing briefly up.

'Just to let you know that we finished processing Mr Balinger, boss.'

'OK, good.'

'And that we've placed him in interview room one.'

'Great.'

'Also, that he's been kicking up a bit of a fuss.'

'Don't they all?'

'He attacked Constable Jenkins, the moment we took his handcuffs off.'

Tanner looked up with a start. 'Seriously?'

'I'm afraid so, boss. He threw a chair at him.'

'Is Jenkins alright?'

'He seems to be, but he's sustained quite a nasty cut to his head.'

'Jesus Christ!' Tanner replied, instinctively reaching up to feel the metal staples running along the top of his own.

'So we've called an ambulance.'

'Yes, of course.'

'Apparently, the suspect doesn't like enclosed spaces.'

'Then he better start getting used to it, hadn't he.'

'Anyway,' Taylor continued, 'we've had to restrain him again, but he's still in interview room one, waiting to see you.'

'Has his solicitor arrived?'

'He says he doesn't need one.'

'Oh, right!' Tanner exclaimed, sending Vicky a presumptuous smile. 'Then I suppose we'd better start interviewing him, just in case he changes his mind.'

- CHAPTER FORTY EIGHT -

'GOOD AFTERNOON, MR Balinger,' said Tanner, in a cheerful tone, following Vicky into the interview room, only to find their way blocked by a broken wooden chair. 'I hear you've taken rather a strong dislike to our furniture.'

Lifting his eyes off of what was left of the chair, he gazed up at the suspect, standing dejectedly in the corner of the windowless room with his hands handcuffed in front of him. 'Or was it the police officer you threw the chair at who you took a dislike to?'

With Balinger staring tight-lipped at the floor, Tanner glanced around at one of his larger-than-average constables, standing to attention by the door. 'Does he speak?'

'He was remarkably vocal earlier, boss.'

'I take it you weren't the one he threw the chair at?'

'No boss. That was Jenkins. And he didn't so much as throw the chair as use it as a sort of multifaceted baseball bat.'

Tanner took the burley constable in with a little more interest. 'Multifaceted?'

'Yes, boss. It means to have many aspects, or sides.'

'Was that your word of the day?'

'No, boss. That was yesterday's word.'

Tanner continued to study the man's angular,

unintelligent-looking face, endeavouring to see if he was being deliberately facetious. 'What was your name again?' he eventually enquired, unable to see anything in his expression but stoic subservience.

'Hicks, boss.'

'Well, Hicks, I think you can return to your duties.'

'Yes, boss.'

'But perhaps you could uncuff our guest before you leave?'

The constable stopped where he was to offer Tanner a doubtful grimace. 'Are you sure about that?'

'Don't worry, I'm confident he'll be on his best behaviour,' Tanner replied, shifting his attention to the suspect. 'You won't attack us with another chair again, will you, Mr Balinger?'

Remaining silent, the suspect continued to stare down at the floor.

'There, you see! He's clearly managed to calm himself down. I'm sure we'll be perfectly safe. Oh, and if you could take this chair with you, on your way out,' Tanner added, as Hicks diligently removed Balinger's handcuffs, 'at least, what's left of it.'

'No problem, boss.'

'Perhaps you could find us another one to replace it?'

'Right you are.'

Waiting for him to leave, Tanner quietly closed the door.

'Sorry about all that, Mr Balinger,' he said, turning to see the man in question rubbing painfully at his wrists. 'Now, where were we?'

Still the suspect remained stubbornly silent.

'I would offer you a chair,' Tanner continued, 'but we seem to be one short.'

'I'm not saying anything!' Balinger finally stated, glancing up with a belligerent glare. 'I know my rights!'

'Well, good for you!'

'Please don't patronise me, Chief Inspector.'

'I wouldn't dare. But you should know that remaining silent won't help you, at least not in the long term. To be honest, it's probably more likely to do your defence more harm than good.'

'Oh, really? And why's that?'

'Because a jury will simply interpret your silence to be a sign of guilt, as an innocent man wouldn't need to be. Of course, you'd know that if you had a lawyer.'

'I don't need some stuck-up, over-priced lawyer, thank you very much!'

'No, of course,' Tanner smiled. 'I must admit, I have always considered them to be a complete waste of someone's hard earned cash.'

A knock at the door had Hicks' face re-appearing. 'I have that chair you asked for, boss.'

'Thank you, Hicks,' Tanner responded, taking it from him. 'Perhaps you could find us some coffee, as well?'

Waiting for him to leave once again, Tanner closed the door to set the chair down on the other side of the table, next to where Balinger was standing. 'Would you care to take a seat?'

'I'm quite happy standing, thank you very much.'

'Suit yourself,' Tanner replied, pulling one out for first Vicky, then himself. 'But we could be a while.'

Balinger eyed up the chair as Tanner and Vicky made themselves comfortable. 'How long is this going to take, exactly?'

'We're legally entitled to hold you for a twenty-four hour period before having to either request an extension, charge you, or let you go.'

'That's not what I asked.'

'Then perhaps I could put it another way. The

sooner we start, the sooner we'll know how long it will take.'

As Balinger resentfully pulled the chair out, Tanner started the wall-mounted recording device to spend a few moments running through the legal formalities. 'If I may,' he eventually said, placing a file on top of the table, 'I'd like to pick up where we left off earlier today.'

'Which was where?'

'Endeavouring to establish your whereabouts this morning, at around half-past seven.'

Balinger locked his arms over his chest. 'Why do I have the feeling that you already know where I was?'

'So, you're not going to deny the fact that you were parked directly opposite the offices of Morgan & Naylor at the time in question?'

'Why should I deny it?'

'You did the first time we asked. Actually, that's not true. From memory, you went so far as to lie to us about your whereabouts.'

'I seem to recall saying something more along the lines of that I didn't know.'

'For the record,' Tanner asked Vicky, 'I don't suppose you could recall what the suspect *did* say when he was first asked?'

Taking a quiet moment to refer to her notebook, she eventually replied, 'The suspect said he was, "Getting ready to go to work"'.

Balinger leaned forward to catch Tanner's eye. 'I seem to remember my response was more of a question than an actual statement of fact.'

'You mean, you *weren't* in the process of getting ready for work?'

'I'm not sure how I could have been, not if I was parked directly outside Morgan & Naylor's offices.'

'Then may I ask what you were doing there?'

'I can tell you what I *wasn't* doing there.'

'Are you about to deny setting fire to their offices?'

'How very astute of you.'

'If you weren't there to start the fire, then what were you doing?'

'If you must know, I had a business meeting with the owner, Mr Richard Naylor.'

'At half-past seven in the morning?'

'That's correct.'

'Isn't that a tad early for a so-called "business meeting"?'

Balinger shrugged. 'As I think I mentioned to you before, I'm a busy man. That just happened to be the only time I could do that day.'

'Half-past seven in the morning?' Tanner repeated.

Balinger replied by sitting back in his chair to offer Tanner a thin, calculating smile.

'May I ask what the meeting was supposed to be about?'

'I wanted to discuss a book deal with him.'

'A book deal?'

Balinger folded his arms over his chest. 'Is it really necessary to repeat everything I say all the time?'

'Only when what you say seems unfathomably difficult to believe.'

'Whether or not you believe me is hardly my fault.'

'Are you honestly trying to tell us that you're in the process of having a book published?'

'I'm not *trying* to tell you, Chief Inspector. I *am* telling you.'

'And you wanted to meet Mr Naylor at half-past seven in the morning to discuss it?'

'Correct again!'

'I don't suppose there's any chance we could see a copy of this alleged book?'

'Unfortunately, that won't be possible.'

'Any particular reason why not?'

'Because, I haven't written it yet.'

Tanner snorted with uncontrolled laughter. 'Sorry about that,' he spluttered, quickly wiping at his nose. 'That really was quite unforgivable.'

'Laugh away, Chief Inspector, but I'm the one who's about to have the next Sunday Times Best Seller.'

'We are still talking about your book, the one you haven't written yet?'

Ballinger sneered back at him with brooding menace.

'Could you at least tell us what it will be about?'

'It's going to be a self-help book.'

'Right, yes, of course it is,' Tanner replied, doing his best to keep a straight face. 'And what's it going to be called. How to Lose Friends and Murder People?'

'I haven't come up with a title yet.'

'Oh, right. Well, feel free to use that one, if you like.'

'That's exceptionally kind of you.'

'Putting your future bestselling book to one side for now, may I ask what happened *after* you pulled up onto the kerb outside Morgan & Naylor's offices?

'Nothing happened.'

'Nothing?'

'That's what I said.'

'The video footage shows you at least getting out. What happened after that?'

'I got back inside and drove away.'

'You didn't set fire to the place before doing so?'

'Strangely enough, no, I didn't.'

'Even though we've been advised that the fire started at pretty much the exact same time?'

'Not by me it wasn't.'

'I'm sorry, Mr Balinger, but if you really expect us to believe you, I really think you need to at least *try* to be a little more convincing.'

'I know it wasn't me because the fire had already started when I arrived. That's why I got back into my car and drove away.'

'So, you arrived to find the place was already burning down, leaving you free to drive off without a care in the world?'

'Not exactly.'

'Then what, exactly?'

'I dialled 999 before moving my car to a safe distance. If you check the emergency recording, I think you'll find that it was my voice on the end of the line.'

DAVID BLAKE

- CHAPTER FORTY NINE -

WITH BALINGER GRINNING at him like a demented Cheshire Cat, and with nobody appearing with the coffee he'd asked for, Tanner decided it was probably a good time to take a break.

'Sounds to me like he could be telling the truth,' he heard Vicky mutter, whilst ushering her out into the corridor.

'What makes you think that?' Tanner demanded, in an irritable tone, as he quickly closed the interview room door. 'Because he *says* he was the one who reported the fire?'

'As he said, it's easy enough to check if he did or not.'

'But even if he did, it doesn't mean anything. All it proves is that he's slightly more intelligent than I gave him credit for.'

'But why would he call the fire department for a fire he started himself?'

'I can only assume that he must have been confident enough to know that they wouldn't arrive in time to stop it, probably because he'd covered half the ground floor in petrol. If he *did* make the call, it also does a surprisingly good job of making him appear to be nothing more than a victim of circumstance, someone who just happened to be at the wrong place at the wrong time, as he is alleging.'

'What about the whole thing about his self-help book?'

'That's probably more plausible than you might think.'

Reaching the end of the corridor, Vicky came to an abrupt halt. 'You're not being serious?'

'Not the part about him writing one, obviously. More about him having had the idea, then using it as an excuse to lure Richard Naylor into his office at a time when it was unlikely anyone else would have been there.'

Pushing their way through to the station's reception area, Tanner saw Sally scurrying out from the main office to glance furtively about, before making a b-line straight for them.

'Yes, Sally, what is it?'

'We've finally been granted access to Mr Balinger's finances.'

'OK, and...? Anything of interest?'

'Gina's started going through them now,' she continued, flipping over the pages of her notepad, 'but she's already found the evidence that the suicide victim, Sammuel Brogan, must have unearthed. A series of substantial payments to a company owned by a man called Jeremy Southcott, who just happens to be the chairman of the local council's planning and housing committee.'

'OK, well, that's good, I suppose, but we're really looking for something connecting him to either Professor Baxendale or Richard Naylor – preferably both!'

'Well, we haven't discovered anything linking him to Richard Naylor.'

'Does that mean that you *have* found something in reference to Professor Baxendale?'

A broad smile appeared over Sally's full red lips.

'I've been going through Balinger's phone records.'

'And...?' Tanner prompted, with curt impatience.

'It looks like he called the professor from his mobile phone, two days before he was found murdered in his study.'

- CHAPTER FIFTY -

W ITH THREE COFFEES being carried between them, finding himself in a far more optimistic frame of mind, Tanner led Vicky back into the interview room to see Simon Balinger, pacing up and down with an irritated scowl.

'Just how much longer am I going to be trussed up in here for?' the man demanded, stomping to a halt behind his chair.

'Not long now,' Tanner smiled, placing a coffee mug onto the table for him. 'Milk, no sugar. I hope that's OK?'

Balinger glared belligerently down at it with his hands clasped around the back of the chair. 'I'd have preferred sugar,' he eventually said, 'but it will do.'

'Our pleasure,' Tanner replied, waiting for Vicky to take a seat before pulling one out for himself.

Recommencing the interview, he returned to the table's surface the same file they'd brought in with them before, to begin flicking inattentively at one of its corners. 'You were telling us before about your self-help book.'

'Sorry, was there a question there?'

'And how you'd arranged to meet Richard Naylor, the now deceased owner and CEO of Morgan & Naylor Publishing, only to discover someone had set fire to the building you were supposed to be meeting him in.'

'I'm still waiting for an actual question.'

'I'd now like to move the conversation on to Professor Baxendale?'

'Who?'

'You remember. The man found in his study with his throat cut.'

'What about him?'

'Had you arranged to meet *him* at all?'

'Why the hell would I have wanted to do that?'

'Does that mean you didn't?'

'Didn't what?'

'Meet him?'

'I thought I'd already told you that I didn't know the man, which makes me wonder how on earth I could have arranged to meet him.'

'Well, that is rather peculiar,' Tanner replied, opening the file to remove a single A4 sheet of paper that listed row-upon-row of numbers, dates, and times, one of which had been highlighted. 'That *is* your mobile phone number, isn't it?' he enquired, rotating the piece of paper around.

Balinger leaned forward to study the number emboldened at the very top of the page.

'Was that a yes?'

'Yes, it is,' he eventually confirmed. 'So what?'

'Do you recognise *that* number?' Tanner continued, pointing to the highlighted row.

'Not off the top of my head.'

'It belongs to the previously mentioned Professor Baxendale.'

Balinger's eyes lifted off the page to dart erratically between Tanner's.

'The date the call was made is even more interesting, being that it was the day before his body was found.'

'I d-don't understand,' Balinger stuttered, tracing

his finger along the row, from the number, all the way to the date in question.

'I'd be willing to offer the suggestion that you may have dialled it by accident,' Tanner proposed, 'had it not been for the fact that the call lasted for a fraction under twenty minutes.'

'There must be some sort of mistake.'

'I suppose it's possible for someone to have stolen your phone in order to call him.'

Tanner watched Balinger reach an instinctive hand up to his suit jacket's inside breast pocket.

'Is your phone still there?'

By the look on his face, it was obvious that it was, even if he wished it wasn't.

'Someone must have used it to call him, without my knowledge.'

'You're suggesting someone's endeavouring to frame you for Professor Baxendale's murder?'

'Yes! That must be it!'

'Even though you've already admitted to seeking a meeting with his publisher.'

Baxendale's expression turned from agitated fear to that of befuddled confusion. 'Whose publisher?'

'I hope you're not trying to tell me that you didn't know about Professor Baxendale's latest book; what is, apparently, a fascinating examination of Norfolk's involvement in the Cold War?'

As scales of confusion seemed to fall from Balinger's eyes, he leaned back in his chair to present Tanner with a look of gleeful mirth.

'Don't tell me you've read it?' Tanner queried, with a feeling of unsettled curiosity.

The suspect leaned forward to bring his hands together on top of the table. 'I haven't, no. Nor do I have any intention of.'

'But you have heard of it, though?'

'I have indeed! When I first spoke to Mr Naylor about publishing my own work, he mentioned it to me. He even told me to contact its author, to ask him any questions, or maybe to raise any concerns I might have had about using their publishing services.'

'So you *did* call Professor Baxendale, the day before he was killed?'

'Yes, I did.'

It was Tanner's turn to look confused. 'Then why have you spent the last ten minutes denying it?'

'Because I didn't know it was Professor Baxendale I was speaking to. Mr Naylor only ever referred to him by what I can now safely assume must have been his pen name, Mr Clive Chapman.'

- CHAPTER FIFTY ONE -

STANDING IN FRONT of his office window with his hands shoved down into his pockets, Tanner glared indignantly out at the carpark beyond. With an oblique view of the station's entrance, he watched in brooding silence as Balinger hurried out into another torrential downpour, to jump immediately into a waiting taxi.

A knock at the door had him glancing fitfully about to see Vicky's head emerge cautiously around from the other side.

'I just thought you'd like to know that Balinger's gone, boss.'

'Yes, I can see, thank you.'

A moment of silence followed, as Vicky stepped inside. 'Are you really sure that was the right thing to do?' she eventually asked, closing the door quietly behind her.

'There was no point keeping him.'

'We still had another eighteen hours. Something might have come up.'

'Like what?'

'I don't know. But if we need to arrest him again, we won't be able to use the same evidence.'

'And what evidence was that?' Tanner questioned, his voice rising with angry frustration. 'According to the forensic report that Sally so kindly brought to our attention, neither his DNA, nor fingerprints, were found at the scene where Professor Baxendale's body was discovered. There's also no real evidence to suggest that he *did* set fire to the publishing house. He doesn't have a single motive for having wished either the Professor or Mr Naylor harm in any way, let alone want to murder them, and his reasons for having phoned one up, and having been caught on camera outside the building of the other, seemed nothing less than completely plausible.'

'What about his bank records – that he bribed a local government official?'

Dragging his hands out of his pockets, Tanner returned to his desk to let out a dispirited sigh. 'To be honest, Vicky, I'm really not sure I care all that much. Not when I'm in the middle of a double-murder investigation. Certainly not when I have a wedding to go to tomorrow. My own, in fact!'

'Then let me handle it!'

'What, my wedding, or the financial dealings of some dodgy local property developer?'

'The latter, obviously. Besides, I don't think Christine would be too pleased to find me waiting at the end of the aisle for her, instead of the man she agreed to marry.'

'Who knows?' Tanner mused, staring at his monitor. 'Maybe she'd prefer it. Maybe I would, as well.'

Glancing up to find Vicky scowling at him with a distinctly unamused expression, he shifted in his seat to offer her an apologetic grin. 'Only joking.'

'I'm not.'

'You're not, what?'

'Joking about me, going after Balinger for his dodgy financial dealings.'

'Look, if you really want to head up what I can assure you will be an insanely tedious investigation, one that will probably end up with Balinger's lawyers convincing a jury that the money their client sent to some local councillor was nothing more felonious than a short-term loan, then you're more than welcome to.'

'Oh – right.'

'But not before we've found out who killed Professor Baxendale!' he stated, glaring over at her.

As Tanner returned his attention back to his screen, the office fell into an uncomfortable silence.

'So, what's the plan?' Vicky eventually asked, shifting her weight from one foot to the other.

'If there's nothing else, then I'm going to go home,' he announced, rapidly closing various windows on his computer screen.

'Yes, of course.'

'I hope you're still able to come tomorrow?'

'I wouldn't miss it for the world!' she replied, offering him an earnest grin.

'OK, good.'

'What about afterwards? Are you still going away?'

'Assuming you're referring to my honeymoon; at this stage, I'm not sure how I can.'

'I don't see why you shouldn't. You can always cut it short if something does come up.'

'I'm not sure Superintendent Forrester will see it that way, nor the press parked outside.'

'When will you decide?'

Turning off his monitor, he stood up to begin glancing furtively about his desk. 'About five minutes before leaving for the airport, probably,' he replied, fetching up first his phone, then his keys.

'If you think there's a chance that you will be going, don't you think it would be a good idea to brief the office, before you leave?'

Tanner stared over at her with a look of evasive

reluctance.

'It may be wise to appoint someone to stand in for you, as well.'

'I suppose you'd like to volunteer for the role?'

'Better me than Cooper, don't you think?'

Tanner shook his head dismissively as he whipped his jacket off the back of the chair. 'Either way, the honeymoon is in Spain, not the North Pole. I really don't think you'll have any trouble contacting me, should you need to.'

'What if someone has to make a statement to the press?'

'You mean, to explain why I'm lying beside a private swimming pool on the coast of Spain, instead of spearheading a double-murder investigation in the middle of Norfolk?'

'Something like that.'

Tanner cast his eyes out of his window towards the various news vans, littering the road outside. 'I suggest we cross that bridge when we come to it. That's if we ever have to.'

'OK, fine, but don't expect me to do it.'

Tanner smiled over at her. 'I suppose you'd prefer not to brief the office, either, whilst I slip quietly out the back?'

'Not particularly.'

'Fair enough, but you can't pick and choose, Vicky. If you do end up taking over, you'll have to do *everything* the job entails, not just the parts you enjoy.'

'Tell you what. If you leave me in charge, then I will.'

'You'll brief the office, or hold the press conference?'

'Both!'

Tanner held her robust gaze for a moment before

letting out a heavy sigh. 'I'll think about it. Meanwhile, I suppose I'd better do what you suggested.'

'What's that?'

'Brief the office, in case I do decide to go,' he replied, sinking slowly down into his chair to turn his monitor back on.

Vicky waited for a moment before eventually asking, 'Do you want me to do anything?'

'If you can give everyone a heads-up, just in case they're all about to leave for the day, that would be useful, thank you.'

- CHAPTER FIFTY TWO -

'OK, EVERYONE, IF I can have your attention, please!' Tanner called out, in much the same way Forrester used to, when endeavouring to prise an office full of people from their phones, or the conversation they were having with the person next to them.

Giving his audience a moment to settle, he placed his hands together to take them all in. 'As I'm sure you all know,' he eventually began, 'I'm getting married tomorrow.'

A lacklustre cheer came back in response, followed by an equally uninspiring round of applause.

'Thank you. You're too kind. Now, I know that I was only able to invite a handful of you, so I wanted to take this opportunity to apologise to those of you I was unfortunately unable to include. However, I can assure you, you won't be missing much.'

A polite ripple of laughter followed.

'If you are desperately keen to go, send me an email, and I'll make sure to invite you to the next one.'

That comment brought a more appreciative response.

'Whether or not I'll be going on the holiday that's supposed to follow, something I believe is commonly referred to as a honeymoon, depends largely on you. If you want me out of your hair for the next two weeks, then we're going to have to find the person responsible for the murder of Professor Baxendale, as well as the fire that resulted in the death of Morgan & Naylor's CEO, Richard Naylor. However, as there's only about thirty-six hours between now and when I'm supposed to be boarding my flight, it looks increasingly unlikely that I'll be able to go.'

'What happened about Simon Balinger?' he heard Cooper call out, from the very back of the office.

'With regret,' Tanner replied, directing his answer to the room in general, 'despite the fact that Mr Balinger was in the immediate vicinity when the fire was thought to have started, and that he was also found to have spoken to Professor Baxendale the day before he was found dead, questioning revealed him to be an unlikely candidate for either, leaving me little choice but to let him go. That leaves us without a prime suspect, at least not a realistic one, which, in turn, means whoever *is* responsible remains roaming Norfolk, as free as a bird. As long as that's the case, I think it's unlikely that neither the press, nor the local population, would take kindly to the idea of me spending the next two weeks doing nothing more productive than lying beside a swimming pool in Spain. I'm not sure HQ would be particularly keen for me to be, either.

'Anyway, back to the wedding. For those of you unluckily enough to have been invited, and stupid enough to have decided to come, I look forward to seeing you loitering outside a church tomorrow morning.

'For those of you forced to work over the weekend, just a reminder that we're looking for someone with a realistic motive for wanting Professor Baxendale dead, something that potentially relates to either the publishing of his latest book, or maybe the publisher's CEO, Richard Naylor. As things currently stand, the only half-decent lead we have is the person the professor's sister claims to have seen, the day before her brother was murdered. According to her, he was a tall, thin man with short-cropped hair, wearing a suit and tie, and a pair of highly polished black office shoes. The description, combined with the method used to kill the victim, leads us to believe that the person we're looking for may have a military background, possibly with special forces training.

'The only other lead we have is the word bluebell, which was what she thought she overheard one of them say at the time. Whether or not that was in reference to Bluebell Wood, we simply don't know. What I do know is that every path we've so far uncovered has led us straight there. Unfortunately, each one has eventually ended up being a complete dead end.

'The only other idea I was hoping would bear fruit concerned Professor Baxendale's as-yet unpublished book, the manuscript of which someone reportedly stole from the publisher's office. However, that would also appear to be a dead end, being that not a single one of our suspects was mentioned, and the only reference to either bluebells or Bluebell Wood was an old military base, one that was demolished back in the nineties to be replaced by the Millbank Shopping Centre.

'So, there we have it!' Tanner concluded, his voice sounding tired and drained. 'Unless something else comes up, I'm not sure what else we can do. To be completely honest, I'm not even sure what our next step should be. Whatever it is, I'm fairly sure it can wait till Monday.'

- CHAPTER FIFTY THREE -

NIGEL MELLOR LET out a frustrated sigh, as yet another grubby plastic hire boat came motoring down the River Bure towards him. Lifting his head, just enough to see from under the peak of his brand new fisherman's cap, he rested a scornful eye on the red-faced man he could see slouched behind its wheel, sipping gleefully at what he'd put money on was a can of Stella Artois.

'Bloody tourists,' he muttered bitterly to himself, shifting his gaze to his fishing line's small orange float, bobbing gently on the water about ten feet out from the bank. 'At this rate, I may as well be fishing next door to the bloody M11!'

Having not had a single bite all day, he stubbornly buried his chin into the warmth of his khaki green coat's felt-lined collar to stare resolutely ahead, only to realise that the stupid tourist's boat was now heading straight for the end of his line, at what must have been more than double the river's speed limit.

Jumping up from his camping chair, he drew in a lungful of air to yell a tirade of abuse at the driver, only to see the red-faced man had been replaced by a small boy with a round angelic face, struggling to see over the boat's over-sized steering wheel.

Catching his words before they could escape from his grimacing mouth, he yelled out instead, 'Excuse me! Could you steer away from my fishing line, please?'

But the boy's only response was to stare unblinkingly back at him, like a young buck caught in a car's rapidly approaching headlights.

He was about to ask again, when the boy suddenly whipped his little blond head around to promptly disappear, leaving the boat charging along without a single person behind the wheel.

As the boat immediately began altering course to start heading straight for him, Nigel stared frantically about. With the speed the boat was travelling at, he'd barely have time to retrieve his carbon fibre fishing rod, let alone to remove the keep net he had hanging over the bank's side, before it came crashing into both.

Wasting not a second more, he lunged forward to snatch up first the rod, then the keep net. With both in hand, he stumbled backwards, dragging each along with him, only for his wading boots to slip on the wet muddy grass.

Falling hard on his side, he pushed himself onto his elbow to see the red-faced man was back behind the wheel, gesturing down at him with an apologetic nod of his fat bald shiny head, as the boat swept harmlessly past.

With his elbow sinking into the soggy ground, he was left to watch in furious dismay as the hire boat blasted effortlessly away, until all that was left of it was its turbulent wake, sending wave after wave crashing against the bank.

Deciding right then and there that this was his very last fishing trip, and that he was going to put all his ridiculously over-priced equipment onto eBay the moment he got home, he pushed himself up to begin clambering to his feet.

As the river returned to its previous state of

tranquil serenity, he dropped the keep net to take hold of the rod with both hands. Still cursing under his breath, he began reeling the line in, only to feel the hook on the end suddenly catch on something.

With all thoughts of the plastic hire boat, its moronic driver, and selling all his gear on eBay instantly obliterated from his mind, he began pulling enthusiastically back on the line. 'There's something there,' he murmured quietly to himself, doing his best to control his growing excitement. After all, it would hardly be the first time his line had caught on something, only for it to end up being nothing more rewarding than a rusty bicycle, or, in one particular instance, a discarded shopping trolley.

Placing one foot firmly behind the other, he let the line run out a little before reeling it back in. 'There's definitely something there!' he repeated with more confidence, as his heart began pounding deep inside his chest.

Pulling back again, he leaned forward to reel in the slack before hauling back once more.

'Jesus Christ!' he exclaimed through gritted teeth. 'Just how big is this thing?'

As beads of sweat erupted over his brow, he let the line go slack again to gasp desperately at the air.

Planting his feet firmly down onto the waterlogged grassy bank, he heaved back on the line with all his strength. *There's no way this can be a fish*, he began telling himself. *The damned thing's just too bloody big!*

He was on the verge of giving up when something huge finally broke through the surface, its sleek glistening body as black as pitch.

'What the hell is *that*?' he asked himself, in a tone filled with growing resentment.

He was just coming to terms with the fact that the

catch of his life was nothing more than a binbag full of old clothes, or something equally as dull, when the object suddenly twitched before his eyes, sending ripples of water spiralling out in every direction.

With renewed hope that it may have been some sort of massive fish after all, he discarded his rod to scurry over to the water's edge.

Clambering carefully down the steep grassy bank, he slowly immersed himself into the swirling river below.

As muddy brown water began creeping up his chest-high waders, and with his feet sinking steadily down into the river's silty bed, he held his arms high above his head to begin making his way carefully out towards what continued to float in the middle of the river, albeit now with an unsettling stillness.

The moment he was in arm's reach, he leaned gradually forward, just enough to touch it, but not enough for the water that was already up to his chest to spill over the top of his waders.

The second he was able to lay a hand on it, he knew it wasn't a fish. Nor was it anything living. It was as he'd previously thought. Nothing but a stupid binbag stuffed full of discarded clothes. What had made it spasm before, he'd no idea. Probably a log, or maybe a branch, knocking against it through the gently ebbing tide.

Questioning what the hell he was doing in the middle of a cold unwelcoming river, for no other reason than to rescue a bag of old clothes, he was about to pivot around to wade back to the bank when something brushed against the top of his thigh.

Jumping with a start, he peered cautiously down through the murky depths. There he saw what looked to be some sort of a peculiar colourless crab, somehow managing to maintain its position against the river's natural flow.

Consumed by curiosity, he slipped a hand under the water to touch it. The moment he did, he instinctively knew what it was. It wasn't a crab. It was a human hand, suspended in the water just inches from his legs.

It took him another full moment to realise what that must have meant: that the object in front of him wasn't a binbag full of clothes, but was a lifeless corpse, floating on the surface with its head facing down.

Having never so much as seen a dead body before, let alone find himself standing next to one, consumed with morbid curiosity, he took a gentle hold of the flaccid, rubbery hand. Grimacing, he lifted it through the water, rotating the body attached to it as he did. As the body rolled slowly over, he tilted his head down to see first a nose, then a mouth. It was only when he saw a pair of lifeless blue eyes did it occur to him that he was holding hands with a floating corpse.

Shuddering in revulsion, he instantly let go to spend a voyeuristic moment watching the body slowly rotate itself back to where it had been before.

The distant sound of a motorboat came rumbling through the air, its thumping diesel engine drifting over the river like rolling thunder.

Unable to leave the poor man just floating there like that, ready to be mown down by every passing boat, Nigel took a firm hold of the man's coat with the aim of hauling him back to the bank. But when he tried lifting one of his boots from the river's heavily silted base, the bloody thing wouldn't budge!

Trying not to panic, he shifted his weight to pull the other one out, but that too was stuck fast.

'Shit!' he cursed, his heart picking up a beat as his mind spun around in circles, desperately trying to think what to do.

With the sound of the boat growing steadily louder, he had an idea.

Viewing the corpse as some sort of a macabre floatation device, he threw his arms over it, hoping that by doing so would allow him to pull out his boots. But the moment he did, the body simply rolled towards him, leaving him in the same position as when he'd started.

Catching a glimpse of the boat out of the corner of his eye, he tried again, only for the exact same thing to happen, this time resulting in a gallon of freezing cold water surging over the top of his waders, down into the very boots he was trying to free.

Having to take shallow rapid breaths, he lifted a hand to wave madly at the rapidly approaching boat, but it was too close to catch the driver's eye. All he could see was its looming white hull, growing wider and higher with every passing second.

As the noise of the engine became a deafening roar, he knew he had no choice. He *had* to free himself from the riverbed's deadly grip!

With the last of his ebbing strength, he launched himself up as high as he could, flinging his arms over the corpse for one final time. But just as before, the moment he did, the body simply rolled back towards him, this time taking him all the way under.

As his head plunged beneath the surface, he closed his eyes to claw violently at the body that seemed to be deliberately trying to hold him down.

With the water boiling around him like a steaming cauldron, he opened his eyes to see the body's pale, ghostly face, hanging above his own like a shimmering ghost. But the dead man's eyes weren't lifeless and vacant as they had been before. They were bright and alive, staring into his with malicious intent.

Using what was left of the air in his lungs, he shoved the body away to force himself up.

Breaking free of the surface, he gasped madly at the air, only for the speeding boat's hull to smash hard into his skull, instantly ploughing over the rest of him, leaving its spinning propellor to spew out what remained, nothing but a twisted mass of lacerated limbs and splintered bone, pitching and rolling in the boat's gradually disappearing wake.

- CHAPTER FIFTY FOUR -

'HONEY, I'M HOME!' Tanner called out in a frivolous tone, nudging open the door to his modest riverside bungalow only to find his way was being blocked by a larger-than-average suitcase.

'I'm in the bedroom!' came Christine's high-pitched response.

'That's a first,' he muttered, quietly to himself, his eyes remaining fixed on the suitcase.

Wondering exactly how he was going to break the news to her that they were going to have to cancel their honeymoon, he stepped over the suitcase to close the door behind him. 'I don't suppose there's anything I can help you with?'

'I don't have time for that!' came her chiding response.

'I didn't mean...' he began, before thinking that maybe he had, at least at a subliminal level. After all, it had been a while.

Reminding himself that there was a good reason why they hadn't had sex in such a long time, he dumped his keys on the counter to begin peeling off his coat.

'You're not allowed to come in, either!' he heard her continue.

'Any particular reason why not?'

'Because I'm trying on my wedding dress, or at

least I'm endeavouring to.'

'Fair enough.'

'I only had the waist taken out last week, but the bloody thing already doesn't fit!'

'Oh dear,' he laughed, making his way quietly down the hall.

'At this precise moment in time,' came her voice again, 'I'm beginning to think that perhaps we should have postponed the wedding until *after* Kung Fu Ken arrived.'

'Too late now.'

'Anyway, as long as I don't eat anything between now and our honeymoon, I should be alright.'

'*Speaking of which,*' he mumbled to himself, knocking gingerly on the bedroom door.

'I said, don't come in!'

'I know. That's why I'm knocking.'

'OK, hold on.'

Listening to the muffled sound of rustling clothes, Tanner waited patiently beside the door, his hand resting gently on the handle.

'You can come in now.'

Tanner drew in a fortifying breath to inch it slowly open. 'Are you decent?' he asked, peering through the gap to see his bride-to-be standing sideways in front of the mirror, wearing nothing but a bra and pants.

'I'm not sure I've been decent since the eighties,' she replied, arching her back with a painful grimace as her hands wandered over her bulging abdomen. 'Less so now that I've been knocked up by some reprehensible policeman, a man who I'm fairly sure has only ever been interested in one thing.'

Stepping inside to stand immediately behind her, Tanner wrapped his arms around her thin narrow shoulders. 'That's not true,' he whispered, gently into her ear, as his hands wondered down to encircle her breasts. 'I can think of two more things, for a start.'

'No time for that, I'm afraid,' she replied, nudging him away to pick a towel up from the floor.

Tanner stuffed his hands into his pockets to look dejectedly at himself in the mirror. 'To be honest, I didn't think there would be.'

'I've left a suitcase on the bed for you to pack.'

'Ah, yes. About that.'

Christine spun around to glare at him. 'Please don't tell me that you can't go.'

'I'm sorry, honey,' he shrugged, 'but I really don't see how I can.'

'I thought I saw what's-his-name being taken into custody on the news?'

'Simon Balinger, and yes, he was.'

'But not anymore?'

'Unfortunately, at least for us, he lacked motive. He also had an alibi, or at least a sensible enough reason for being where we already knew he was. On top of that, we didn't have any physical evidence, leaving me with little choice but to let him go, which, in turn, means I don't have a suspect.'

'Don't you have any more leads?'

'Nothing worth chasing.'

'Then why can't you come? I mean, it is our honeymoon, or at least it was supposed to be.'

'Because if the press found out I was lying beside a private swimming pool in Spain, instead of spearheading a double-murder investigation in Norfolk, they'd be demanding my head, and I'm not particularly convinced Forrester wouldn't give it to them.'

'But if there's nothing for you to do, you may as well come? I mean, it's not as if nobody will be able to get hold of you. The villa *does* have wi-fi. I checked before I booked. There's also something which I believe is called a mobile phone, one of which you have.'

'Only my old one,' he replied, digging it out to check for messages, 'the battery of which is virtually useless.'

'I'm not sure that's a problem. I'm fairly sure Spain has electricity, being that it's not the Eighteenth Century. I've already packed your phone's charger, as well as a universal plug socket.'

'That's not the problem.'

'Then what is?'

'The British press!'

'Since when have you given a rat's arse what the British press thinks?'

'Since I became a DCI.'

'Really?' she questioned, in an incredulous tone.

'OK, perhaps not. But it doesn't alter the fact that I'm in the middle of a double-murder investigation.'

'For which you just said you have neither suspects, nor leads, leaving you with nothing to do but to sit behind your desk with your feet up.'

'That's not exactly true.'

'I see. And what else were you planning on doing?'

'Well, I've got that book of crosswords for a start, the one you bought me for Christmas. Then there's the Norfolk Herald to read, of course. It comes out every day. Did you know that?'

Christine locked her arms over her chest to present Tanner with a look of unamused indignation.

'I suppose I could ask Forrester if it would be OK if I went.'

'Yes, I suppose you could.'

With Christine still glaring at him, Tanner waited awkwardly with his phone still in his hand. 'Er...' he cautiously began, 'do you want me to call him now?'

'Yes please!' she replied, remaining resolutely

where she was.

'Right. Hold on.'

Dialling his number, he listened to it ring before it clicked through to voicemail.

'He's not picking up,' he whispered.

'Then leave him a message!'

Tanner gave her a subservient nod. 'Good evening, sir, it's Tanner calling. Do you think it would be possible to call me back, when you get a chance? Thanks. Bye!'

'Whilst you're waiting for him to do so,' Christine continued, plonking herself down at the dressing table to start prodding at her hair in the mirror, 'you can start packing that suitcase of yours.'

'And what if he says no?'

'Then you can tell him not to bother coming to our wedding.'

'But – he's my best man!'

Christine glared up at him through the mirror's reflection. 'Do I look like I give a shit?'

'I suppose not,' he replied, turning to look down at the empty suitcase, just as his phone sprang to life in his hand.

'I assume that's him?'

'Sadly not,' he replied, staring down at the screen. 'It's Vicky.'

Hearing nothing more from Christine, he turned away to answer the call. 'Yes, Vicky. What's up?'

'Sorry to bother you, boss. I know it's the night before your wedding, and everything, but something's come up.'

Tanner could almost feel Christine's eyes burning into the back of his head. 'Go on.'

'I'm afraid not one, but two bodies have been found floating down the river Ant, just up from Barton Broad.'

'Right!' came his fractious response.

'It sounds like one might be a fisherman who got into trouble.'

'And the other?'

'We don't know.'

Tanner took a moment to think.

'I'm happy to handle it myself. I just wanted to ask your permission?'

'No, it's fine. Text me the location. I'll be there as soon as I can.'

- CHAPTER FIFTY FIVE -

EAVING HIS CAR parked on a grass verge behind Dr Johnstone's beaten-up old Volvo Estate, Tanner climbed wearily out to feel the wind instantly whip around his head. Closing the door behind him, he took a contemplative moment to watch a line of ominous-looking clouds, chasing themselves over Norfolk's wide open horizon, as if playing some sort of never ending game.

When he heard his name being tossed about by the buffeting breeze, he turned to see Vicky, stomping over the thick, lush grass towards him, a hand held half in the air to help garner his attention.

'You didn't have to come,' he heard her call, as his eyes were drawn to the river Ant behind her, its surface illuminated by a billion shards of light from a fast-setting sun.

'So you said,' he absently replied, as she came to a breathless halt beside him.

'I hope Christine wasn't too upset?'

'More so about our honeymoon. She'd only just persuaded me to go, as well.'

'I'm sorry again. You deserved some time off.'

'It doesn't matter. It was only a holiday. We'll just have to go another time.'

Forcing a smile at her, he deliberately changed the subject. 'Has anything else turned up since your call?'

'The bodies have only just been pulled out,' she

replied, leading him back the way she'd come, where the normal collection of uniformed policeman and overall-clad forensic personnel could be seen, all surrounded by a long line of flickering blue and white tape. 'Dr Johnstone is taking a look now.'

'Was that a yes, or a no?'

'We've found ID on both,' she continued, pulling out her notes. 'One would appear to be someone by the name of Nigel Mellor.'

'Which one was that?'

'The one we think was a fisherman.'

'And the other?'

Vicky cast a wary eye at him before returning to her notepad. 'If the ID matches the body, then it looks likely to be someone we all know and love, or at least you do.'

Tanner gave her an anxious glance. 'Are you going to tell me or not?'

'It looks like it's that reporter from the Norfolk Herald. Sidney Fletcher.'

Tanner's pace slowed to a crawl as the bodies gradually crept into view, their eyes gazing forever up at the darkening sky above. 'Would I be correct in assuming that he didn't drown?'

'The cause of death has yet to be confirmed, but if he did, I doubt if it would have been accidental.'

Coming to a standstill behind Dr Johnstone, Tanner discreetly cleared his throat.

'Ah, Chief Inspector!' came the medical examiner's surprised response. 'Don't you have a wedding to go to?'

'I do?' he queried, with a curious frown.

'I'm fairly sure you have, being that you're the one who invited me. My wife, as well!'

'Ah – you're thinking about the one that's tomorrow.'

'Of course. Silly me. But a word of warning,' he added, in a low, conspiratorial tone. 'When the vicar invites you to say the words, "I do", it may be wise to use them without the question mark at the end.'

'Yes, of course. I'll just have to keep practicing.'

'With regards to what we have here,' Johnstone continued, turning to take in the two bodies, 'at this precise moment in time, I'm afraid I don't have a great deal for you, but in my defence, I haven't been here all that long myself. I'm also more used to dealing with one body at a time.'

'It's a special offer,' Tanner replied. 'Murder one, get another murdered for free.'

'Very droll, Tanner, but sadly inaccurate. I don't think they were both murdered, although each were likely to have been killed by a blow to the head, albeit by two very different objects.

'Looking at the man wearing what's left of the fishing waders, the entire top of his skull has been crushed by something substantial. If you take into account the location his body was found, together with the parallel lacerations running the length of his body, I'd say he was most likely run over by a boat, one that must have been going far faster than the designated speed limit.

'The other man's head injury looks more likely to have been caused by a hammer, or something similar.'

'I don't suppose it's possible that one killed the other during some sort of fight, perhaps a squabble over who'd caught the biggest fish?'

'I've heard fisherman to be passionate about their hobby, but I doubt it extends to murder, at least not over a dead fish. Certainly not with a hammer. A fish knife, perhaps?'

Tanner folded his arms to continue taking in the

scene. 'Is there anything else you can tell me?'

'Judging by how challenging the divers said it was to pull the fisherman's boots out from the riverbed, and how his remains were found entangled with the other victim, I'd say it's likely that he was trying to retrieve the body when he realised he'd become stuck, at which point a passing boat ran straight over the top of him.'

'Time of death?'

'For the fisherman, it must have happened within the last hour. As for the other chap, I'd say it was more likely between six and nine hours ago. He's certainly been in the water for about that sort of time.'

'OK, thank you. Let me know if you find anything else.'

'No problem, but I doubt it will be before your wedding, I'm afraid.'

'Don't worry. Monday will do. I'm not exactly going anywhere.'

'I thought you were jetting off to Spain for your honeymoon?'

'So did Christine,' Tanner laughed, with an unamused grimace.

Johnstone offered him a sympathetic shrug. 'I suppose you do have a fair amount on your plate at the moment.'

'You could say that. Anyway, as I said. Let me know if you find out anything else.'

'Will do.'

Stepping away, Tanner glanced about to see Vicky, busily chatting to an elderly man, a dog lying patiently by his feet.

Catching her eye, just as he began leading his dog away, he stepped quickly over. 'I assume that was the person who found them?'

'He says he was walking his dog when he saw

something floating against the tide. When he found the abandoned fishing gear, he gave us a call. I told him he could go. I hope that's OK?'

'You took down his details?'

'Of course.'

'Then I'm sure that's fine.'

Tanner took a quiet moment to watch the old man wander away, his dog following with obedient devotion.

'What do you want to do now?' he heard Vicky ask.

'Go to bed,' came his honest reply.

'I meant, about the bodies?'

'Which ones? There have been so many, I'm beginning to lose count.'

With Vicky remaining stoically silent beside him, he turned to offer her an apologetic grimace. 'Sorry. That was hardly professional.'

'Don't worry. If I was getting married tomorrow, I wouldn't want to be here either. In fact, I wouldn't be!'

'No, well, fair enough.'

'But as you are, what's the plan?'

'I think the first thing is to find out where Mr Fletcher was last seen alive, then to establish his movements leading up to that point.'

'That's if it *is* Sidney Fletcher.'

'Oh, it's him, alright. I'd recognise that face a mile off, even if it has spent nine hours floating in a river whilst being run over by every passing motorboat. Maybe start by asking his editor what he was currently working on. The chances are that he'd discovered something that someone wasn't too keen for him to write a story about.'

Pleased to see her taking notes, Tanner's gaze drifted sagaciously over to the river again. 'It may also be worth trying to work out where his body entered the water, approximately at least, but that's something I can ask Christine about.'

'Is that really a subject you want to bring up with your fiancée, the night before your wedding?'

Tanner shrugged with indifference. 'I'm not sure she'll mind. Besides, it will give us something to do together, other than unpacking, of course.'

- CHAPTER FIFTY SIX -

Saturday, 13th June

FEELING FAR MORE nervous than he'd been expecting to, Tanner found a place to park outside Ranworth Village Hall to climb slowly out. With one hand resting on top of his car's door, he gazed up at St. Helen's church's ancient rectangular stone tower, stretching high into the menacing grey sky above. 'Please, God,' he whispered quietly to himself, 'don't let it rain. At least not for the next hour or so.'

Clasping his hands together in front of him, he was about to say, 'Amen,' when a single drop of water landed squarely in the middle of his forehead.

Sending the supreme being in question a derisive scowl, he remained where he was, praying that it might just be that one single drop. But as a rapidly increasing number began thudding into the ground around him, he quickly gave up, turning to grab an umbrella from inside his car before closing the door.

Wrestling the umbrella open, he discreetly joined the back of a group of smartly dressed people to follow the lane leading up to the church. When he eventually reached its entrance, he quickly scanned the faces of those who'd already arrived to spy a group he recognised; the members of his CID team, taking shelter from the rain under a sprawling beech tree.

'Nice day for it,' he said, stepping up to them to shake his umbrella closed.

'There you are, Tanner!' boomed Forrester, slapping him hard on the back. 'We were about to start taking bets on whether or not you were going to show up. Cooper, here, was about to offer me fifty British pounds that you wouldn't.'

Jamming a skinny elbow into her uncle's ribs, Sally caught Tanner's eye with a beguiling smile. 'Don't listen to him. He's making it up.'

'She's right,' Cooper announced, with a sardonic smirk. 'I was only going to offer a tenner.'

'I had twenty pounds that you wouldn't!' Henderson suddenly called out, with a wholly misplaced grin.

'Then we must be paying you too much,' Tanner replied, kindly filling in the awkward silence that seemed to follow what he assumed to be the young DC's rather poor attempt at humour.

'Shame about the weather,' came Gina's voice, the elegant features of her face appearing from under a wide, lavender-coloured hat.

'I suspect that was my fault,' Tanner lamented. 'I rather stupidly asked for it not to rain, only for it to start pouring down about three-and-a-half seconds later.'

'That'll teach you,' laughed Townsend, standing beside Sally.

Glancing down to see they were discreetly holding hands, Tanner smiled gently at them both. 'I must admit, I should have known better. Hopefully, it will pass, before Christine arrives.'

'That's if she turns up,' Cooper muttered, from out of the corner of his mouth.

'If you're not careful, Cooper,' came Forrester's berating voice, 'we'll be asking you for that fifty pounds, whether she shows up or not.'

With Cooper snapping his mouth closed, Tanner glanced over his shoulder to see their medical examiner, Dr Johnstone, puffing his way along the path, a black umbrella held between himself and the petite middle-aged woman he was walking beside.

Raising a hand to attract his attention, Tanner watched him pass the umbrella to the lady before lolloping his way over.

'Morning, gents!' the medical examiner eventually announced, attempting to share the shelter of the same tree. 'Nice day for it.'

'That's what the groom said,' Forrester remarked.

Johnstone glanced about at them all through a pair of misted-up glasses. 'And where is he?'

'I'm right here!' Tanner stated, rolling his eyes.

'So you are,' he replied, peeling off his glasses to start wiping them with a tissue. 'Any sign of the bride?'

'Not yet,' smirked Cooper.

Tanner dug his hands dejectedly down into his pockets. 'May I ask why everyone seems to be assuming that the bride-to-be is in the process of doing a runner?'

'Er...no reason in particular,' came Johnstone's somewhat hesitant response, glancing surreptitiously around at the others in the group.

Forrester's face cracked into a beaming grin. 'Don't worry, Tanner. She'll show up!'

'I wasn't aware I was worried.'

'Oh, right,' Forrester replied, returning a look of surprised concern. 'Don't you think you should be?'

Shaking his head, Tanner found himself glancing anxiously over at the now empty path.

'Anyway,' he heard Forrester continue, 'may I suggest we make our way inside. I think the idea is for the groom to be waiting at the end of the aisle for the bride to arrive, not fretting about outside worried that she won't, or perhaps worse still, that she will.'

Hearing everyone snicker around him, Tanner glanced down at his watch. 'Don't worry. It's only quarter to eleven. There's still plenty of time.'

'For her not to show up, or for you to change your mind?' Forrester enquired, with a look of earnest curiosity.

Realising that the only way to stop the seemingly endless banter was to change the subject, Tanner returned his attention to Johnstone. 'Any more news on those two bodies?'

'Only what I told Vicky, but to be honest, I barely had a chance to look at them after you left.'

'Er...excuse me,' came Forrester's inquiring voice, his eyes endeavouring to drill down into Tanner's, 'but what bodies are those?'

'They were found yesterday evening,' Tanner replied, glancing absently around, 'one we believe to be a reporter for the Norfolk Herald. I'm sorry if I didn't mention anything about it before, but as I hope you can appreciate, I've been a little preoccupied of late.'

Without giving him the chance to respond, Tanner cast an enquiring eye at his team. 'Has anyone seen Vicky?'

The question left them all gawping around at each other.

'She *said* she was coming,' came Gina's eventual reply.

'That's what she told me as well.'

'I assume she relayed to you what I told her,' enquired Johnstone, 'about what I found on the murder victim's hand?'

'The *murder* victim?' came Forrester's demanding

voice again.

Continuing to ignore him, Tanner kept his attention firmly fixed on the medical examiner. 'I haven't spoken to her since I left.'

'There was something written on it,' Johnstone continued. 'I've no idea what it meant, but she certainly seemed to find it interesting.'

'I don't suppose you can remember what it was?'

The question left Johnstone digging out his phone to begin swiping at the screen. 'Just some random letters and numbers. Unfortunately, they were all rather badly smudged. C, A, 4, 3?' he eventually proposed, squinting down at his phone over the top of his glasses, 'followed by what could be a D, H, and maybe a 7?'

As he rotated the phone for Tanner to see, everyone began gathering around.

'I don't think that's an A,' commented Townsend, pointing down. 'It looks more like an H to me. And the line underneath. I'd say that's a P, not a D.'

'It's an acronym for chapter forty-three, paragraph six,' stated Tanner, searching the group for Henderson's goat-like face. 'I don't suppose you still have a copy of that book?'

'You mean, the one about Norfolk's role in the Cold War?'

'I was actually thinking about Winnie-the-Poo and the Blustery Day,' came Tanner's biting response.

Watching Henderson blush with confused consternation, Tanner drew in an apologetic breath. 'Yes, sorry. I did mean the one about the Cold War.'

'Oh, right.'

'Do you have it?'

'I gave it to Vicky.'

'And why, may I ask, did you do that?'

'Because she asked me for it.'

'You didn't make a copy for yourself?'

'I didn't think I was supposed to.'

Tanner tore his eyes from Henderson's face with a look of frustrated annoyance.

'But that chapter and paragraph,' he heard the young DC continue. 'I'm fairly sure it was one of the ones I emailed to you; the ones relating to Bluebell Wood.'

- CHAPTER FIFTY SEVEN -

PLUNGING A HAND into one of his pockets, Tanner tugged out his old mobile phone, only to remember that he'd forgotten to charge it the night before. Hoping to God that it was going to work, he turned it on to end up having to wait for what felt like a week and a day for it to creep slowly into life. 'Bloody thing,' he cursed, swiping restlessly at the screen, only to be forced to wait once again.

'Don't you think it's time for a new phone?' he heard Johnstone remark.

'I already have a new phone,' he grimaced, 'at least, I did.'

'It was stolen,' Sally explained. 'He was mugged, a couple of days ago.'

'I'm sorry to hear that,' Johnstone replied, offering Tanner a sympathetic frown. 'But – didn't you tell them who you were?'

Tanner shook his head with incredulous consternation, whilst the bulk of his attention remained fixed on his phone. 'OK, here it is. Chapter forty-three, paragraph six.'

The group fell silent as he began reading it through to himself.

'Well?' came Forrester's impatient demand.

'It doesn't say anything!' Tanner eventually stated, reading it through again. 'It just says about how the Bluebell Wood research facility was closed, two years after the collapse of the Berlin Wall.'

Showing Forrester the screen, he heard Townsend say, 'Then it must be in reference to another book.'

'No doubt, but as the only book that's even remotely relevant to this investigation is the one about Norfolk's involvement in the Cold War, I'm not sure how that helps.'

'Who's this Major Campbell guy?' asked Forrester, his eyes transfixed by the screen.

Tanner stared at him with a look of distracted bewilderment.

'His name's mentioned twice,' the superintendent continued, glancing up.

Tanner took the phone back to re-read the passage again. 'It just says he was in charge of the facility when it was closed down.'

'Could he be relevant?'

'I don't *think* so. As far as I know, we don't have anyone by that name who's considered to be a...'

As Tanner's voice trailed away, his eyes drifted slowly off into space. 'I'm an absolute idiot!' he eventually said, returning to look back at the phone.

'Can't argue with that,' muttered Cooper.

'Samuel Brogan,' Tanner continued, 'the teenager who hanged himself. His father's name is Campbell. His biological father, that is. He abandoned him when he was a baby. He came in to see me the other day, to ask if he was needed.'

'You think he's this Major Campbell guy?' questioned Forrester.

'It's too much of a coincidence for it not to be, don't you think?'

'I don't know. There must be a fair few Campbells knocking about the place.'

'But for a reference to the chapter and paragraph naming him to be found on a journalist's hand, the same journalist whose body was discovered floating down the river Ant yesterday, and now with Vicky going missing, shortly after being told about the very same reference?'

'It's a little too early to say that she's gone missing, don't you think?

'Are we really willing to take that chance?'

A disturbing silence fell over the group.

'Has anyone tried getting hold of her?' Forrester eventually asked, staring around at them all.

'I texted her earlier,' Gina replied, digging out her phone.

'And...?'

'She didn't come back.'

'Can you try calling her now?'

Leaving her to spin away with her phone pressed against her ear, Forrester looked back at those remaining. 'What about this Campbell character? Does anyone know where he lives?'

'If he came into the station,' Sally replied, 'then his address should be in the system.'

'Can you give the office a call to find out?'

'No problem,' she smiled, as Gina stepped back into the group.

'I can't get hold of Vicky. It keeps going through to voicemail. I can drive around to her flat, if you like?'

Forrester turned to Tanner. 'What do you think? I mean, this *is* your wedding. I don't particularly wish to be responsible for telling half your guests that they need to leave. It's also your investigation, of course.'

Tanner gave him an appreciative nod. Standing tall, he glanced around to find everyone staring attentively back. 'Cooper and Gina, as soon as we've found his address, I want you two to go straight over there. Townsend, take Sally around to Vicky's flat. It could be that she's simply late. If she is, then tell her to hurry up! Henderson, I want you back at the station. We need to find out all we can about Campbell, starting with what car he drives. The moment you have a numberplate, I want you to plug it into the ANPR. Then get an All Ports Warning out, just in case he's thinking about leaving the country.'

As the group quickly disbanded, Forrester was left looking at Tanner. 'What about me?' he asked, with a questioning frown.

'You're the best man. I need you here.'

'You don't need a best man to get married. Just the bride and groom, and a vicar, of course,' he added, gesturing towards the church's entrance, where the vicar in question could be seen gazing over at them with a hand resting discreetly over his watch.

Acknowledging the fact that he was clearly waiting for him, Tanner offered him what he hope would be a pacifying nod.

'Looks like the bride's here as well,' he heard Forrester say.

Turning to follow his gaze, he saw Christine making her way along the path, a gaggle of bridesmaids enveloping her, one holding an umbrella above her head, the other two attempting to keep the hem of her modest off-white wedding dress from dragging along the wet, muddy ground.

'Would you mind driving over to Wroxham Station?' he asked, looking back at Forrester. 'Henderson could probably do with a hand.'

'I can go one better than that. I can get every available officer in Norfolk out looking for them.'

'Thank you, sir. I'd appreciate that.'

- CHAPTER FIFTY EIGHT -

WATCHING FORRESTER HURRY past his approaching bride to offer her nothing more than an apologetic nod, Tanner opened his umbrella to hurry over to where the vicar was waiting.

'Sorry about that,' he breathlessly said, joining him under the shelter of the church's arched stone entrance. 'The bride's just coming.'

'So I can see,' the vicar mused. 'Just a shame to see so many others leaving.'

'Unfortunately, something important came up at work.'

'More important than your wedding?'

'I'm afraid so.'

'And what about your best man. Am I correct in thinking that he's had to leave as well?'

'Er...' Tanner replied, with an apologetic grimace, 'do I need one?'

'Well, it would have been nice, but no doubt we'll get by. Shall we go inside?

'Before I do, I don't suppose I could have a very quick word with the bride?'

The vicar turned to face him with a look of parental concern. 'My dear boy, I do hope you're not having second thoughts?'

'Not at all. I just think I'd better explain to her why all of my guests have just left, the best man included.'

The vicar continued to study his face, but now with a look of dubious suspicion. 'Very well,' he eventually said, 'but don't put it off for too long. Procrastination can be a dangerous thing. Besides, I have another wedding at one o'clock.'

Watching the vicar head inside with a benevolent smile, Tanner was left to face a rapidly approaching Christine, whose face appeared to be considerably less amenable.

'You look amazing!' he said, as she came storming up to him.

'Never mind that! What the hell's going on?' she demanded, batting her bridesmaids away like irritating flies. 'I've just seen your entire CID team leaving, the best man included!'

'I'm afraid something came up.'

'Let me guess. Something to do with work?'

'We think Vicky may have gone missing.'

Christine opened her mouth, only to immediately close it again.

'We also think we know who's responsible for Professor Baxendale's murder, possibly everything else as well.'

As Tanner talked, her expression changed from agitated irritation to one of curious intrigue. 'Anyone I know?'

'You remember I told you last night about the bodies found floating in the river, and that we thought one was a reporter from the Norfolk Herold?'

'Shortly before you announced that we were going to have to cancel our honeymoon. Yes, I remember!'

'Johnstone found something written on his hand, a few minutes after I left. We think it was in reference to a passage from Professor Baxendale's unpublished book. It named the person responsible for closing down the Bluebell Wood research facility.'

'What's this got to do with Vicky going missing, and Professor Baxendale's murder?'

Tanner followed her eyes as they darted furtively around at their remaining wedding guests, all of whom were now staring at them with curious intrigue. 'The man's name was Major Campbell. It's the same surname as Samuel Brogan's biological father.'

'OK, now I'm even more confused. Are you saying the father murdered his own son?'

'I'm not sure about that, but I *do* think it's possible that he killed Professor Baxendale.'

'But why?'

'Because of what the professor said about him in his book.'

'Which was...?'

'Well, nothing really,' Tanner was forced to admit. 'Only that he was in charge of the military facility when it was closed down.'

'Then I don't mean to be rude,' she said, in an ominously low tone, 'but why the *hell* are we standing outside a church talking about it on the day of our wedding, with all my friends and family staring at us, no doubt trying to decide which one of us has had a change of heart?'

'Because the reporter who had the passage highlighted on his hand is now dead, and the last time anyone heard from Vicky was when Dr Johnstone showed it to her.'

Tanner's words were left hanging in the air as Christine stared silently back.

'What are you doing to find her?' she eventually asked.

'Sally and Townsend are heading over to her flat as we speak. With any luck, she's just running late.'

'And the person mentioned in the book?'

'Cooper and Gina are trying to locate his house, Henderson's gone back to the office to see if he can find his car, and Forrester's headed off to get every police officer in Norfolk out on the streets looking for both him and Vicky.'

'Is anyone looking into where he works?'

'I'm fairly sure he's retired,' Tanner replied, leaving him wondering what had made him think that. 'Even if he hasn't, and we knew where he did, I think the fact that it's the weekend would make it unlikely that he'd be there.'

'Well, if he *has* decided to hole up somewhere with Vicky, I think it's highly unlikely he'd be doing so from the comfort of his own home.'

It was at that moment Tanner remembered the reason for assuming Campbell to have been retired. It was that ridiculous cap he'd been wearing when he'd met him, and what he'd gone on to say after Tanner had brought his attention to it. 'He's got a boat,' he suddenly announced, fixing Christine's eyes. 'He mentioned something about it when he came into the station.'

'Do you know where it is?'

'I don't even know *what* it is, let alone where!'

Christine thought for a moment. 'Have you got your phone on you?'

'Somewhere,' he replied, searching his pockets. 'Don't you have yours?'

'Strangely enough, I didn't think I'd need it. I'm not sure where I'd have put it, either.'

'Here,' Tanner said, handing his over.

'What was the suspect's name again?' she asked, swiping at the screen.

'Campbell.'

'First name?'

'I can't remember.'

'OK, I'm calling the Broads Authority,' she continued, lifting the phone to her ear. 'If he does have a boat, then they should have a record of what it is and where it's moored. That's assuming it's been registered.'

Tanner stood quietly by as he listened to someone answer.

'Hello, I wonder if you can help?' Christine began. 'My name's Christine Halliday. I'm a Broads Ranger, calling on behalf of Norfolk Police. We're looking for a boat belonging to someone by the name of Campbell. I'm afraid we don't know his first name, nor the type of boat.'

There was a long pause before she covered the mouthpiece to look up at Tanner. 'They have four Campbells listed, all with boats on the Broads. Shall I ask them to email their names to you?'

'Can you see if any are listed as belonging to a *Major* Campbell?'

Tanner listened to her repeat the question to the person on the other end of the line before waiting again.

'I know where that is,' Christine eventually said, the corners of her mouth creasing into a smile. 'Thank you for your help.'

'What did they say?' asked Tanner, taking back his phone.

'If it's the same guy, then he has a boat moored up along Fleet Dyke, just up from South Walsham Broad.'

'But – that's just down the road!' Tanner exclaimed, staring over Christine's shoulder, to the path leading back to where he'd left his car.

'You're not seriously thinking about leaving your pregnant bride at the altar, are you?' she demanded, reading his mind as if it was an open book.

'Well, no...' he began, shifting his weight from one foot to the other, 'although, it could be argued, at least technically, that you're not at the altar, at least not yet. You're still standing outside the church.'

Christine planted her hands firmly down on her hips to glare at him with a look of dangerous foreboding.

'I did say technically.'

After spending a sultry moment shaking her head, she leaned towards him to whisper, 'What the hell am I going to tell the vicar, my family, and all my bloody friends?'

'Maybe you could tell them that I forgot to buy you a wedding ring, and that I'll be back in a jiffy.'

'If you did forget, I'm not sure how you could possibly be back in a jiffy.'

'Does that mean I can go?'

'You can't ask someone else?'

'Well, I could, but...'

Christine let out an exasperated sigh. 'Go on then. But if you're not back in half-an-hour, don't expect to find me here. I'll be at home, stuffing your clothes into the bin, whilst endeavouring to seduce some handsome young man as he changes all the locks.'

- CHAPTER FIFTY NINE -

A RRIVING AT A small deserted carpark to the side of Fleet Dyke, Tanner stepped out of his car to immediately open his still dripping umbrella. Instantly holding it up against the unrelenting rain, he began scanning the river's windswept banks, looking for what he hoped would be Campbell's boat. But there wasn't a single one there. Both sides of the river were empty. The only thing that could even be vaguely described as a boat was a large ungainly houseboat, moored up just beyond a weeping willow tree, its branches being tossed about by the buffeting breeze.

Realising that it would have been sensible to have asked what sort of boat it was before abandoning his wedding to drive over there, he made his way cautiously along the grass towards first the tree, then the houseboat beyond. As he did, he kept his eyes peeled for something more in keeping with a man who went around wearing a cap with the word "Captain" emblazoned above its peak, something like an over-sized motor cruiser with an unnecessarily high flybridge, from where the owner could stare down at those less worthy than himself.

Skirting his way around the willow trees tangled mesh of dangling wet branches, he stared up at the ungainly houseboat that was in such a poor state of repair, it was a miracle it was still afloat.

'Hello!' he called, his eyes scanning the grimy windows for even the vaguest sign of life. 'Is anyone on board?'

With the only noise being the rain drumming against the top of his umbrella, and the breeze rustling against the tree's branches, something else occurred to him, something that did now appear to be rather obvious. If Campbell *did* own a motor cruiser, and was using it to imprison a police officer, it was a little unlikely that he'd have left it moored up against the banks of a river in plain sight. Glancing down at his watch, it also occurred to him that if he'd stayed at the church with Christine, as he now wished he had, they'd have been married by now.

As a wave of guilt crashed over him, he pulled out his mobile to give her a call, only to remember that she didn't have her phone with her.

Cursing with frustration, he dialled Townsend's number instead, hoping to at least find out if there'd been any sign of Vicky. When it clicked through to voicemail, he became even more annoyed when he realised that his phone's battery was about to die.

To save what was left, he was about to turn it off when it rang suddenly in his hand. 'Tanner speaking!' he replied, lifting it to his ear.

'Hello, er...boss, it's Henderson. I don't suppose you have a minute?'

'Just about, but make it quick. My battery's about to die.'

'I didn't know if I should call, what with you getting married, and everything.'

'As I said, Henderson, make it quick!'

'Sorry, of course. I just thought I should let you know that I've found Campbell's car. It's an old blue C-Class Mercedes.'

'I don't suppose you've been able to trace it?'

'Not with ANPR. The last time the cameras picked it up was two months ago, driving along the A47.'

'OK, well, thanks for letting me know. I don't suppose there's been any news about Vicky?'

'Not that I've heard. Superintendent Forrester is in your office. He's more likely to know than me. Shall I put you through?'

'Don't worry. He'd have called if there had been.'

'There's something else as well,' Henderson continued, 'about the suspect. I'm not sure its relevant.'

'OK, but be quick.'

'I've just started to do some background research on him. Did you know that he was a co-operating witness during the Adlington trial?'

Tanner raised a curious eyebrow. 'I don't suppose you know why?'

'I don't know the specifics. Do you want me to find out?'

'If you could, but when you do, don't call me. Tell Forrester.'

Ending the call to immediately turn off his phone, Tanner gazed back at the houseboat. Without it looking as if anyone had so much as touched it in years, he was about to head back to the car when he heard a loud muffled thud coming from somewhere inside.

Remaining completely still, he tuned his ears for the slightest of sounds. But all he could hear was the persistent rain and the buffeting wind.

Putting the sound down to the boat's rotten, creaking frame, he turned to leave when he heard it again, but this time, instead of a single thud there came three in short succession.

As his eyes continued to scan it's ungainly structure, hc listened intently to hear another thud, to be eventually followed by two more, with a longer interval between each. When another three followed in quick succession, his heart leapt into his mouth. There was no doubt about it. Someone was thumping out the SOS signal in morse code.

- CHAPTER SIXTY -

WASTING NOT ANOTHER moment, Tanner scrambled up onto the houseboat's narrow walkway, down into the boat's main entrance to begin staring earnestly about. When the thudding sound came again, he brought his eyes down to the rotting grey wooden floor. It was coming from its shallow rectangular hull. How to gain access, he had no idea. 'There must be a hatchway around here somewhere,' he told himself, turning slowly around.

Unable to see any latches set into the floor, he slowly slid open a grubby glass patio door to creep cautiously inside.

'Hello!' he called out again, choking at the pungent odour of damp rotting wood.

Staring about at the musty, dust-covered saloon he found himself in, he stopped to listen again. When another three loud thuds came from directly underneath, he stared wildly around at the floor. There, at the base of a set of crooked wooden steps that led up to the floor above, was a small narrow hatchway.

Launching himself over to it, he heaved it open to find another set of steps, leading down to an inky blackness below. Pulling in a breath against the thick, nauseating smell of diesel fumes, he began creeping down to find himself stepping on to a bevelled wooden floor, covered in at least two inches of dark oily water. Crouching down, he stared underneath the floor of the saloon, into what he assumed to be the houseboat's engine room. 'Vicky? Are you down here?'

As his voice echoed around the dark confined space, he heard the unmistakable sound of a woman's muffled cry.

Turning his head to the sound, he could just about see the outline of a figure, huddled against what had to be the engine, the person's arms held awkwardly above their head.

'Hold on,' he said, ducking under the floor to begin making his way down, the sound of his shoes splashing in the water, reverberating around the cramped inhospitable space.

By the time he'd reached the figure, his eyes had adjusted to the low level of light, enough at least to recognise Vicky's voluminous head of dark red hair, and the black gaffer tape that had been flattened over her mouth. 'Are you alright?' he asked, examining her more closely for any signs that she'd been injured.

Seeing her nod back in response, her teary-blue eyes shimmering up at his, he crouched down beside her. 'I'm going to take the tape off your mouth,' he said, using the tips of his fingers to take hold of one of its corners. 'Now, this may hurt a little.'

Without waiting for her to respond, he ripped the tape off to discard over his shoulder.

'Ow!' stated Vicky, rubbing her lips together. 'You could have warned me.'

'Sorry. I thought I did.'

'Aren't you supposed to be at a wedding?'

'I decided to visit you instead.'

'That's exceptionally kind of you. Whilst you're here, I don't suppose you'd be kind enough to undo my hands?'

'Already on it,' he replied, picking at the corners of more of the same gaffer tape that bound her wrists to what appeared to be the engine's crank shaft.

'Any chance you could hurry up. That deranged lunatic will be back in a minute.'

'By "deranged lunatic", I assume you're referring to Mr Campbell?'

'He calls himself Major.'

'I thought he called himself Captain?'

'I assume you're referring to the cap?'

'I take it he's still wearing it?'

'Apparently so.'

'So are you going to tell me how you ended up down here, or am I going to have to wait to read it in your report?'

'Dr Johnstone found something written on that dead reporter's hand.'

'Chapter forty-three, paragraph six,' Tanner commented, his mind recalling the image on the medical examiner's phone.

'I assumed it was in relation to Professor Baxendale's book,' Vicky nodded, 'so I looked it up to find the name of a certain Major Campbell.'

'How did you know it was Samuel Brogan's biological father?'

'He is?'

Tanner briefly stopped what he was doing to stare down at her. 'Who did *you* think he was?'

'I'd no idea. I just phoned up the Norfolk Herald to tell them that we thought we'd found Sidney Fletcher's body, and to ask if they knew what he'd been working on. They told me it was about some guy called Major Campbell. The reporter had somehow managed to get hold of Professor Baxendale's notes from his book. Apparently, Campbell had been dishonourably discharged from the Army, shortly after the Bluebell Wood Research Facility was closed.'

'Did it say *why* he'd been dishonourably discharged?'

'He was found guilty of sexually assaulting a young male Army Cadet, after the victim registered a complaint against him.'

'That may help to explain why he was a co-operating witness during the Adlington trial,' Tanner mused, half to himself.

'Are you nearly done up there?' Vicky queried, staring up at her hands.

'I don't suppose you've got a knife on you, by any chance?'

'Not on me, no.'

'Don't worry. I'm just about done,' he said, unwinding what was left of the tape from her wrists to leave her flexing her arms as he helped her to her feet.

Guiding her back through the engine bay to the stairs, Tanner climbed up before holding a hand down for her.

As she emerged safely out from under the floor, he turned to begin leading her out, only to find none other than Major Campbell, smiling at them from just inside the patio door.

'I was wondering whose car that was,' Campbell said, placing a green plastic petrol can by his feet.

'If that petrol's for me,' Tanner said, glancing down at it, 'then I'm OK. I filled up last night.'

'It wasn't for you, specifically.'

'Still got that sailing cap on, I see?' Tanner commented, pulling Vicky closer towards him. 'You do know that it's illegal to hold people against their will, don't you?'

'I didn't think police officers counted.'

'I'd have to check, but I'm fairly sure they do.'

'OK, well. Good to know, I suppose.'

'I've just been hearing about your time in the Army. Specifically about how you were dishonourably discharged.'

Pulling his shoulders back, Campbell locked his steel blue eyes onto Tanner's. 'I was what I believe is called a scapegoat.'

'So you *didn't* molest a young Army Cadet?'

'He was sixteen years old, and the sex was consensual.'

'Then why did he accuse you of rape?'

'I can only assume my superiors forced him to, as a way of getting rid of me.'

'And why would they have wanted to do that?'

'Because of the project we'd been working on inside the Bluebell Wood facility: creating chemical weapons to use against what was then called the Soviet Union.'

'And what chemical weapons were those, may I ask?'

Campbell's eyes narrowed, as if trying to decide just exactly how much he should be saying. 'We were working on something that could affect a human's amygdala,' he eventually replied, 'the part of the brain responsible for processing emotion. The idea was to make our enemy become so aggressive that they'd struggle to make logical, reasoned decisions, ideally resulting in them turning on each other. Unfortunately, it proved far harder than we'd expected. It also led to some unfortunate mind-altering side effects. We'd only just come up with something ready for human testing, when the Cold War came to a regrettable end, which was when I came in. Out of the blue, I was promoted up to the rank of major, forced to sign the Official Secrets Act, to then be put in charge of the entire facility, with the strict orders to destroy every shred of evidence as to what we'd been doing before closing the whole place down. Easy enough, you might think. The problem was the chemicals we'd been manufacturing. By that time we'd produced gallons of the stuff, or at least attempts at making it, and it wasn't the sort of thing you could simply flush down the toilet. So I ordered it placed into chemical waste containers and buried. It was only about a month later when the rape charge was brought against me, leaving me out of a job, with little chance of ever getting one.'

'May I ask where you buried it?'

'In what we used to refer to as our back garden.'

'You mean, Bluebell Wood?'

Campbell nodded in response. 'We dug a trench in the middle of it. At the time the whole place was just an overgrown forest, one that nobody really knew about. It was only after the research facility was converted into a shopping centre that it became a popular place for dog walkers and the like.'

'May I ask when Professor Baxendale came onto the scene?'

Campbell cast a wary eye over at the two police officers.

'I'm not looking for a confession,' Tanner lied. 'I'm just curious to know what happened.'

'Fair enough,' Campbell eventually replied, his face cracking into a helpful smile. 'The professor first contacted me about three months ago. He said he was writing a book about the Cold War, and that he wanted to interview me about the Bluebell Wood facility. At first I gracefully declined, but he wouldn't give up. So I eventually agreed to meet him at his house. That was when he told me exactly what he knew about me, specifically that I'd been responsible for covering up what happened at the facility, but more about the rape charge. He also relayed the real reason why he'd been so keen to meet; that he'd included everything he knew about me in his latest book, and that he'd only be willing to take it out if I paid him the somewhat hefty sum of fifty-thousand pounds. Unfortunately for him, what he didn't know was that prior to my appointment at the Bluebell Wood facility, I was a Royal Marine Commando, and that a significant part of my training was how to silence people, something I took a particular pride in doing during the Falklands War.'

'I assume it was only after you killed him that you realised the book had already gone to the publishers.'

'I didn't know, but I thought it was a possibility. That's why I broke into their offices, to have a look around.'

'Which was when you found the manuscript?'

'I must admit,' Campbell nodded, 'I'm a little behind the times with regards to computer technology. I thought having the manuscript would solve the problem. It was only when I got home that I realised it was probably also kept on a computer file somewhere. That's when I decided to stop by at your offices to have a chat, to see how you were getting on.'

'And that was when you saw one of my officer's hand the flash drive containing the book to me.'

Campbell shrugged. 'I guess I got lucky.'

'It *was* you who mugged me, wasn't it?'

Campbell smiled again. 'I've always been good with accents. And it's remarkably easy to make yourself appear bigger than you actually are.'

'After that, I assume you decided to set fire to the publishing house, presumably to avoid taking any chances that another copy existed.'

'Well yes, naturally, although I must admit, I had

no idea the company's CEO was inside at the time.'

'Tell me, where does the Adlington case come into all this?'

Campbell looked momentarily confused. 'The *Adlington* case?'

'You know, the one where you were a co-operating witness.'

'That's got nothing to do with this!'

'May I ask *why* you were a co-operating witness?'

'As I just said...'

'Was it because you were one of over a dozen men who paid the Adlingtons to have sexual intercourse with their son?'

Becoming stubbornly silent, Campbell's eyes drilled menacingly down into Tanner's.

'What was that poor boy's name again?' Tanner asked, his eyes lifting to the houseboat's rotten wooden ceiling. 'Samuel Adlington, wasn't it?'

With Campbell remaining unresponsive, Tanner gave his shoulders a dismissive shrug. 'I assume you didn't know that the Adlingtons had formally adopted him. If you had, then I doubt you'd have been quite so dismissive when I mentioned their name to you just now. I suppose it wasn't something you were ever asked about during the trial, probably being that it wasn't considered relevant. Had anyone done so, then you'd have known that his name was originally Pickford.'

Tanner watched with reticent glee as Campbell's face suddenly paled.

'I'm going to bet that you also didn't know where they lived, again being that it was irrelevant to the proceedings: a cottage in the middle of Bluebell Wood, not far from where their adopted son was found hanging by his neck earlier this week.'

With tears now appearing at the corners of

Campbell's shadow-filled eyes, Tanner offered him a gleeful grimace. 'To be honest, I'm not surprised you're upset. If I'd just discovered that I'd spent year-upon-year paying to have sex with my own son, I probably would be as well.'

Campbell's head fell slowly forward to leave him staring vacantly at the floor. 'I – I didn't know,' he eventually said, his voice nothing more than a faltering whisper.

'Let me guess. Next you're going to tell me that none of it was your fault, that you're nothing but a helpless victim. It was the Adlingtons who forced their son into prostitution, not you. It was their actions that left him so mentally imbalanced that he eventually came to the decision to take his own life.'

As Campbell's entire body began trembling, he lifted his head to offer Tanner a look of pleading desperation, as if a single word of forgiveness could instantly eliminate his all-consuming sense of sickening self-loathing.

'And if it wasn't for the orders you gave during the closure of the Bluebell Wood research facility, you could well have been right,' Tanner continued, holding the man's tear-filled eyes with an unrelenting gaze.

'My orders?'

'To dispose of the facility's produce by having it poured into hazardous waste containers, to then be buried in the middle of Bluebell Wood. From my own personal experience, I strongly suspect that at least one of those containers has developed a leak, possibly since the time it was dumped there. If that is the case, it would go a long way to explain what happened to the Adlingtons corrupted state of mind; how they changed from being a loving young couple to placing their adopted son into the predatory hands of sick, deranged paedophiles, such as yourself, a decision that ultimately led to the father hanging himself, whilst the mother was left so mentally deranged, she's now a permanent resident of a local mental institution.

'It would explain a few other things as well,' Tanner continued. 'Bluebell Wood's distinct lack of wildlife, why people's dogs seem to become instantly deranged the moment they're let loose inside the place, and perhaps most disturbing of all, why more people have committed suicide there than anywhere else in the whole of Norfolk, your biological son sadly being amongst them.'

With his eyes still fixed on Campbell's face, he watched him wipe at an escaping tear before reaching down for the petrol can.

'You know,' the major began, as he lifted his chin to look Tanner dementedly in the eye, 'I bought this for you – well – not you, exactly. I thought I had a reasonable enough chance of getting away with the murder of some fossilised professor, even some loathsome reporter, but I knew it would be a different story with a police officer, especially an attractive female one, like your colleague here.'

With his tears already drying up, he offered Vicky an acidic smile. 'So, my original plan was to use my somewhat dilapidated houseboat as a funeral pyre for her. That would at least give me time to leave the country before anyone was able to identify her body. But now...' he continued, his attention drifting wistfully off into space, 'there really isn't much point. I can't run away from what I've done. Not to my own son. Nor do I deserve to.'

As if reaching an irreversible decision that had been handed down to him by both a judge and jury, he spun the lid off the petrol can to start pouring its contents over the top of his head.

'STOP!' yelled Tanner, leaping forward, only to be brought skidding to a halt by the sight of a chrome zippo lighter being held towards him.

As the petrol continued tumbling out of the can, Campbell flipped open the lighter. 'I'm sorry,' he eventually said, calmly igniting it with the single roll of his thumb, 'but I've no particular wish to continue with this existence. I think I'll just take my chances with the next one.'

The moment he saw the flickering lighter slip through Campbell's fingers to begin spiralling its way down to the floor, Tanner lurched forward in a desperate bid to stop it. But he'd barely managed to take a single step when the man standing in peaceful reconciliation in front of him was suddenly transformed into a twisting vortex of flickering flame.

Forced back by the heat, Tanner and Vicky were left staring open-mouthed as the man's twisted agonised face seem to first ripple, then melt before their very eyes. As his burning body began to sink slowly to the floor, the flames above his head stretched themselves up to the cabin's low wooden ceiling, growing with intensity as they did.

Pushed further back to the steps leading up to the floor above, with the realisation that the man's burning effigy was blocking the only way out, they each began to stare frantically about.

'There must be another way off this damned boat,' Tanner muttered, his eyes becoming transfixed by the flames creeping inexorably over the ceiling towards them.

'Could we break one of the windows?' asked Vicky, staring over at them.

Tanner turned to follow her gaze, only to see the cabin's slatted wooden walls were already blistering in the heat. 'It's too late for that. I think we're better off heading up to the floor above. There may be a way off from there.'

'And if there isn't?'

'Then we should be able to get out through a window. Either way, we're running out of time.'

With the decision made, Tanner helped Vicky up the stairs to instantly begin following her, when the entire boat lurched violently to the side.

As Vicky lost her footing to come tumbling down, Tanner managed to catch her, just in time before her head smashed against the floor.

'I didn't know you cared,' she said, batting her eyelashes sardonically up at him.

'No time for mucking about, Vicky. If that was the hull burning through, then we really need to get out of here.'

'And we didn't before?'

With the agonising sound of the houseboat creaking and groaning around them, as if the whole thing were trying to tear itself apart, Tanner grabbed Vicky's hand to drag her up the steps.

- CHAPTER SIXTY ONE -

REACHING THE FLOOR above, they found themselves in what appeared to be a disused ballroom, in the middle of which was a large rectangular dancefloor, surrounded by a collection of broken chairs and empty tables.

Spying a door at its furthest end, they glanced up to see the room was fast filling up with searing hot smoke, billowing above their heads like a gathering storm.

Already choking at the air, they charged towards the dancefloor to be instantly forced back. The surface was alive with rippling blue flames, dancing to the tune of the burning boat.

'The floor's caught fire,' Tanner said. 'It's not safe to cross.'

'Then how are we going to get out?'

Over the noise of the raging fire came the distant sound of a single siren, floating on the buffeting breeze from somewhere outside.

With the slim hope of being rescued, Tanner dragged Vicky over to the nearest window. Fetching up a chair, he hurled it at the soot-blackened glass. The moment it shattered, they leapt forward, shoving their heads through the jagged hole to begin sucking frantically at the cool clean air beyond.

Able to hear the approaching siren more clearly, Tanner blinked his eyes open to see two shadowy figures, a man and a woman, waving at them from the grassy bank below.

'Sally? Townsend?' he called, as their features came more sharply into focus.

'Can you get out?' he heard Townsend shout.

'All the exits are blocked.'

'Then you have to jump!'

Nodding in acknowledgment, Tanner stared at the riverbank. It was a drop of at least fifteen feet, and the boat itself was about six, maybe seven feet from the bank itself. It was doable, but it wouldn't be easy, not when they'd be jumping from the narrow ledge of a burning houseboat, one that was tilting further away from the bank with every passing moment.

A tumultuous crashing sound immediately behind had them spinning around to see the dancefloor disappear to be instantly replaced by a raging inferno.

Looking back at Townsend, Tanner called, 'We're going to jump!'

'We are?' he heard Vicky ask.

'We don't have a choice, I'm afraid, and you're going first.'

'Can't we go together?'

'No chance,' Tanner replied, examining the ledge. 'The window isn't big enough.'

Vicky's entire face creased with fear and uncertainty.

'You'll be alright,' Tanner said, offering her a reassuring smile, 'but you have to go now. If you don't, then neither of us are going to make it.'

Watching her return a reluctant nod, Tanner held his sleeve over his mouth to bring his head back inside the burning room, giving Vicky the space to climb out onto the window's narrow ledge.

Choking madly at the air, Tanner could feel his brain spin around inside his skull as he watched her clamber ever-so slowly to her feet. He knew he didn't have long. If she didn't jump soon, he was likely to lose consciousness, leaving his body to be consumed by the encroaching flames.

With what was left of the air inside his lungs, he was about to scream at her to jump, when he looked to see her body flutter away, like a fledgling bird taking flight for the very first time.

Plunging his head back through the window, he gasped at the untainted air to see Sally and Townsend haul Vicky to her feet on the grassy bank below.

Hearing Townsend beckon his name, he knew it was his turn.

Dragging himself out, he climbed unsteadily to his feet. As he clung to the sides of the window frame, he stared down at the bank for his head to immediately spin. It was far higher than he'd thought, and with the boat continuing to tilt away from the bank, he was further out as well.

His mind briefly entertained the idea of remaining where he was, only to realise that would mean he'd be left stranded on top of what would become his own funeral pyre.

With the noise of the fire raging behind him, the sound of his heart thumping inside his chest, and the wail of a siren drifting listlessly in the air, he pulled in a ragged breath and jumped.

- CHAPTER SIXTY TWO -

W AKING UP TO find himself lying on a sloping grass bank, his body cold and numb, his head pounding with pain, Tanner glanced about with his eyes to see nothing but a myriad of boots, clomping around him as if he didn't exist.

As a pair of black office shoes came into view, he tilted his head up to see Townsend, crouching beside him with a concerned frown.

'Where am I?' he asked, his mouth as dry as sandpaper.

'Don't you remember?'

As the memories of the last few hours began flooding back into his mind, he lifted himself up onto his elbows to begin staring earnestly about. 'Where's Vicky?'

'With Sally, waiting for the ambulance.'

'But...she's OK?'

'She seems to be. More to the point, how are you?'

Tanner sent a mental probe along the length of his body. 'My head hurts, and I would appear to be soaking wet. Is it still raining?'

Townsend shook his head. 'It stopped a while ago.'

'I assume that means I didn't make it to the bank.'

'Your head did! The rest of you ended up in the river.'

'That would explain why I'm so wet.'

'Can you tell me what happened?' Townsend asked. 'Inside the boat?'

'Major Campbell is what happened,' Tanner replied, with a resentful scowl, taking a moment to watch two burly firemen direct a hose at the houseboat's smouldering remains. 'I think he's still onboard.'

Townsend whipped his head around to follow his gaze. 'Is he alright?'

'I doubt it,' Tanner mused, sitting painfully up to find a foil blanket draped over his shoulders. 'After confessing to the murder of Professor Baxendale, stealing my phone, setting fire to Morgan & Naylor Publishing house, and killing that reporter from the Norfolk Herald, he decided to pour a can of petrol over his head to set fire to himself.'

'Why the hell did he do that?'

'Probably something to do with the fact that he'd just found out he'd spent five years paying for the privilege of having homosexual relations with his own son.'

Townsend glanced away with a look of sickening disgust. 'Anyway, the ambulance will be here any minute. I suggest you stay still until they can take a look at that head of yours.'

'Not again,' Tanner muttered, reaching a hand up to find warm sticky blood, running down the side of his face.

'Looks like Christine's beaten them to it,' Townsend continued, staring over Tanner's shoulder towards the carpark.

'Shit!' he cursed, closing his eyes to imagine what she'd say to him about failing to show up to their wedding, at least the most important part of it.

'Considering its supposed to be the happiest day of her life, she doesn't look like she's enjoying herself very much.'

Tanner turned to see her stomping her way over the grass towards them, the hem of her bedraggled wet wedding dress gathered up in her clenched, white-knuckled hands.

'If you don't mind,' he heard Townsend mutter, 'I think I'll leave you two to it.'

As the young DC slunk discreetly away, Tanner climbed painfully to his feet to force a smile at his rapidly approaching bride.

'Are you alright?' she demanded, stopping to offer him an anxious frown.

'Just about,' he replied, taking a moment to adjust his tie. 'Listen, I'm really sorry I didn't make it back for our wedding.'

'Don't be daft! I heard what happened. We all did!' she exclaimed, glancing back over her shoulder, where the vicar and her bridesmaids could be seen. 'From what I heard, you're lucky to be alive!'

Tanner turned again to look at what was left of the houseboat. 'I managed to jump off, before the whole thing went up. Vicky as well.'

'Is she OK?'

'I think so. At least she made it to the bank.'

'And you didn't?'

'Only the top half, apparently. The rest ended up in the river.'

Christine looked down to take in his suit, and how it was sticking to his body like clingfilm.

'At least it's stopped raining,' Tanner continued, casting his eyes up at the overcast sky.

'Judging by the state of you, I'm not sure it would have made much difference if it hadn't.'

'No, I suppose not,' he shrugged.

'Have you been given the all-clear by the paramedics.'

'We're still waiting for the ambulance.'

'Then maybe I should take you home, before you freeze to death.'

'What about our wedding?'

'I think that can wait for another day, don't you?' she replied, her gaze shifting down to her feet.

'Er, no, I don't!' Tanner stated, tilting his head down to see that she was crying.

Hooking a finger under her chin, he lifted her face to gaze down into her tear-filled eyes. 'Listen, Christine. I love you, and I want to marry you. I promised I'd do that today, and I've got no intention of going back on my word, certainly not because some deranged psychotic paedophile decided that today was the day he was going to set himself on fire.'

'Is that what happened?'

'Something like that.'

Christine wiped at her tears to present Tanner with a wavering smile. 'It doesn't matter,' she eventually said. 'It's too late, anyway. The vicar's got to get back for another wedding.'

'Then we'll do it now.'

'Now?'

'Why not? Everyone's here.'

'The best man isn't.'

'But the vicar is, as are the bridesmaids.'

Christine glanced undecidedly around at them. 'Do you think the vicar would mind?'

'I don't see why not. He's probably over there right now, furious with himself for not having married us when he had the chance.'

Christine snorted with laughter.

'Besides, all he has to do is to ask if we take each other as husband and wife, and then for us to say the words that I've spent the last twenty-four hours practicing.'

'And what words are those?'

Taking her hands in his, Tanner cleared his throat to look deep into her shimmering green eyes. 'I do.'

- EPILOGUE -

'ANY IDEA WHAT you want to do tomorrow?' asked Christine, lying back on a luxuriously padded sun lounger, as her fingers flicked lazily through a tourist's guidebook to Valencia.

Sitting up on an identical sun lounger beside her, Tanner shielded his eyes from the morning sun to glance over at her from his laptop. 'What did you have in mind?'

'We could go to the Llotja de la Seda?'

'Remind me what that was again?'

'The Silk Exchange. Apparently, it's one of the finest examples of gothic architecture in existence today.'

'So, it's an old building, then,' Tanner replied, his interest instantly returning to his laptop.

'What about the Bioparc?'

'You mean, the zoo?'

'It's not just a zoo!'

'Doesn't it keep animals inside enclosed environments, ones which they can't escape from?'

'Yes, but...'

'Then it's a zoo,' Tanner concluded.

'Well, we have to do something.'

'Is there any particular reason why we can't just lie here, enjoying the sun?'

'Because we go home tomorrow evening. Besides, we've been doing nothing but lying here, enjoying the sun, for the last three days.'

Tanner gazed over at their private swimming pool to spend a pensive moment watching its cobalt blue water sparkle with enticing serenity. 'I thought it was two?' he eventually asked.

'It's three. At least, it will be after today.'

'Then I suggest we make it four,' he yawned, stretching his arms above his head before returning his fingers to his laptop's keyboard.

A sullen silence followed, leaving Tanner thinking that his total lack of interest in doing anything at all was probably beginning to wind Christine up, and not for the first time. 'Tell you what. How about we go down to the marina after lunch?'

'That's the same place we went to the day we arrived!'

'Then it's high time we went back, don't you think?'

Tanner glanced over to see Christine considering his proposal with a distinct lack of enthusiasm. 'We could then have dinner at the Marina Beach Club,' he continued, endeavouring to sell her on the idea. 'After that, we could enjoy a few glasses of Sangria whilst watching the sun set slowly over the Mediterranean Sea.'

'You do remember that I can't drink, I hope,' she replied, resting a hand on her curving abdomen.

'Sorry, I meant a few glasses of ice-cold, instantly refreshing sparkling water.'

'Don't worry, you had me at dinner,' she smiled back.

'So, we can stay here today?'

'As long as we can go out somewhere tonight.'

'OK, sounds good,' Tanner replied, typing something on the laptop's keyboard.

'Please God, tell me you're not working again?'

'Not at all. I'm just checking my emails.'

'I think most people would consider that to be working.'

'It's only working when you reply,' he muttered, typing again.

'Sounds to me like that's exactly what you're doing.'

'Only to the essential ones.'

Christine shook her head. 'Any news from home?'

'Not much. Vicky's moaning about Cooper, Cooper's moaning about Townsend, and Townsend's broken up with Sally.'

'Not again!'

'Don't worry. I'm sure they'll be back in each other's beds by the time we get back.'

'Don't you mean, in each other's arms?'

Tanner took a pensive moment to gaze up at the cloudless cobalt blue sky. 'You know, I really don't think I do,' he eventually replied, returning his attention back to the screen. 'Meanwhile, in other news, the building plans for the Bluebell Wood housing development have been withdrawn.'

Christine sat up with interest. 'How come?'

'They found over a dozen hazardous waste containers buried near the tree where Samuel Brogan was found. They've sealed off the entire wood whilst trying to work out what's inside them.'

'It's that chemical waste Major Campbell dumped there, surely?'

'The government's denying all knowledge, as is the military.'

'No surprises there.'

'Simon Balinger is furious.'

'Really? How strange.'

'He says he's going to sue the council for breach of contract.'

Christine snorted with disdain. 'He'll probably make more money doing that then he would have done if he'd built all those bloody houses.'

'Undoubtedly.'

'Anything else?'

'The Norfolk Herald's running a story that there's some sort of giant rabid ghost dog, praying on cavorting young couples in the dead of the night. They're calling it The Hound of Bluebell Wood.'

'Sally and Townsend better watch out, then.'

'Maybe that's why they broke up; it just became too dangerous to be caught canoodling in public.'

'You know what really worries me?' Christine asked, staring over at Tanner's laptop.

'What's that?'

'Why you're scrolling through the Norfolk Herald's website?'

Tanner shrugged. 'I must admit, it's more entertaining than I thought. They've even posted a picture of it.' Tanner held the laptop up for Christine to see the blurry image of a dog, strolling innocently past a tree.

Christine tugged her sunglasses down her nose to squint at it. 'When they said ghostly, I assume they meant out-of-focus?'

'Very possibly, but more importantly, I think it might actually be a Rottweiler.'

'And why's that more important than it being an out-of-focus dog with rabies?'

'Because, from memory, it's the same breed as that dog that went missing in Bluebell Wood, the one that found Samuel Brogan. Assuming it is, you know what that means?'

'Do tell.'

Tanner turned to offer her a triumphant grin. 'That I've just solved a missing dog case, whilst doing nothing more arduous than lying beside a private swimming pool on the coast of sunny Spain.'

'Congrats.'

'Thanks! I better email Vicky, to let her know.'

As Tanner started typing with a smile of smug self-satisfaction, Christine became strangely quiet beside him.

'Er...when you've finished,' she eventually said, 'I don't suppose you could do me a favour?'

'What's that?' he asked, somewhat absently.

'Could you call me a doctor?'

Tanner stopped what he was doing to offer her a bemused frown. 'Why on earth do you need a doctor?'

'Because, if I'm not very much mistaken, my waters just broke,' she replied, staring back at him with a petrified grimace.

DCI John Tanner
will return in
Swanton Morley

- A LETTER FROM DAVID -

Dear Reader,

I just wanted to say a huge thank you for deciding to read *Bluebell Wood*. If you enjoyed it, I'd be really grateful if you could leave a review on Amazon, or mention it to your friends and family. Word-of-mouth recommendations are just so important to an author's success, and doing so will help new readers discover my work.

It would be great to hear from you as well, either on Facebook, Twitter, Goodreads or via my website. There are plenty more books to come, so I sincerely hope you'll be able to stick around for what will continue to be an exciting adventure!

All the very best,

David

- ABOUT THE AUTHOR -

David Blake is an international bestselling author who lives in North London. At time of going to print he has written twenty-three books, along with a collection of short stories. When not writing, David likes to spend his time mucking about in boats, often in the Norfolk Broads, where his crime fiction books are based.

Printed in Great Britain
by Amazon